Dear Reader,

When someone we love is ill, we want to do something tangible to help them. Like Mary in this story, we feel the frustration of our ineffectiveness. Physical activity serves an important role in those situations, both as a distraction and as a source of comfort. "Doing something"—even if it's not directly related to the patient—can help us feel we have accomplished something useful.

Often we find, as Mary did, that the one thing we can do best is pray. No matter where we are or what we are doing, God is always listening. He chooses to answer our prayers. James 5:16 tells us "the effective prayer of a righteous man can accomplish much."

Mary's reliance on Scripture to comfort her is one of her character traits that blesses me. It reminds me of how God draws us closer to Him through His Word and our communication with Him through prayer. So even if you're in a situation where you can't get out like Mary and solve mysteries, stay in close touch with God and keep in mind that you can still accomplish much through prayer.

Happy reading!
Susan Page Davis

Secrets of Mary's Bookshop

A New Chapter
Rewriting History
Reading the Clues
The Writing on the Wall
By Word of Mouth
A Book by Its Cover
Poetry in Motion
Missing Pages
Between the Lines
By the Book
Disappearing Acts
A Classic Case
Cover Story
A Thousand Words
The Lost Noel
Work in Progress
Words of Wisdom
Lost for Words
Cooking the Books
Snowbound
Digging Up Clues

SECRETS *of* MARY'S
BOOKSHOP

Shady Characters

Susan Page Davis

Guideposts

New York

Published by Guideposts Books & Inspirational Media
110 William Street
New York, New York 10038
Guideposts.org

Acknowledgments

Every attempt has been made to credit the sources of copyrighted material used in this book. If any such acknowledgment has been inadvertently omitted or miscredited, receipt of such information would be appreciated.

"From the Guideposts Archives" originally appeared in *Daily Guideposts,* 1981. Copyright © 1980 by Guideposts. All rights reserved.

Cover and interior design by Müllerhaus
Cover illustration by Ross Jones, represented by Deborah Wolfe, Ltd.
Typeset by Aptara, Inc.

Printed and bound in the United States of America
10 9 8 7 6 5 4 3 2 1

Shady Characters

ONE

Mary Fisher arranged a new batch of mystery books on a shelf in her bookshop, placing the volumes in the order of the series. The author had created a Cape Cod saga with fascinating characters and a challenging mystery in each book. The Plymouth Riddles series had become a new favorite that Mary recommended often to customers.

She went over to the counter and gathered the loose, crumpled paper that the publishing company had used for shipping and tucked it into the empty box. Gus, her long-haired gray cat, leaped up onto the counter and batted a paw at a wad of paper peeking out the top of the carton.

"Well, hello, Gus." Mary stroked his silky fur. "Have a nice nap?"

Mary's employee Rebecca looked over from where she was working in the classics section. "He's ready to play now."

"So am I!" Rebecca's daughter Ashley popped up out of the claw-footed, carpeted bathtub in the children's nook, where she had been reading. "Come on, Gus."

The cat didn't deign to obey her summons, but neither did he object when Ashley came over to the counter and lifted him into her arms.

"Do you really want to play with that boring paper? I know where your toy is," Ashley said confidentially as she carried Gus toward the seating area at the back of the store.

"Sometimes paper makes a good toy," Rebecca called after her.

Mary smiled as she watched them. Since school had let out for the summer, Ashley was able to come to the store most days with her mother. The little girl had a soul wise beyond her seven years, and she was an asset to the shop. Mary considered her a top salesperson in the children's area especially, although she'd made plenty of sales of adult mysteries too.

The bell on the door jingled, and Tess Bailey came in, smiling broadly. "Good afternoon, ladies!"

"Hi, Tess," Rebecca called.

"Hi there," Mary said. "How's business at Bailey's?"

"Booming, with this warm weather."

Mary grinned. "Nothing better than ice cream on a hot day."

"People really go for that peanut butter caramel you came up with this month, but it's time to think about the July flavor. Have you got a recipe for me yet?" Tess leaned on the counter. Her auburn hair, which she usually kept tied back while serving behind the counter at the ice-cream shop, flowed over her shoulders this morning.

"I confess I haven't," Mary said. "We've been busy too. But maybe something with blackberries?"

"*Mmm.* Blackberry-flavored ice cream, or whole berries in vanilla, or what?" Tess asked.

Mary couldn't help laughing. "That's way more than I've decided yet."

"Let me know." Tess straightened. "But I really came to get a book. Last night, I actually had an evening off, and there was nothing good on TV. I looked around and realized I had nothing new to read."

"We can certainly help you there." Mary came out from behind the counter and walked with Tess toward the display of recent arrivals. "We've got some wonderful cozy mysteries, or if you want a little more excitement, there's a suspense line I really like."

They chatted a few minutes longer while Tess selected the newest volume in the Cape Cod series Mary had been shelving. More customers came in, and Rebecca went to help them.

When Tess was ready to check out, she and Mary strolled back to the counter, and Mary rang up her purchase.

"I hope you like it," Mary said.

"I'm sure I will. Now, don't forget about the ice cream. It's early, I know, but Blake likes extra time to order the supplies ahead if you use something unusual."

"I'll try to give it some thought tonight."

Tess's green eyes twinkled. "I had an idea for a flavor. It's a little off-the-wall, but it might be good for business."

"What is it?" Mary's interest was piqued. Tess did most of the ice-cream manufacturing at Bailey's, and she was a talented ice-cream developer. Though Mary usually provided the flavor of the month recipe now, Tess still created some scrumptious treats of her own.

"I'm still working on it, but it has to do with raspberries."

"Yum," Mary said. She thought it would be nice if Tess had the spotlight more often.

Tess laughed. "Maybe I'll give you some competition this month."

"Maybe you should do next month's flavor."

Tess shook her head. "People come in wanting to know what you've come up with. We need you to keep on creating, or we'd have some very upset customers." Suddenly, Tess's face lit up. "We should have a contest. A taste-off!"

Mary eyed her dubiously. "I've heard of bake-offs, but I don't know about a taste-off."

Lynn Teagarden, who was a member of Mary's prayer group, had come to the counter holding two books. She smiled at them. "Sounds good to me!"

Tess smiled at Lynn. "Yes, and we could involve the whole community to vote on which was best." She was on a roll, and Mary was charmed.

"Something new for Ivy Bay. You may have something here," Mary said.

"It's a wonderful idea," Lynn said. "Two new flavors of the month. Or"—she looked from Tess to Mary and back again—"what if you let other people enter their flavors?"

Tess frowned. "Maybe…. Let me think about it. Oh, I know! Anyone who wanted could enter a new flavor. Or a new recipe, at least. We'd have to narrow it down to a few finalists." Tess looked eagerly at Mary. "What do you think?"

"It sounds like a lot of work…but a lot of fun too."

Rebecca came over to join the debate. "I love the idea, Tess. You could offer a special on a double-dip cone with competing flavors."

"Or a sampler dish." Tess's eyes focused on something outside the bookshop. "A community-wide contest would be great publicity. Especially if we did it on the Fourth of July."

"Whoa!" Mary stared at her. "Do you really think you could put it together that fast? That's only—what? Two weeks away."

"Yeah. I need to talk to Blake. But think of it. Thousands of tourists are in town every year around the Fourth. We'd have the parade in the morning, and immediately after it disbanded, we'd have the ice cream available in the park."

"The park?" Mary frowned. The more Tess talked, the more complicated the idea sounded.

"Sure, the Albert Paddington Park. We could set up a booth near the gazebo."

"I don't know, Tess. That's awfully short notice to get publicity and recipes and ingredients." Mary doubted even the Bailey family could pull it off.

"I'll run it by Blake and the girls. But you wouldn't mind if we opened it to the public and asked everyone to submit their best recipe?"

"Not a bit," Mary said. "And you could feature the winning flavor all month."

"Of course, we want you to enter."

"I wouldn't need to. You'd get a lot of people with great ideas."

"People will want to see one of your flavors on the roster."

"I'm flattered," Mary said. "All right. I'll try to think of something exciting. And if you really think you can do all the work—the organizing and publicity and production, all of that—then I think it's a great idea. You'll sell thousands of cones that day." Mary slid Tess's book into a brown bag with a sticker that said, "Mary's Mystery Bookshop."

Tess nodded, smiling. "And the customers can vote for the flavor they like best. We'll get back to you with the details as soon as we work them out."

"Sounds good," Mary said. "And may the best flavor win!"

Tess took the bag with her book in it and left the shop, grinning. Mary rang up Lynn's books and waved as she left.

Rebecca came to the counter to join Mary. "Sounds like a fun event."

"It really does," Mary said.

"They'll sell a lot of ice cream, however they work it," a voice behind Mary said. She whirled to find Bernice Foster, who had been browsing the shelves, standing near the counter with two books in her hands.

Mary took Bernice's books and keyed in the prices on the cash register. "I guess I need to come up with an extra-special flavor this month. It takes time to test it and perfect the recipe." She bagged Bernice's books and handed them to her. "Thanks, Bernice. You should enter the contest too."

"Not me, but if you need any volunteer tasters, let me know," Bernice replied with a wink.

When Bernice had left and the other customers in the store were still browsing, Mary sat down at the computer and pulled up her inventory program. "Do you think we need to order more classic mysteries? We've sold quite a few this month, and Bernice just walked out with another Dorothy Sayers."

"Maybe. They're always steady sellers, even if they're not at the top of the list." Rebecca chuckled. "You're going to have a blast with this taste-off thing."

"Only if I come up with a super flavor idea. Maybe I could come up with a mystery flavor."

"That would be good for cross-promotion between us and Bailey's," Rebecca said.

"Mystery berry?" Mary closed the inventory file and opened the cash drawer. They still had two hours until closing, but she could start making out the bank-deposit slip for the checks they had received that day. "I hope Tess does enter. I don't have a problem with that since the customers will be voting, not the staff of Bailey's."

"Wouldn't it be wild if she won?" Rebecca said.

"I think it would be great," Mary said. "But I doubt she'll even enter because she'll be the one making all that ice cream they'll sell."

Ashley ambled over, with Gus limp in her arms and purring loudly. "Is there going to be an ice-cream-making contest?"

"That's right," her mother said.

Mary nodded. "And now I have to come up with a super new flavor. Any ideas, Ashley?"

Ashley screwed up her face into a thoughtful frown as she teased Gus with the end of one of her braids. "How about licorice fudge?"

"Licorice fudge." Mary couldn't help feeling a little skeptical about that one. "I'll think about it."

"You know, licorice ice cream with chunks of chocolate fudge," Ashley said brightly.

"*Ew*," said Rebecca. "It gives me a stomachache just thinking about it."

The phone rang, and Mary reached to pick up the receiver. "Mary's Mystery Bookshop."

"Hi, Mary. It's Henry."

She smiled. "Well, hi. How was the antique car show?"

"Terrific." Henry's voice held a deep contentment. "Mary, I bought something, and I want you to see it."

Mary's jaw dropped. "You mean...at the car show?"

He laughed. "That's right. I'm not telling you what it is, but it might involve an evening drive to Bailey's for some ice cream. Can you have dinner at my place?"

"I'd love to." Mary's excitement mounted. Henry had driven his blue-and-white 1953 Bel Air for more years than she cared to count. Had he finally bought a newer—or older—car? "What can I bring?"

"Not a thing. I picked up some bay scallops and salad greens, and I stopped at Sweet Susan's for fresh dinner rolls."

"Oh stop! I'm already drooling." Mary rolled her eyes at Rebecca, who burst out in laughter. She stifled it quickly as three customers entered the shop. One of the women had a little girl with her, so Ashley hurried into the children's area, ready as always to serve the shop's young customers while her mom and Mary helped the grown-ups.

"I'll be there," Mary said into the phone. "What time?"

"Just come over when you close up," Henry said. "Unless you want to go home first."

"I should probably take Gus home," she said. Mary took her cat back and forth in his carrier, and Gus loved going to work with her, but it could make things awkward if she wanted to run errands after the shop closed.

"Okay, just come as soon as you can."

"Thanks. Can't wait to see your new acquisition. I'll see you later."

The rest of the afternoon flew by, the anticipation staying with Mary. She hadn't heard such a lilt in Henry's voice in a while. She snatched a moment to call her sister Betty and tell her about her plans for the evening.

"Have a great time," Betty said. "I'm going out with Eleanor."

"Oh? Where?"

"To a charity auction." Betty named an auction house in the next town. "They get some classy merchandise there. It might be fun."

"I hope it is." Mary knew that outings Betty took with her sister-in-law could go either way.

More customers arrived, and she hastily ended her phone call. Tourists flocked the charming village of Ivy Bay in the summer, and the warm June day had lured them from their cottages and boats to browse the shops. Mary's local-interest books were severely depleted by the time she closed for the night.

"Good thing you ordered extras on that new police series," Rebecca said when she turned off the vacuum after a quick cleanup.

"I'll say. And I'm sending for more Cape Cod cozies right...now." Mary clicked the Checkout button on the computer screen, where she had hastily put in her order on a regional publisher's Web site. "We'll get those in tomorrow or Monday."

They finished their closing routine, and Mary let Ashley put Gus into his carrier. She locked up, and they all headed home.

Betty had already left the house when Mary arrived home with Gus. She released him from his carrier, and he rubbed against her legs while she filled his dishes with fresh food and water.

She dashed upstairs to her room to run a brush through her short, curly gray hair and freshen her lipstick. This would definitely be a casual evening, so she kept on her dark pants and slipped a print sweater over her blouse. Henry's home was right on the bay, and a cool breeze usually teased the shore in the evening. As an afterthought, she tucked a scarf into her bag. Perhaps Henry had bought another convertible, like the Bel Air, so she'd best be prepared.

"Now you be good while I'm gone," she said to Gus as she passed through the kitchen on the way out to her car. Mary smiled to herself. As if Gus would misbehave. He would probably curl up on the sofa and sleep the entire evening.

Ten minutes later, she parked in Henry's driveway, got out of her car, and paused to look out over the shore. The view from Henry's front windows was unparalleled. The waves broke gently tonight on the shore below, and the breeze ruffled her hair as she watched the sky darken over the bay. Off to her right, a worn path and wooden steps led down to the dock where Henry kept his small motorboat tied in the summer. His larger fishing boat, the *Misty Horizon*, was berthed at the marina, but Henry liked to have a smaller open boat handy, and he often took it to the marina instead of driving. The sun was setting behind her, and when she turned toward the house, she could see streaks of peach and rose staining the clouds to the west.

The door opened, and Henry came out onto the front steps.

"Hi! I thought we'd eat out on the screened porch." Henry stood tall and straight, smiling at her comfortably. He wore khaki pants and a short-sleeved print shirt. The skin of his forearms and face was tanned from his hours on the water, and the corners of his eyes crinkled when he smiled, which he did often.

Mary tucked her car keys and phone in her pocket and walked up onto the porch. "Sounds heavenly."

"Everything's almost ready, but I thought maybe we'd take a peek in the garage first." His sea-green eyes lit up, and his boyish smile infected her with his eagerness.

"Yes, let's. I can hardly wait." She glanced toward the garage, but the overhead doors were closed.

"Come on in this way then." He led her through the living room to the kitchen, where he had the breaded scallops ready to fry, and opened the connecting door to the garage. He stood aside and let Mary enter first.

She stopped at the top of the three steps and gazed at a gleaming white-on-red machine, so perfect she would have sworn it had just rolled out of the showroom.

"Oh, Henry, it's beautiful!"

He grinned and put his hand under her elbow, guiding her down the steps. "I think so. Careful—not as much room in here as there used to be."

His Bel Air was parked in the second bay of the garage, which he normally used as a workshop. He had moved some of his woodworking machinery aside to accommodate it and give the new car the slot nearest the kitchen door.

"Tell me about it."

"It's a 1955 Buick Century."

"Oh, so you've upgraded."

He chuckled. "Yeah, it's two years newer."

"Not by much then." Mary glanced over at the Bel Air.

"No, but it's an important difference. See, a lot of companies went with a V-8 in '55, Chevy included. I've always had six cylinders."

"More powerful. That's an impressive change."

"Yeah. And it's the convertible, of course. I don't think I'd have bought it otherwise. And it's got the wire wheels and fender skirts, and…do you like the color?" He looked at her anxiously.

"Very dashing! I can't wait to be seen in it."

He laughed in delight. "Within the hour, madam! But we'd better eat first."

"Yes, I've been anticipating that too."

They went back into the kitchen. It still bore the stamp of Misty's creative hand in decorating, with blue-and-white-striped wallpaper, starched white eyelet curtains, cobalt-blue dishes on display, and antique kitchen utensils hanging on the walls. Henry went to the range.

"What can I do?" Mary asked, setting her purse on the counter.

"These scallops will only take a minute. You can get the salad out of the fridge and take it to the porch. Oh, and the rolls."

Mary followed his instructions and returned to ice their water glasses just as he scooped the fried scallops out of the pan.

They carried everything out through the back kitchen door, onto the porch. Three walls were lined with screens from about two feet off the floor to six feet up. The fourth wall was the outside of the house, from which hung oars, several multicolored lobster fishing buoys, and a "sailor's valentine," made from seashells. Henry had set up a card table for two, with a few wild roses stuck in a vase. They grew above the rocks on the shore, and the bright pink blooms cheered up the whole porch.

"This is wonderful. I love it out here, where we can see the water and hear the waves, without having to worry about bugs." Mary set down the water glasses she carried and took her seat.

Henry asked the blessing and scooped half the scallops onto her plate. "Here you go. Enjoy."

The first bite was so tender and succulent that she closed her eyes. "*Mmm.* These are *so* good."

"Thank you." Henry smiled and helped himself to a yeast roll.

"You're one of the few men I know who can make the whole meal turn out ready at the same time," she said.

"Well, I only cooked one thing," he noted with a laugh.

They ate and watched the water turn from silvery to mysterious gray and black as the light faded. Mary loved the peaceful spot. Henry and Misty had chosen well when they bought the house years ago. Though the next neighbor was not far away, their position away from the road, between the water and a patch of pinewoods, guaranteed privacy.

"You know I love my old car," Henry said, leaning back in his chair.

"Of course." She gave him her full attention.

"It's served me well for a long time, but, Mary, this new one—it's great! Dan owned it for three or four years, and he babied that thing. Restored it to near-mint condition."

"Dan is the former owner?"

"Yes. He's in the antique auto club. I've known him a few years, since before he got the Buick. He's fanatical about the work he does on old cars."

Mary could see Henry's enthusiasm in his animated face. "I guess he knows you'll take good care of it."

"Sure I will."

"Are you going to keep the Bel Air?" she asked.

"Oh ·yeah. I won't want to drive the Buick everywhere. I might keep it for Sunday best." He laughed. "On the other hand, I just spent a pile of money on a car, and I should drive it, right?"

"Yes," Mary said, "but I'm probably not the best person to give advice, since I'm not up on how quickly antique cars depreciate from everyday use."

"Condition is everything. But if you can't enjoy it, what's the point? That's what I say."

"I think you're right. No point in keeping it in the garage all the time."

"I was kind of surprised when I saw what Dan was offering at the show today. I didn't think he'd want to part with this one, but he told me—" Henry broke off and cocked his head toward the kitchen. "Did you hear that?"

"What?" Mary asked.

She heard a sound then, over the gentle surf. It wasn't loud, but the thump sounded as though it came from beyond the kitchen.

"Stay here." Henry rose and strode inside.

Mary heard him open the door to the garage and then call, "Hey!" Muffled sounds followed, and then a *thwack*.

She shoved back her chair and ran through the kitchen, her adrenaline pumping and lending her speed. The door stood halfway open, and she pushed it wider and looked into the garage. The small main door stood wide open onto the driveway, and she thought she heard hastily retreating footsteps on the gravel. The garage light wasn't on, but in the dimness, she made out Henry's still form, lying beside the Buick on the concrete floor.

TWO

Ignoring her instincts, Mary leaped down the steps and ran past Henry to the open door. The footsteps had faded into the darkness, and a moment later, she heard a car engine start out near the road. A car's taillights appeared and faded into the distance, headed toward town. She fumbled for the light switch inside the garage door and ran back to Henry's side, noting that the passenger door of the Buick was open.

Kneeling on the garage floor, she touched his shoulder.

"Henry? Henry, can you hear me?"

He lay on his back, rolled a little on his right side. She caught her breath when she noticed the skin high on his left cheek was broken, and a bruise was forming beside his eye. His chest rose and fell, but each short, quick breath sent a pang to her heart. She took his wrist and looked at her watch so she could count his pulse. Her own heartbeat drummed in her ears, and she had to calm herself to distinguish Henry's rapid pulse. So far, so good. She bent over him and brushed back his silver hair, but the bruise reached to his hairline, and she couldn't tell where the discoloration ended.

"Oh, Henry!"

Her cell phone was in her pocket, and she shifted so she could pull it out. She had the local police dispatcher's number programmed into her contacts.

"What is your emergency?" came an efficient voice.

Quickly, she told the dispatcher Henry's situation. Since she was calling on her cell phone, she gave Henry's address.

"Please tell them to hurry."

"Yes, ma'am. Don't hang up. I'm dispatching EMTs now. I'd like you to stay on the line with me and give me a little more information. Do you know the patient's age?"

"Yes, he's sixty-three."

Mary sat down on the cold floor and held the phone to her ear with one hand, grasping Henry's hand with the other. In between answers to the dispatcher's questions, she prayed silently. Though the overhead fixture didn't give her as much light as she would have liked, she could see enough. She didn't like the color of Henry's face or the bruise that seemed to take on more color and grow larger as she watched.

The wait for the ambulance to arrive couldn't have been more than ten minutes, but it seemed to take forever. At last, Mary heard the distant wail of its siren, and soon, the vehicle rolled into the driveway, lights flashing, and parked behind her Impala.

She stood and hurried out to meet the two uniformed EMTs, a man and a woman, on the driveway.

"He's in there, on the floor. I think someone struck him on the temple."

They strode past her, carrying bags of equipment. Mary stood in the doorway, clutching her phone and trying to stay calm. She noticed a wad of paper on the floor and stooped to pick it up. When she had smoothed it out, she saw that it was a program from the Ivy Bay Wheelers' antique auto show. Henry must have dropped it. She idly shoved it into her pocket.

After a couple of minutes, the female EMT went out to the ambulance and opened the back. Mary followed her.

"Can you tell me anything?" Mary asked.

"We'll take him right in to the hospital. Did you see what happened?"

"No. I was on the porch."

"Could he have fallen on the steps?"

"I don't think so, though I suppose it's possible. Henry yelled at someone. I heard a noise, and when I got to the door, I heard someone run away, and then a car started. I didn't see the other person, but I know someone was out here."

The EMT nodded. "Okay."

"Is he going to be all right?"

"We're stabilizing him now for transport. Are you his wife?"

"No, a friend. He's widowed."

"Good thing you were here. But you can't ride with us."

"I'll take my car," Mary said.

"Does he have family nearby?"

"No nearer than Boston, I'm afraid."

"Can you check him in? Give the information they'll need at the hospital?"

Mary nodded. "I'll call his daughters too."

"That would be good. Thanks."

The EMT pulled a wheeled stretcher from the back of the ambulance and took it to the garage. The technicians loaded Henry and secured him to the stretcher, then wheeled it out.

The male EMT was talking on his radio, giving the hospital data as they worked. Mary gathered they would start an IV drip on the way. She caught the words *possible skull fracture* and gritted her teeth.

Dear Lord, watch over them! Give the EMTs wisdom in caring for him. Her chest ached at her utter helplessness.

A police car drove up and parked at the end of the driveway, leaving the ambulance room to drive out. Officer Tilton got out of the squad car. Mary was glad someone she knew had arrived, and she hurried to meet him.

"Hello, Mrs. Fisher. What happened?" Officer Tilton asked.

"It's Henry Woodrow. I think someone assaulted him in the garage. I was on the back porch, and I didn't see it." She looked over her shoulder. One EMT was climbing into the driver's seat of the ambulance. "I'm going to the hospital. Can you come there if you need more information from me?"

"Sure. You go. And don't worry—we'll secure the house before we leave."

Mary pulled her keys from her pants pocket. "Thank you." She walked past the ambulance as it began to roll and got into her car.

The drive to the hospital seemed both fleeting and eternal. She found to her dismay that tears streamed down her cheeks. With shaking fingers, she pulled a tissue from the leather holder on the visor and mopped the worst of them away. She had to blink several times to clear her vision as she followed the ambulance.

She pulled into the hospital lot right behind the unit, but had to park in the visitors' section. By the time she walked to the emergency entrance, the EMTs and Henry had already disappeared through the special entrance for ambulance crews and their patients.

Inside, she approached the clerk's window and explained that she had just come in with the emergency patient. The clerk asked her to sit down and provide her with some information about Henry. Because Mary wasn't a relative, she couldn't sign the forms.

"I'll call his daughter Kim right away," Mary said. Kim lived closest and could probably come quicker. "She'll probably come tonight or first thing in the morning."

"I'll have her sign these when she gets here then." The clerk directed Mary to the waiting area. "The doctor will examine him right away, and someone will come for you when he's finished."

Mary went into the hall just outside and called Betty first. Her sister's phone was apparently turned off, and Mary remembered her auction date with Eleanor. She left a message. "Bets, I'm at the hospital. Henry's been injured. Please call me as soon as you get this."

She was crying again, and she went into the ladies' room and washed her face before stepping up to a wall-mounted phone in the hallway. She opened the fat Boston directory and found a number for Gregory and Kimberly Allen. Kim was one of Henry's twin daughters. She was geographically closest, and Mary was sure she could count on her to inform her sister Karen. She punched the number into her cell phone, saved it, and then pushed Send.

When Kim answered, Mary said, "Kim, it's Mary Fisher. I'm afraid your father's been injured, dear. I'm at the Ivy Bay Hospital now, waiting to hear what the doctor has to say."

"Oh my goodness! What happened? Is he going to be okay?"

Mary told her everything she knew.

"Wow." Kim blew out a deep breath filled with worry. "I'll come tonight, but I'll have to talk to Greg and see if his folks can take the boys."

"Will you call Karen and tell her?" Mary asked.

"Of course. And let me give you my cell phone number."

Mary had barely signed off with Kim when her phone rang, and the display said Betty.

"Hi, Bets."

"Is he going to be okay?" Betty asked without preamble.

"I don't know yet. I'm in the emergency waiting room—well, in the hall outside—and they haven't told me anything yet. We've only been here a few minutes."

"What happened?"

"Someone hit him on the head." Mary realized how bizarre that must sound and sucked in a deep breath. "We were eating supper, and we heard a noise. Henry went to see what it was, and the next thing I know, he's out cold, lying on the floor in the garage."

"Are you sure he didn't just fall and hit his head?" Betty asked.

"I'm sure."

"I'll be there in half an hour," Betty said.

"Oh no, you're with Eleanor." Mary glanced at her watch. It was after eight o'clock, but she knew the auction would probably go on for some time.

"Sweetie, Henry is much more important than this event. Did you call Kim?"

"Yes. She's driving down tonight, but it may be a while before she gets here."

"Well, you just sit tight, and I'll be there soon." Betty's tone forbade arguing, so Mary relented.

"Thanks. A lot." Her voice broke, and she dabbed at the fresh tears flowing down her cheeks.

"I'll be praying," Betty said gently. "See you real soon."

Betty closed the connection, and Mary drew in a ragged breath. She needed to get hold of herself, so that she could help Henry. She wasn't sure yet how she could do that, but whatever opportunity presented itself, she had to be ready.

After taking several deep, slow breaths, she walked into the waiting room. She found a seat among fifteen or so other people. Some were waiting to see a doctor, but most seemed to be relatives waiting for news. She picked up a magazine and flipped through it, not seeing the pages. Across the room, a television mounted near the ceiling was tuned to a reality show that had contestants performing outrageous stunts. Mary leaned back and closed her eyes, praying silently.

Sometime later—the program had changed to a police drama—a nurse came out of the emergency room and said, "Henry Woodrow's companion."

Mary jumped up, wondering what people would think that meant, but only for an instant. She didn't care, really.

The nurse ushered her inside the trauma area and spoke calmly. "You're Henry's neighbor?"

"His friend. I'm Mary Fisher."

"And his family isn't here?"

"His daughter is coming, but it will be a couple of hours, I'm assuming. I told her I'd call again if I had any news."

The nurse nodded. "We're sending him over to the Imaging Department for a CT scan, Mrs. Fisher. If you want to walk over there, you'll find a smaller waiting room that's more private. I'll tell the receptionist in Imaging to look after you."

"Thank you so much," Mary said.

The nurse smiled and nodded. "We're moving him now, and the scan won't take long—maybe twenty minutes in all. Just tell them at the desk that you're with him."

"Is he awake?" Mary asked.

"Not yet."

Mary followed the nurse's directions down the hall, around a corner, and down another long passageway. At last, she came to an opening on the left with a sign that read Imaging hanging over the lintel. She stopped at the desk to identify herself and then sat down in the cozy waiting room. It was much nicer than the ER waiting room, mostly because it was smaller, and only two other people waited there. An older man sat staring blankly at the wall opposite him, and a middle-aged woman sat serenely reading a novel. Mary couldn't help noticing that it was a cozy mystery.

She texted Betty to tell her she had changed her location.

"Thanks. Just parked," Betty replied a few seconds later.

Mary leaned her head back and closed her eyes. Memories flooded her mind of the time when she had lost her husband, John. That same helpless feeling had come over her then— the need to do something constructive, something that would make a difference. To calm herself, she repeated one of the many Scripture verses she had memorized over the years: "Keep me as the apple of Your eye; hide me in the shadow of Your wings" (Psalm 17:8). Then she changed it to a silent prayer, placing Henry's name where the *me's* had been. *Keep Henry as the apple of Your eye, Lord. Hide him in the shadow of Your wings.*

When her sister arrived a few minutes later, Mary flew into her arms. "Thank you so much for coming!"

Betty hugged her close. "Was it awful, being alone with him until the ambulance came?"

Mary nodded. "I don't want to go through anything like that again."

"Any word yet?"

"Not really."

Betty sat down with her in padded chairs in the corner. The man was called in for his exam, and the woman who had been reading had left. For a while, the two of them were alone.

Mary told Betty everything she could remember. She touched her fingertips to her temple. "The bruise is here, all purple and blue."

"Let's pray while it's quiet in here." Betty reached for Mary's hands and prayed softly, fervently for Henry's recovery. "And thank You, Lord, that Mary was there when it happened, so that Henry wasn't alone with no one to call for help."

Mary shuddered at the thought that if she hadn't gone for dinner, or if the intruder had come after she'd left, Henry might still be lying there now—all night, even.

"Thank You," she whispered.

Betty patted her arm. "I called Pastor Miles on the way over. I hope you don't mind. Tricia said he was counseling tonight, but he'll come in a little while."

Mary nodded. The door to the inner chambers of the imaging department opened, and a woman in blue scrubs came out.

"Mrs. Fisher?" She looked at them expectantly.

"Yes." Mary rose and walked toward her.

"We're finished with Henry, and they're taking him up to the ICU. The doctor will be up there in a few minutes. You can go up, if you like, but it will take them a little while to get him settled."

"Can you tell us anything about his condition?" Mary asked. Betty stepped up beside her and slipped an arm around her.

"Dr. Brady should be there soon, and I'm sure he'll update you. Second floor. Turn left off the elevator, and you'll see the sign for ICU."

They went up the elevator together and found the Intensive Care Unit easily enough. Mary spoke to the woman at the nurses' station, who guided them to a small waiting room and promised to tell the doctor they were there.

This waiting room was less stark than the others, with walls the color of terra cotta and pristine white woodwork. Two watercolor seascapes hung on the walls, and Mary recognized them as the work of a well-known Cape Cod artist. A small table held a coffeemaker and cups, and the hospital had also provided a water cooler, a snack vending machine, an array of magazines, and a television with a DVD player and a selection of movies.

Betty fixed each of them a cup of coffee, and they sat talking quietly for about ten minutes. A dark-haired man of about forty, wearing scrubs and a stethoscope, appeared in the doorway. He glanced at the clipboard in his hand.

"Hello, ladies. You're here with Henry Woodrow?"

"Yes." Mary stood as he walked closer.

"I'm Dr. Brady, and I'm on call in the ER tonight. We've had a look at Henry's wound. It's not pretty, but there doesn't seem to be any fracture."

Mary exhaled deeply. "Thank God."

"Yes. Unfortunately, there is a serious concussion, and he's got a lot of blood pooling on the left side."

"I noticed the bruising," Mary said.

Dr. Brady nodded. "It's more serious than a regular bruise. Unfortunately, he's remained unconscious. I understand you were there when it happened?"

"Yes—well, I was on the back porch, and Henry went out to the garage."

"He wasn't conscious when you found him?"

"No. People asked me if he could have just fallen on the steps, but I heard him yell and then someone running away."

Dr. Brady frowned. "He did hit his head on something— on the back of the skull, that is. He has a bump there. But there's also the wound on his temple. Was he lying on steps?"

Mary shook her head. "He was down on the floor, lying on his back. It's concrete. I did look at the steps, but his head was a foot or so away from them, and I didn't see any blood or anything like that."

"It had to be two impacts," the doctor said. "I'd say the one on the back of his head was from when he hit the floor. The other...well, we don't know, do we? I guess it's up to the police to look into that. Anyway, I've admitted Mr. Woodrow to the ICU because of the head injuries. We like to do constant monitoring on a case like this. You can go in and see him, but we limit visitors."

"His daughter and his pastor are on their way." Mary glanced at Betty. "This is my sister."

"Let's have one person at a time in the room with him for now." Dr. Brady made a note on the chart. "His personal-care physician will take over his treatment first thing in the morning."

"You do think Henry will wake up, don't you?" Mary studied the doctor's face for any clues that would offer her hope.

"Oh yes, but it may not be for some time. He could stay in a coma for a while—several days, even—or he could slip into natural sleep. But I do expect him to recover. Of course, we can't see everything that's going on inside, but the indications are good. Now, when you go into his room, you'll see several apparatuses hooked to him. That's so we can monitor several vital signs—heart rate, blood pressure, blood oxygen, and so on. He's getting fluids too, and we'll administer his medications intravenously. The nurses will also go into the room at least every fifteen minutes. We find that it's not always enough to have machines telling you the basics. It's important for a trained person to observe the patient often. Sometimes, small changes aren't picked up by the machinery."

Mary nodded soberly, still trying to get past the word *coma* and take in all he had said.

"Any questions?" Dr. Brady asked.

"I feel better knowing what you're doing for him, and that there's no skull fracture. But he's not out of danger, is he?"

Dr. Brady touched her shoulder gently. "Every head injury is serious. There's always danger of permanent brain damage, or of clots. Residual effects can include loss of memory, loss of motor skills—lots of things. But let's not borrow trouble. When he wakes up, we'll see how he's doing."

"You're sure he will wake up then." She realized he had answered that question, but this was her biggest fear—that Henry had left them and would never regain consciousness.

"I've seen a lot of head injuries, and as I said, the unexpected can happen. But yes, I do think he'll wake up. Meanwhile, we'll do everything we can to make sure there's no further damage."

"Thank you," Mary whispered.

Dr. Brady smiled. "You can go in anytime—one at a time."

"Should we talk to him?" Betty asked.

"It can't hurt. And I see his regular physician is Dr. Teagarden. He'll be in good hands."

Mary nodded, knowing that was true.

Dr. Brady left them, and Betty put her arm around Mary. "Are you all right?"

Mary nodded. "I want to go in and see him."

"Of course. I'll be right here, praying. Stay in there as long as you like."

The nurse drew back a curtain on the front of Henry's room, so that his bed was visible from the nurses' station, through the glass wall. At least three other patients' rooms were situated around the unit, but Henry's was closest to the desk. Mary didn't know if that was because his injury was most critical or because he was their only current patient. Perhaps it was simply the only vacant room when he arrived.

She managed a wobbly smile to the woman at the desk, who nodded and said, "Go right in, and tell us if you need anything."

The nurse was still in the room when Mary entered. She smiled and said, "Hello. We only have one seat in here because Dr. Brady limited the visitors, but you can stay in here as long as you like. I'm Rhonda, and I'll be Henry's nurse until eleven o'clock."

"Thank you. I'm Mary. I'm his friend, and his daughter will be coming in later, as well as his pastor."

"There's a call button right here." Rhonda showed her the device on the rail of Henry's bed. "You can push that if you need me, or just go to the door and speak to whoever's on the desk."

Mary approached the bed. Henry's muscular form looked odd, lying so still, and his tanned face seemed pale. The bruise on the left side of his face had darkened even more since she'd last seen him. His breathing, though, had a more natural rhythm now than it had an hour ago, in the dim garage. She sank onto the stool Rhonda had provided and reached for his hand. It was warm, but Henry didn't respond to her touch. She cradled her fingers around his hand and leaned toward him.

"Henry, I'm here. I'm so sorry this happened to you." She wished his eyes would flutter open and he'd give her the slightly crooked smile she loved. Henry was always active, always eager to do something, to have an adventure. Who had taken that from him?

"I hope you're resting," she said softly. "But when you wake up, I hope you can tell us who did this to you."

"Mary?"

She looked up. Betty stood in the doorway, frowning slightly.

"There's a police officer here. He'd like to speak to you."

THREE

---◆◆◆---

Mary walked out to meet the police officer near the nurses' station. The man in uniform was one she had seen a few times but didn't know personally. He looked young—early twenties, she guessed, with sandy hair, freckles, and blue eyes. He towered over Mary's five-foot-one stature, being almost as tall as Henry.

"Mrs. Fisher?"

She nodded.

"I'm Officer Reed. I'm here to take your statement about the assault on Bayshore Road."

"Certainly. Won't you come sit down?" Mary gestured toward the waiting room.

"If you'll excuse me, I'll just go in and sit with Henry while you're doing that," Betty said softly.

"Thank you." Mary squeezed her sister's hand and then led the officer to the waiting area.

"Tell me what happened to Mr. Woodrow," Officer Reed said when they were settled.

"We were eating dinner on the screened porch." Mary clapped a hand to her mouth. "Oh, the food! I should go back and clean up the kitchen."

"Don't worry about that right now, Mrs. Fisher. An officer is still at the house. If you want to go back later, I'm sure it will be all right."

She nodded. "I'm sorry. It's just been so...so unnerving."

"How was Mr. Woodrow hurt?"

"We were sitting out on the porch, and Henry heard something. We both listened, and then I heard it too. A noise that seemed to be coming from the garage—somewhere beyond the kitchen, anyway. Henry told me to stay, and he went in through the kitchen and opened the garage door. I heard him yell, and that scared me a little."

"What did he say?"

"I don't know. 'Hey, you,' or something like that."

"Did he sound alarmed?"

"Yes, I'd say so. It wasn't as if someone he knew was out there."

"Could it have been an animal?"

"I don't see how. We'd been in the garage before dinner. Henry was showing me the new car he'd bought today at the antique auto show—the 1955 Buick, that is. And the overhead doors and the smaller door were closed then. But after I heard him yell, I looked out there, and the smaller door was open."

"The main door that goes from the garage to outside?"

"Yes. And Henry was lying on the floor, unconscious." She caught her breath. "Dr. Brady said—"

"Yes, I spoke to the doctor in the ER just now. Did you see anyone else?"

"No, but I heard footsteps."

"Can you describe them?"

Mary nodded. "It sounded like someone outside was running away."

"You're sure no one else went into the house?"

"Pretty sure."

"All right. I'll ask the officers on the scene to search inside, just in case." Officer Reed wrote steadily in his notebook for several seconds. "Did you see or hear anything else?" he asked.

"A car. I went outside, just for a second. I hoped I could see the person who was running, but he had a head start on me. Then I heard an engine start, up near the road. I think he must have parked up there. If your men check—"

"Oh, we will. Now, Mrs. Fisher, I'll need your address, in case we need to speak to you again."

"Of course, though Chief McArthur knows me well."

"Chief McArthur is out of town."

"Oh?" Mary didn't like that—not with Henry having been struck down by some prowler. Chief McArthur was good at crime solving, and she would have felt better if he'd been on the job tonight.

"Yes," Officer Reed said. "It's my understanding he's put off this vacation for a long time, and he's finally taking it."

"That sounds like him. I'm sure it's much deserved." Still, Mary felt uneasy. This was a bad time for the chief to be out of town. "So, who's in charge over at the police station while he's gone?"

She thought she saw a flicker of something—distaste?—before the patrolman resumed his neutral expression. "Oh, the state police are taking care of us, ma'am. They've sent a man out as a replacement, and he'll be here another two weeks. Chief McIntosh."

"Oh. That's good, I guess." She eyed him carefully, but didn't see any reaction to her comment.

"So, do you have any idea who may have done this?" he asked.

"No. It seemed odd that a burglar would break in while there were people in the house."

"Do you think he actually broke in then?"

"I suppose not," Mary said. "The garage door probably wasn't locked, though I can't be certain. Henry and I planned to go for a ride after supper, and I don't think he had locked up."

Officer Reed wrote in his notebook.

"I did notice that the passenger door of the car was open," Mary added, remembering how that fact had stood out to her, as though she were looking at a "What Is Wrong with This Picture?" activity.

"Yes, we saw that. Can you tell me anything about the person Mr. Woodrow bought this antique car from?"

"Not much, I'm afraid. His name was Dan. Henry mentioned that he's known him a while through the antique-car club. That's the Ivy Bay Wheelers. They're sponsoring the show this weekend, and that's where Henry bought the car."

"Do you know Dan's last name?"

"Sorry, I don't."

"Well, he should be easy enough to find. Is there anything else you remember, or anything you think might be important?"

"I can't think of anything." Only Henry's ashen face with the frightening bruise filled her mind.

Officer Reed smiled and put his notebook away. "All right then. We'll do everything we can to find out what happened. Thank you very much, and if you think of anything else, do let us know."

"I will."

The officer left the ICU, and Mary exhaled deeply. She wished they had a strong lead and could assure her that Henry's assailant would be caught. Knowing that their only clues were those she provided disheartened her. There ought to be something more.

She walked out of the waiting room, to the glass wall, and gazed into Henry's room. Betty saw her and came out to join her.

"He looks ghostly pale for Henry, doesn't he?"

Mary nodded, her throat tightening. "It's awful to see someone so fit looking so vulnerable."

Betty put her hand on Mary's shoulder.

The door from the outer hallway opened, and Pastor Miles walked in. Mary turned to greet him with a rush of relief. Here was a reminder that God was in control, and that when all was done, good would prevail.

"Mary, Betty." The pastor grasped both their hands. "I'm so sorry about Henry. How is he?"

"No change since I spoke to you," Betty said.

"He's hooked up to everything short of a lie detector," Mary said. "This is his room."

Pastor Miles peered through the glass. "Oh my. So sad. May I go in?"

"Go ahead," Mary said. "We'll wait here."

She and Betty watched Pastor Miles go in and sit on the stool next to the bedside. His lips moved as he patted Henry's hand.

The young woman at the desk was watching them, so Mary went over and smiled at her. "That's Pastor Miles who just went in. He's Henry's pastor."

The woman nodded. "Thank you. I've met Pastor Miles. He comes in here often."

Mary went back to stand beside Betty, joining her silent prayers with the pastor's.

After a few minutes, he came out, his face sober. "Let's find a place where we can talk and pray together."

"Right over here," Betty said.

They went into the waiting room and sat down. Mary told her story again and barely managed not to cry.

"I'm so sorry you had to go through that," Pastor Miles said. "It sounds as if you did all the right things, though."

"I tried, but there wasn't much I could do." Mary reached for Betty's hand.

The pastor prayed with them, and Mary began to feel almost normal again, though a dull ache persisted near her heart.

"If you don't mind, I'll go back into Henry's room," she said.

"Of course." The pastor patted her hand. "I'll stay a little while, until the family gets here."

"You go right ahead in, Mar," Betty said. "Pastor Miles and I will be fine."

Mary had only been at Henry's side a few minutes when Rhonda, the nurse, came in. She observed Henry carefully and checked all his monitors.

"Anything new?" Mary asked.

"He's stable," the nurse said. "That's a good thing, but there's no change in his condition. These things take time."

While the nurse made notes on the chart, Mary looked up and saw three people on the other side of the glass: Betty, Pastor Miles, and Kim Allen.

She jumped up and said to the nurse, "Henry's daughter is here. I'll go out now and let her come in to see him. She'll want to hear about his condition from you, I'm sure."

She went into the hallway, and Kim gave her a hug.

"Mary, thank you so much for helping Dad. I'm sorry you were in the middle of it, though. You could have been hurt."

"I'm glad I was with him," Mary said. "You go in and see him. Stay as long as you like."

Mary, Betty, and the pastor retreated to the waiting area. About fifteen minutes later, Kim came out, her face streaked with tears.

"The on-call doctor just examined Dad," she said. "He's going off duty, and someone else will be available for the rest of the night. There's nothing new, and he says rest is the best thing for Dad. I want to stay with him, and they're going to put a recliner in there for me."

"Oh, good," Betty said. "I think I'll head on home now that you're here, Kim."

"I'll go home too," Pastor Miles said. "Let's pray first, shall we?"

Kim sat down on the sofa next to Betty. "Thank you—and pray for Karen too. She has booked a flight, and she'll be here tomorrow. She's awfully anxious. I'll call her before I go back into Dad's room, just to reassure her that he's stable and the doctors think he'll make a complete recovery."

After they prayed, the pastor and Betty took their leave.

"I probably should go too," Mary said to Kim. She looked around for a moment, feeling suddenly at a loss. "You know, I think I've left my purse at your father's house. Either that or in my car, but..." She racked her brains for a moment, trying to remember those last minutes at the house with the EMTs working on Henry and Officer Tilton questioning her. "No, I don't think I had it when I left to come here. My keys were in my pocket, and I didn't go back into the house. Do you mind if I go and get it?"

"You go ahead," Kim said. "I'll be right here."

Mary squeezed her hand. "Call me if you need anything. I'll come back in the morning."

She drove through the quiet streets of Ivy Bay and onto Bayshore Road to Henry's house. As she approached, the solitude of the location, beautiful as it was, sent a shiver of uneasiness over her. To her relief, she saw a patrol car still parked at the end of the driveway, and she pulled in near it. Officer Tilton left the car and walked over to her as she got out of her Impala.

"Mrs. Fisher."

"Hello, Officer Tilton. I realized I'd left my purse here earlier, and I'd like to go in and get it." *And to clean up after dinner*, Mary thought.

"Of course. How's Henry?"

"The same," Mary said as they walked toward the garage. "His daughter Kim is with him now. The doctor thinks he'll recover, but he hasn't regained consciousness yet."

"Concussion?" Tilton asked.

"Yes. No fracture, thank the Lord." Mary paused near the smaller door. "Is this still unlocked?"

"Yes. We searched the garage and the two cars. I believe you indicated the intruder didn't get into the house?"

"Not as far as I know."

He nodded. "Officer Reed said as much, but we did a quick search inside, just to be sure no one was in there. When you pulled up just now, I was sitting in the car making my report, and I thought I'd lock up just before I left."

"I'll go in this way then." Mary knew where Henry kept his extra house key—it was very cleverly hidden, she thought—but she saw no need to reveal that to Officer Tilton. "I'll only be a minute."

He went into the garage with her and turned on the overhead light. Mary noticed that someone had shut the door of the Buick. She went into the kitchen and found her purse in a corner of the counter, where she had left it. Nearby were a few papers, and she bent over them.

The top one was an official-looking document. She hadn't seen it earlier, but now it caught her eye, and she picked it up. It was the title to the Buick Century. Daniel York had signed it over to Henry that day. She made a mental note of the previous owner's address—Jonquil Lane was part of a neighborhood on the outskirts of Ivy Bay. The houses were very nice, but not palatial, and they didn't have a water view.

Under the title was a program from the antique auto show. She frowned and took the one she had found in the garage from her pocket. It was wrinkled and dirty, but the one on the counter was in perfect condition, which she would expect of Henry. Why would he have two programs? She examined the crumpled one carefully, but found no writing or markings on it. Still, it was odd enough to make her decide she should give it to Officer Tilton.

She bustled around the kitchen and screened porch to put the leftover food away. They had eaten most of the main course, and their dessert was going to be ice cream from Bailey's, so there wasn't much to do. She slid the dishes into the dishwasher, turned it on, and went out through the garage.

Tilton was standing in the driveway, gazing out at the moonlit bay. "Pretty here," he said as she approached.

"Yes. Shall I turn out the garage light?"

"I'll get it."

"I wanted to show you this." Mary held out the wrinkled program. "I found it in the garage earlier, but I assumed Henry had dropped it there, so I didn't mention it."

"What is it?" Tilton held it toward the light, so he could read it.

"It's the program from the car show, and it lists all the exhibitors. I didn't think anything of it until just now, but I saw that Henry has another one on the kitchen counter. What if he didn't drop this one?"

The policeman nodded slowly. "You think the intruder dropped it?"

"It's possible, isn't it? In which case, that person had something to do with the car show." Mary hesitated. "Officer Tilton, what do you think that burglar was after?"

"We're not sure. It did seem highly coincidental that he came just hours after Mr. Woodrow bought that antique car, and this could be a definite tie-in. Could be he was trying to steal the car."

Mary thought about that. "Really? I mean, we were right here in the house, and the lights were on. Wouldn't a car thief wait until there was no one around, or at least until Henry was asleep?"

Officer Tilton shrugged. "We don't know that he dropped this, and you can't often get fingerprints from paper. It could have nothing to do with the prowler. This whole thing could have been a random job—maybe some drug addict looking for cash or something he could sell quickly. Your car hadn't been tampered with, had it?"

"No, I don't think so," Mary said. "I keep change in the ashtray, and that's still there. I didn't lock up when I was here, but I don't keep much of value in my car either."

"We'll look into it; don't worry. Tomorrow we'll be talking to the car-show people and the fellow who sold the car."

"You haven't talked to Daniel York yet?" It seemed to her that the person who sold Henry the car would be one of the first they'd talk to, so they could ask if he had any contact with Henry later in the day, or if he knew anyone else intensely interested in the car.

"I believe Chief McIntosh sent someone around to his address, but he wasn't home. We'll talk to him tomorrow, though. I guess it's possible someone else wanted to buy the car from him, and Mr. Woodrow beat him to it. If the other customer wanted it badly enough, he could have come here to take it, though it's an awfully large item to steal and hide. But don't you worry, Mrs. Fisher. We'll find out what happened."

Mary left him with thoughts whirling through her mind. She glanced at her watch. It was after ten o'clock, far too late to drive to Jonquil Lane and see if Mr. York was home. *Tomorrow*, she thought. It couldn't hurt for her to talk to him herself.

She wondered if the acting chief would handle the case as well as Chief McArthur would have. This was Henry! He deserved the best. He and Chief McArthur knew each other well, and if he was here, Chief McArthur would make sure every lead was followed until they got to the bottom of this and arrested the person who attacked Henry. She wasn't so sure about Chief McIntosh. Maybe when she met the man, she would feel more confidence in him.

She drove home. The lights were out except for a small one in the kitchen. When she let herself in, Gus appeared in the living room doorway, stretching.

"Hi, buddy." Mary bent to fluff his gray fur. "Are you taking care of Betty?"

She tiptoed up to her room, and Gus followed her. As she prepared for bed, Mary realized her heart was back at the hospital. But it was right for Kim to be at Henry's side now. His daughters would have first priority in the ICU. Mary wondered if she could do something for Henry in a different way. The police hadn't located Daniel York. Mary could follow up on that. Maybe she could catch him at his house in the morning.

The Buick was the only link she had between Henry and his assailant, she reasoned. The intruder seemed to have some interest in the car. But she had no clues to lead her to the person who had hurt Henry. The car's former owner was the only path she could see to follow. Tomorrow, if she hadn't heard anything positive from the police, she would go and see Daniel York.

That thought set her more at ease, as it meant she could *do* something. She drifted off to sleep with Gus purring beside her and prayers for Henry cycling in her mind.

FOUR

The morning newspaper carried a front-page story, with photos, about the antique auto show. Mary read it during breakfast on Saturday morning. There was no article about the intruder at Henry's house, for which she was glad. She was sure that Henry wouldn't appreciate having his misfortune spread all over the front page.

On page 4, however, there was a brief entry toward the end of the police log column: *7:10 PM, assault on Bayshore Rd., officers responded.* That was all, and Mary stared at it bleakly. She supposed the item was accurate. As far as she knew, there had been no theft, and the garage wasn't officially broken into, since the door was probably unlocked. What else could the police charge the intruder with? Trespassing, maybe.

She sighed, passed the front section across the table to Betty, and took a sip of her tea. The second section of the *Bugle* lay on the chair next to her, and Gus sprawled on top of it. She hated to disturb him. She almost let him be, but he stood, arched his back, and hopped to the floor.

"Why, thank you. So glad you're finished with it." Mary picked up the section and unfolded it. "Oh, look. There's a picture from the auction you went to last night."

Betty looked up from her reading. "Let me guess who's in it."

"You think you know?"

"Eleanor?"

Mary chuckled. "No, and not you either."

"That's a relief."

Mary was surprised Eleanor, who had helped organize the auction, hadn't found a way to get her picture in there somehow, but she didn't voice the thought.

"Who is it?" Betty asked.

"A Mr. and Mrs. Erick Saxon."

Betty's brow wrinkled. "Do I know them? Let me see."

Mary passed her the paper, and Betty studied the photo. "I remember seeing her. She bought a painting last night—an expensive one. But I don't think I noticed that man with her. Of course, I left early."

"Yes, I'm sorry about that."

"Don't be." Betty squinted at the print. "Her husband. Huh." She laid the section aside. "Are you going to the hospital this morning?"

"Yes, but I'll drop by the shop first, and I have an errand to run." She glanced at the clock. It was after eight. Surely it wasn't too early to call at Mr. York's address.

Betty picked up her tea mug. "Well, I'm going to putter around in the garden this morning, but I'll keep my phone with me."

Mary gathered her things and put Gus in his carrier. She was glad Betty felt well these days. Sometimes her rheumatoid arthritis kept her from the activities she loved, but she hadn't had a bad day for nearly two weeks.

She drove to the address on Jonquil Lane first. The house had a well-kept yard and looked a little more high-end than she had expected. The garage door was down, so she couldn't tell if there was a car inside. She walked to the front door and rang the bell.

The woman who opened the door wore a pink silk robe with wine-colored trim. She looked about forty-five or fifty, and seemed slightly familiar. Her blonde hair hung limply about her shoulders, and the dark shadows beneath her eyes told Mary she hadn't yet applied her makeup. Maybe eight o'clock *was* too early to call on a Saturday.

"I'm sorry to bother you," Mary began. "I was hoping to speak to Daniel York."

The woman frowned. "Daniel hasn't lived here for the last six months."

"Oh, I'm so sorry." Mary took a step back. "Please forgive me. A mutual friend has been injured, and I wanted to tell him."

The woman's shoulders sagged. "He's my ex-husband. Who's the friend, if I may ask? It might be someone I know."

"Henry Woodrow." At her blank look, Mary added, "From the car club."

"Oh." The woman hesitated. "Dan does enjoy the club and working on his old cars. I guess I can give you his new address, if that will help you."

"Thank you very much."

As the woman opened the door wider for Mary to enter, she said, "I'm Dee Saxon."

"Mary Fisher. Nice to meet you."

"Just a minute and I'll get it for you."

Mary was standing in a very modern, well-appointed kitchen with glass-fronted walnut cabinets and a center island with a marble top. Copper pans hung from a rack overhead, and the window at the breakfast nook looked out on a spacious backyard.

The name Saxon wasn't lost on Mary. She wondered if Dee was the same woman whose picture had appeared in this morning's *Bugle*. She hadn't paid much attention to it, but from what she recalled, there seemed to be a resemblance. Of course, in the photo Mrs. Erick Saxon was dressed for a night out and had on her makeup. This woman looked older and less polished, but that was understandable, first thing in the morning.

Dee returned, holding out a sheet of memo paper. "Here you go."

"Thanks," Mary said, still feeling a little embarrassed for her blunder. "Sorry I bothered you so early. I'm sure Daniel will want to know about my friend's injury."

"No problem," Dee said. "Good-bye."

Mary went out, and the door closed firmly behind her. As she walked to her car, she read the address. It was an apartment unit in a large building constructed a couple of years ago on the edge of town—not a bad neighborhood, but still a large step down from this house. Dee had not included Dan's new phone number, and Mary hesitated, wishing she had asked. She decided not to go back.

She opened her car door, and movement across the street caught her eye. A woman with graying hair was standing in the yard opposite, holding a string trimmer and watching her. Mary smiled and called, "Good morning." The woman nodded soberly.

Mary got into the car and backed into Jonquil Lane. So far, she seemed to be only annoying people this morning. She glanced at the dashboard clock. Plenty of time to swing by the apartment building before she went to the store. Gus meowed in his carrier.

"I know, Gus. You want to get out, don't you? Just a few more minutes."

Daniel York's apartment had an outside entrance, and she rang the bell, but no one came to the door. The large brick building had several setbacks, to give the renters more privacy. The lawn looked new, and the shrubs hadn't reached full growth. Mary rang the bell again but still got no response. Discouraged, she got back in the car and headed for the bookshop. It seemed there wasn't much she could do to help Henry, though she was willing to do anything for him.

At the bookshop, she settled down at the computer for a few minutes and reviewed the week's sales. Not bad. June was always a busy month at the bookshop. She checked her e-mail and was delighted to discover a message from her granddaughter Daisy, detailing her plans for the summer, which included a part-time job and a week at teen camp. Mary wrote back and told her a few snippets of news about herself, Gus, and Betty. Since Daisy had met Henry before, Mary told her that her friend had been injured, and she planned to go to the hospital to visit him that morning. She didn't tell her that Henry had probably been assaulted.

Rebecca and Ashley arrived a few minutes later. Ashley, as usual, was full of energy and eager to help. Mary let her set Gus free from his carrier. After telling Rebecca what had happened the previous evening and making sure she was all set to receive customers, Mary went on to the hospital.

At the glass wall of Henry's room, she waved to Kim, who rose and came out to the ICU waiting room to talk to her.

"Dad's about the same. His doctor was here a half hour ago, and he said I should be encouraged, but it's hard."

"I know." Mary put her arm around Kim and squeezed her. "A lot of people are praying for him."

"Thanks. The staff seems to be very diligent about monitoring him and making sure he's comfortable. I'm glad his personal physician came in to see him. Dad's gone to Dr. Teagarden for years, so he knows his history." Kim stifled a yawn. "Sorry. I confess I hardly slept at all. The good news is, Karen should be here this afternoon."

"Is anyone meeting her at the airport?" Mary asked.

"No. Greg offered, but Karen said it was just as easy for her to rent a car at Logan International Airport and drive down here herself. It's a big help, actually, since Greg will have the boys with him all day."

"You need some rest," Mary said. You're welcome to go to my house and sleep. I can call Betty and—"

She looked up as a man in a natty light-gray suit entered. He looked about her age, with silvery hair and brown eyes, and his mouth was set in what she interpreted as a scowl.

"Ladies," he said. "I'm Police Chief McIntosh. Is one of you Mrs. Fisher?"

"I am." Mary stepped forward. "And this is Kim Allen, Henry Woodrow's daughter."

"Ah, good. How is Mr. Woodrow this morning?"

"No better." Kim's eyes misted. "But no worse either. The doctor says he's holding his own, and he could wake up anytime."

Or not, Mary thought. She understood Kim's discouragement.

"I was wondering if it's all right for my sister and me to stay at my father's house," Kim said. "Are the police still investigating?"

"My men are finished out there," Chief McIntosh said. "You can stay there. I'd just caution you to be careful about locking up, even when you're there. We don't know yet why this fellow attacked your father. He probably had theft in mind, but who knows? He may have wanted to confront your father about something, in which case he could come back again."

"Oh dear," Kim said. "I can't imagine anyone being angry with Dad."

"How often do you see your father?" McIntosh asked.

Kim shrugged. "Once or twice a month. I brought my boys down to visit him for a few days when they got out of school, and Dad brought them home afterward and stayed over one night at my house."

"And to your knowledge, your father doesn't have any enemies?"

"Heavens, no."

"He's very well liked in the community," Mary said. "We're all stumped as to why anyone would do this to him."

Chief McIntosh nodded. "We don't have many leads yet, but don't think we're not doing anything. My men are out there questioning neighbors today, to see if anyone noticed anything last night."

Mary tried to ignore the way he termed the Ivy Bay officers "my men." "You can't see Henry's house very well from the road intentionally," she noted. "Still, the intruder didn't drive down the driveway. I'm sure he left his car up near the road. I heard the engine start afterward. I'm sure we would have heard it if he'd driven any closer when he arrived. Maybe someone noticed it parked on the side of the road last night."

"You were at the house when it happened."

Mary nodded. "We were eating dinner on the screened porch, and sound carries. Of course, we could hear the surf, but it was a quiet evening."

"Well, we're doing all we can," Chief McIntosh said. "I'm sure we'll catch the assailant sooner or later."

He seemed self-assured, Mary thought, and a little too smooth and self-important. She supposed he was trying to prove that he was competent, not just a stopgap substitute. If Chief McArthur were standing there, he'd probably tell her they would do their best, but realistically, if this was a random burglary attempt, they might never catch the intruder. That was Mary's opinion, anyway. But she was still banking on the possibility that it was not a random crime. If it had been random, they would have a much smaller chance of solving the mystery of who had attacked Henry.

She hesitated to say too much. After all, Chief McIntosh didn't know of her relationship with Chief McArthur and the way he tolerated her questions. Mary wasn't getting the impression that Chief McIntosh was open to suggestions from civilians, but she decided to ask one thing.

"Have your men talked to Daniel York?"

"York?" McIntosh's eyes narrowed.

"The man from whom Henry bought the car yesterday."

"Oh. I can't really discuss the case, Mrs. Fisher. Don't you fret about it, though. We'll do a thorough investigation."

She almost asked if they knew Daniel no longer lived on Jonquil Lane, but McIntosh's condescending attitude kept her quiet.

"I hope your father gets better soon," he said to Kim.

"Thank you. We all do."

The chief nodded. "One of my men will interview him when he regains consciousness. I just dropped by to check on his status and to assure you we're doing everything we can to solve this case quickly."

He left the ICU, and Mary exhaled. "Our regular police chief is on vacation. I sort of wish he wasn't."

"You don't like this one?" Kim asked.

"It's not that. But Chief McArthur knows your father well. I can't help feeling he would put his heart into it."

Kim's face wrinkled. "I agree. I know Chief McArthur, and I was hoping he'd be working on this. Chief McIntosh seems a little distant, but that's probably just because we don't know him."

"Maybe so," Mary said. "If you want to go to your dad's house and rest, I'd be happy to stay with him."

"Would you?" Kim turned toward Henry's room, and they walked together. "I hate to leave him, but I know it's foolish to go without sleep when he might be unconscious for days."

"I'll call you immediately if there's any change."

"I know you will." Kim hugged her. "I'll grab my bag and head out. Thanks, Mary."

Mary settled down in the recliner next to Henry's bed. The nurse came in and checked his vital signs, then left them alone. Mary took Henry's hand in hers and stroked it gently.

"I do so hope you're not in pain or having bad dreams," she said. "The doctor seems to think you'll come around soon. I hope he's right. I have a lot of things I'd like to discuss with you."

She talked to him intermittently for half an hour, telling him about mundane happenings at home and at the bookshop. She watched his face carefully when she spoke of Ashley's excitement that morning. The little girl had brought a felt mouse she had made and stuffed with catnip for Gus. Mary knew that Henry would laugh about it if he understood, but his placid features didn't flicker. Mary patted his hand and swallowed back the lump in her throat.

Betty arrived a while later. She stayed only a few minutes, and she and Mary prayed together for Henry's swift recovery.

"You didn't eat much this morning," Betty said, handing her a bottle of iced tea and a small bag.

Mary recognized the yellow bag as one from Sweet Susan's Bakery. She opened it and peered in to see a golden-brown scone flecked with cranberries.

"Oh, thanks. That looks delicious."

Betty smiled. "Susan sends her love for you and prayers for Henry."

Shortly after her sister left, Mary looked up to see Dorothy Johnson's stricken face as she stared in through the glass wall. Mary rose and went to the doorway.

"I just heard about Henry," Dorothy said, tears in her eyes. "This is terrible!"

"Yes." Mary gave her a quick hug. She knew Dorothy had special feelings for Henry, though Henry had never shown any sign of returning them.

"The nurse said only one visitor at a time. Can I go in?" Dorothy's voice trembled.

"Of course. I'm staying until Kim comes back or her sister gets here, but—"

"I could stay with him," Dorothy said. "You must have work to do."

"No, I'm staying here," Mary said. "I told Kim I would, and Rebecca's running the bookshop." Dorothy's face fell. "But you go in for a little while." Mary took her arm and swung her toward the doorway.

Dorothy walked in and stood over the bed, staring down at Henry for several seconds. She took out a tissue and wiped her eyes and then sat down in the chair.

Mary watched from outside, wondering how long she should stand there. After a few minutes, she was beginning to think she should go to the waiting room, when Pastor Miles strode through the double door of the unit.

"Ah, Mary." He glanced through the window. "I see Dorothy is visiting our patient."

"Yes," Mary said. "Thanks for coming."

"I had to see how Henry was doing. About the same, I take it?"

Mary nodded. "He hasn't opened his eyes at all."

"Well, don't get discouraged. The doctor said last night he might need a few days to rest before he's ready to come back to us."

"I know you're right."

"Where's Kim this morning?" the pastor asked.

"She's gone out to Henry's house to get some sleep. She sat up with him all night."

"I figured she would."

Dorothy looked up and saw them standing outside. She got up, though Mary thought she did so with reluctance, and came out of the room.

"Hello, Dorothy," the pastor said. "Henry's a popular fellow this morning. Mind if I go in now?"

"Of course not," Dorothy said. She and Mary stayed by the glass until the pastor came out a few minutes later.

"Shall we go into the waiting room and pray together?" he asked.

"I'd like that." Mary took Dorothy's arm and led her to the small waiting room.

She wasn't sure how Pastor Miles managed it, but when he left a short time later, Dorothy went with him. Mary took advantage of the quiet moment to call Rebecca at the shop.

"Everything's fine here," Rebecca reported. "A few people have asked about Henry. I think the pastor must have sent word around the prayer chain."

"He did," Mary said. "Visitors are limited, though. Folks might want to wait a day or two to try to see him."

"If anyone else asks, I'll tell them that. Oh, and Tess called. The taste-off is definite for the Fourth of July. Blake got permission from the town council. They'll hold it in the park all day, after the parade finishes, and announce the winners late in the afternoon. What do you think?"

"It's ambitious." Mary rubbed her forehead. "To tell you the truth, I haven't given it a lot of thought since yesterday."

"I figured you hadn't. Tess didn't know about Henry, so I told her to double-check with you later. This might not be the best time for ice-cream making."

"Thanks," Mary said. "How's Ashley doing?"

"Great, but I made her put the catnip mouse away when there were a lot of customers. Gus just wouldn't settle down. He's fine now, though—lying in the sun. Ashley is picking out a few books to have handy if any moms come in with little kids."

Mary laughed. "I don't mind if she plays with Gus, but it can be distracting if the store gets too busy."

"Yeah, and he was starting to pounce on people," Rebecca said, and laughed.

"I'll leave it to your discretion." Mary signed off and resumed her place by Henry's side. Her life had certainly grown more complicated in the last twenty-four hours. She wondered if the police had talked to Daniel York yet, or if he had returned home. Part of her wanted to be out there, doing something, but she knew that she would rather be with Henry at this time than anywhere else.

The nurse came into the room, checked the monitors, and replaced the bag of saline on Henry's IV pole.

"Mrs. Fisher, Dr. Teagarden has asked that we limit visitors to family only."

Mary's heart lurched.

"Except for you," the nurse continued. "Henry's daughter specifically named you as someone who should be allowed in here anytime."

"Thank you," Mary said. "That means a lot."

The nurse nodded. "We just got the word at the desk. If more visitors come in, we'll tell them they can't come in

here at this time. You can see them in the waiting room, if
you want. But if not, we'll just ask them to come back when
Henry is out of ICU. We expect him to improve rapidly
once he regains consciousness. Time enough for friends
then."

"You don't think…"

"What?" the nurse asked, pausing beside her.

"I just wondered what happens if he doesn't wake up."

"A neurologist examined him this morning, and they'll be
doing more tests today. Everyone thinks he'll recover and that
he'll wake up within the next couple of days."

"But—"

The nurse patted her shoulder. "Don't borrow trouble."

"You're right. Thank you."

When the nurse had left the room, Mary closed her eyes.
She had needed this reminder. Her worrying wouldn't speed
Henry's healing. A verse from the final chapter of the book of
Job came to mind. *I know that you can do all things; no purpose
of yours can be thwarted* (Job 42:2). "Lord, You know all my
thoughts," she whispered. "Please take away the unhelpful
ones and help me to trust You with Henry."

She kept her vigil through the lunch hour. The scone kept
her hunger at bay, and the prospect of a meal wasn't enough
to draw her away from him. The ward clerk came to the
doorway twice to tell her visitors were outside. She went out
each time to greet members of her church who had come to
inquire about Henry. Dr. Teagarden came in about one o'clock.
Mary left the room, and he drew the curtains while he
examined Henry. When he had finished, he sought her out in
the waiting area. His soft brown eyes were reassuringly calm.

"Vitals are stable, Mary. Everything looks good. I'm having more blood work done, but I'm holding off on another scan. If this coma hasn't broken tomorrow, we'll do more tests, but I think nature is taking its course."

"Thank you," Mary said. "I'll tell his daughters." She felt better, just hearing Dr. Gary Teagarden's soothing voice.

About a half hour later, Mary was sitting placidly beside the bed when she looked up and saw Karen gazing in at Henry. At first, she thought Kim had returned, but in a split second realized the hairstyle was a little different, and this was her twin sister. Mary jumped up and went to the doorway.

"Karen! I'm so glad you're here." Mary hugged her. "How was your flight?"

"Not too bad. Jeff was so thoughtful—he booked my flight for me last night, and he had a rental car waiting for me when I got to Logan. And traffic wasn't as bad as it is on a weekday."

Mary quickly brought her up to date on her father's condition and Dr. Teagarden's visit.

"Thanks," Karen said. "That's comforting. I spoke to Kim on the phone just before I came in. She's had a good rest, and she's coming back here soon."

"I'll leave you with your dad then," Mary said. "The nurses are very helpful, but feel free to call my cell phone if there's anything at all I can do for you." She gave Karen her number and went out to her car.

She made a brief stop at the bookshop, but Mary felt at loose ends. Rebecca and Ashley had things well under control, and Mary was too distracted by Henry's condition to settle down and work. She decided to go by Daniel York's apartment again. If the police had questioned him, he would probably tell her. Seeing him at least would help her to feel that she was doing something active for Henry, even if she couldn't help him directly.

She told Rebecca she would come back later for Gus and went out to her car again. Digging up information was something she was good at, and she might as well put her talent to use.

FIVE

◆◆◆

Mary rang the bell a second time and waited, her frustration mounting. Had Daniel York even been home since the car show yesterday? She knocked on the door, knowing it wouldn't do any good. She had heard the bell faintly through the door. If he was home, he would have answered. Wouldn't he? It was Saturday, and she supposed he might have gone somewhere—anywhere.

The apartment was on the ground level, and a window lay about six feet to the left of where she stood on the steps. As short as she was, Mary thought she could see through it if she moved over there.

She looked around to see if any of Daniel's neighbors watched her. Seeing no one, she edged down the steps and into the grass. The apartment building didn't have much landscaping, and there were no flower beds or shrubs beneath the window. At least the grass had been recently mowed.

She put both hands on the textured brick wall. By stretching to her utmost tiptoes, she was able to peer over the windowsill and into what appeared to be a very messy living room. In his newly found singlehood, Dan York had apparently lapsed in the housekeeping department. Magazines and papers overflowed the coffee table onto the floor. Throw pillows, an overturned coffee mug, and one of the sofa cushions lay in a hodgepodge on the carpet. DVDs spilled out of a cabinet near the television set, and the only picture she could see on the wall—some sort of framed automobile ad—hung crooked.

The sun beat down on her as she turned away from the window. She sighed and got into her car. Was Mr. York really that sloppy? Henry had said he took great pains to restore the antique Buick. Would a man that meticulous live in a pigsty of an apartment? It had looked more as though someone had ransacked the place.

At the end of the driveway to the apartment building, she paused. What else could she do? She didn't have any leads, except the man Henry had bought the car from at the antique auto show, and he was a hard man to contact.

A sudden thought struck her. She was certain the auto show was a two-day event. She wished she had taken the good program from Henry's kitchen. She'd given Officer Tilton the crumpled one, but she was sure it had said Friday *and* Saturday. Maybe Daniel was at the car show again today. With renewed purpose, she turned toward the fairgrounds.

At the gate, a man wearing an Ivy Bay Wheelers button approached her car, and Mary put down her window.

"Is there an entrance fee?" she asked.

"Naw, you can go in for free," he said. "We're nearly done. In an hour, everyone will be gone."

"Thanks. Oh, could you tell me if Daniel York is here?"

The man shook his head. "I don't think so. He was here yesterday, and he had some cars to sell, but I don't think he came back today. Hold on." He walked over to a small wooden stand and picked up a clipboard. Perusing the pages clipped to it, he sauntered back to her car. "Dan was in slot 18, if that helps. Here's a program for you."

"Thanks very much."

Mary drove in and parked in the sparsely populated lot. As the attendant had indicated, things did seem to be winding down. Food and T-shirt vendors still hawked their wares, but exhibitors were loading antique roadsters and touring cars on trailers to haul home, and others seemed to be earnestly engaged in making final deals before they packed things up.

Mary strolled down the grassy aisle between the exhibits, trying to match the numbers in the program with the business signs and automobiles on display.

The biggest exhibit had a large plastic banner overhead that blared Bargain Bill's—For All Your Auto Needs. The vendor had several cars for sale, most of which Mary would not have called antiques. A few, she conceded, were classics, such as the Mustang and the old Pontiac sedan. She recognized the large man wearing a Western shirt and Stetson, laughing loudly and talking to a small group of people. She had seen him on commercials, advertising his used-car business in Barnstable.

The spot she thought should have been Daniel's was empty. Next to it, a man was dismantling his booth and collapsing a folding table while a woman loaded booklets into a box. Mary walked over and smiled.

"Hi. I'm looking for Daniel York. Was that his booth, next to yours?"

The woman nodded. "Yeah, Dan was here yesterday, but he sold all the cars he brought, and he didn't come back today."

"I see." Mary frowned. "How many cars did he have?"

"Three, I think."

The man straightened and came over to her. "That's right. He had three in top shape, and he sold them all in one day."

"That's pretty good, isn't it?" Mary asked.

"It's not the way things usually go."

Mary consulted the program. "You must be Hal Saunders."

"That's right, and this is my wife, Julie."

Mary and Julie smiled at each other.

"A friend of mine bought the Buick Century from him," Mary said.

"Oh, sure." Hal grinned. "Henry Woodrow, right? I know him from the Wheelers club."

"Yes." Mary wasn't sure how much to say, but she assumed Henry knew these folks only superficially. She wasn't sure how much he would want her to reveal. Still, she wondered who had bought Daniel's other two antique cars. Did the attacker also pay them a visit, or did he go only to Henry's house? "Do you know who bought Mr. York's other two vehicles?"

"*Hmm.*" Hal frowned and shook his head. "The first one went early. I didn't recognize the customer."

"I saw Bargain Bill talking to him a couple of times," Julie said. "Is there a problem?"

"No, not with the vehicle," Mary said. "I just need to talk to Mr. York, and I thought maybe someone who dealt with him yesterday would have some idea of where he went this weekend."

"Oh," Hal said. "Well, Dan wouldn't ever sell to Bargain Bill. He likes to go around early and offer a lowball price, hoping to buy out the competition and then resell what he buys—if not here, then at his business in Barnstable."

"But Dan did sell all his cars quickly," Julie said. "I figured he must have sold them pretty cheap to unload them all in one day."

"Maybe, but not to Bargain Bill," her husband said. "The first two I'm pretty sure went to outsiders. Probably people who saw the show advertised and came here specifically looking for a nice antique car. And Dan's were in near-mint condition. I'll bet he got what he was asking, or close to it. That last one—well, Henry's a friend, or at least a fellow Wheeler. Dan might have given him a discount, I suppose."

"He sure left in a hurry after he sold it," Julie said.

"That's true. We were going to ask Dan if he wanted to get supper with us, and he was gone." Hal shrugged. "Maybe he had someplace else to go last night."

Mary thanked them and ambled down the row, chatting briefly with a couple of other exhibitors, but most seemed to have their minds on closing and getting home.

The last man she asked about Daniel said, "I don't know him personally, but you might check with the auto club president. He's right over there." He pointed to a man of about sixty wearing a straw hat, standing outside the announcer's booth with another man. "That's him in the hat—Stan Auger."

"Thank you." Mary took her time walking over to the booth. The air remained warm, and it made her want to do everything in slow motion.

As she approached, the other man left, and the club president turned toward the booth. "Mr. Auger?" she called. "Excuse me."

He faced her and smiled. His green polo shirt had a steering wheel and Ivy Bay Wheelers stitched on the front in gold. "Hello. May I help you?"

Mary introduced herself as a friend of Henry's, and his face lit up. "Glad to meet you, Mary."

He didn't seem to know anything about Henry's injury, and Mary decided to keep quiet about that. If she mentioned it, his friends might delay her with explanations. Besides, she didn't know if any of these people were involved in the assault or not.

She told him of her interest in Daniel York, and he confirmed that Dan had left the previous afternoon, after selling all three of the antique cars he had offered for sale.

"It was a good day for Dan. Not many folks have sold out."

"Is everyone here to sell old cars?" Mary asked.

"No, some just come to show off their babies, or to see what other people have. We get a lot of old auto buffs who just want to look, and some of our exhibitors do it for the fun, and to meet people, not to sell anything."

"But Daniel was selling three cars."

"Yes. His entire inventory, I believe." Stan Auger frowned. "He seemed a little agitated when he left. Can't say as I blame him, though. He'd had a couple of those cars for several years, and he really loved them."

"Why was he selling them, if he cared so much about them?" Mary asked.

"He had to." Stan leaned closer and lowered his voice. "Just between you, me, and the lamppost, Dan's ex-wife pretty much cleaned him out when she divorced him."

"Oh dear," Mary said, thinking of Dee Saxon and the house where Daniel used to live.

"Dan made no secret of the fact that his ex got the house and half his bank account," Stan said. "She kept all her jewelry too, or so the story goes. Dan got the antique cars and another, less valuable piece of property. That's it, so far as I know." He shook his head. "I'm not one to gossip, but I get riled every time I think of his situation. Poor old Daniel really got taken by that gold digger."

Another man poked his head out of the announcer's booth. "Hey, Stan!"

"Oh, excuse me," Stan said to Mary. "Say hello to Henry for me."

"Of course." She walked slowly back to her car, a bit puzzled. Dee Saxon had seemed fairly nice, considering Mary had rung her doorbell so early on a Saturday and she wasn't dressed yet, but Stan Auger painted a different picture. Maybe she should go back to Jonquil Lane and have another talk with her.

On her way to Jonquil Lane, Mary tried to decide what to say to Mrs. Saxon when she encountered her for the second time that day. She parked in the driveway and drew in a deep breath before approaching the house. However, no one responded when she rang the doorbell.

Disappointed, Mary headed back toward her car. Across the street, the woman she had seen that morning was watering a bed of perennials. This time, she returned Mary's wave.

Mary walked over to the neighbor's yard. "I couldn't help admiring your flowers. They're lovely, especially the phlox and the dark iris."

"Thank you."

"I'm Mary Fisher, and I was hoping to see Mrs. Saxon this afternoon."

The woman turned off her garden hose. Her short, graying hair curled about her face, and she wore gold-framed glasses, blue capris, and a striped top. As she considered Mary's comment, her face hardened slightly.

"Are you a friend of Dee's?"

"No," Mary said, "I met her for the first time this morning, when I came in search of Daniel York. I was hoping to speak to her again."

The woman's face cleared. "I'm Gloria. You know Dan then?"

To Mary, it seemed Gloria felt much more kindly toward Daniel than she did toward Dee. "We have a mutual friend, and I was hoping to find Daniel so I could tell him that his friend has been injured."

"Oh, that's too bad."

"Yes, it's very sad, and I know he spent some time with Dan yesterday before it happened. I was sure Dan would want to know he's in the hospital."

Gloria's lips pursed. "I'm sorry about your friend." She glanced across the street. "If you want to talk to Dee, it's hit or miss. She's in and out all the time—at all hours. This would be a quiet street if it wasn't for her comings and goings, and her parties."

"Mrs. Saxon entertains a lot?" Mary asked. Gloria seemed more than ready to talk about her neighbor, and Mary got the feeling it wasn't out of admiration.

Gloria rolled her eyes. "She's a party girl. It's all about friends for her. Too bad she didn't spend more time with her husband. Her last husband, that is. The new one seems to go along with her ways. Maybe she deserves him. But Dan didn't deserve the way she treated him."

"You've known Dan a long time?" Mary said. She wished she had come to Gloria on her first visit. She might have gleaned a lot more information than she had from Dee.

"Well, sure. We've lived across the street from each other for fifteen years. Before my husband, Jonathan, died, he and Dan were good friends. And he was there for me when Jonathan had his heart attack. But then that...that woman sank her claws into Dan. It was a sad day when he married her."

"You don't seem very fond of Mrs. Saxon."

"Ha!" Gloria shook her head. "Dan York is the sweetest guy, but unfortunately, he's also gullible. At least he was before he married her. Maybe he's wiser now. He fell hard for her. Totally lost his head. He hadn't known her more than two or three months when he married her."

"How long were they married?" Mary asked.

"Only about two years. Then she saw something she liked better. And poor Dan lost his house and everything. I just can't stand her. What she did to him was criminal."

Mary blinked. That was a pretty strong statement, but then, Gloria seemed to be a very emotional person.

"Do you know what she did last summer?" Gloria asked.

"No," Mary said, wondering if it was time to shut down the conversation. They seemed to be getting away from useful facts and into gossip, perhaps based on jealousy. Gloria had certainly taken Dan's side when it came to the split.

"She went out of town with some of her girlfriends—at least she *said* it was with girlfriends—over the weekend of Dan's birthday. Can you imagine going off with your friends and leaving your husband alone on his birthday?"

Mary didn't know what to say to that, so she tried for a sympathetic expression.

Gloria nodded emphatically. "That man was doing just fine without her. And now he's turned out of his own home. I could have told him she was only after his money, not that it was so much. But he wasn't in the mood to take advice back then, I'll tell you. And then she up and dumped him for another man. Big surprise."

"So, you were never on friendly terms with her?" Mary ventured.

"Oh, we'd wave and say hi, back when she and Daniel were together, but she never invited me to one of her parties or anything like that." Gloria waved one hand, scowling. "I've had some hard times since Jonathan died, and heaven knows, I can't afford to entertain—not the way she does. Dee's social circle seems to only include people with money. I'm just trying to hang on to this house and get by. And I sure didn't steal any ring from her."

Startled, Mary eyed her keenly. "What do you mean, steal from her?"

Gloria shrugged and seemed for the first time to regret talking so freely. "Well, listen to me rattle on! It was nothing, really. She had some jewelry stolen, and apparently she hinted to the police that I needed money. They came and questioned me. Talk about humiliation!" She stepped away from Mary. "I'd better finish my yard work."

"All right." Mary was tempted to press her for more, but perhaps she had picked up enough for now. She was torn between wanting to learn any scrap that might help and not wanting to encourage Gloria's indiscretion. She decided to end the visit and smiled. "Nice talking to you, Gloria. Have a good evening."

Before Mary's words were out, Gloria had turned on the hose and fixed her attention on the flowers in her front border.

Mary walked over to her car, thinking through the odd conversation. Someone had stolen some jewelry from Dee Saxon, and she had mentioned her neighbor's financial struggles to the police. How did that fit into the picture? Mary wasn't sure that it did. Probably the police had routinely asked Dee if she knew anyone who might steal her things, just as they had asked Mary and Henry's daughters if they knew anyone with a grudge against Henry.

Whatever the circumstances, Mary tended to believe Gloria was telling the truth, at least as far as she knew it. That truth was no doubt colored by her admiration for Daniel and her jealousy of Dee—or maybe it was just her wounded air and an outraged sense of justice. Mary tried to look beyond the emotion. The events of Gloria's lurid tale must be unrelated to Henry's troubles, although Daniel might possibly have something to do with them. Gloria couldn't be mixed up in the attack on Henry, but Mary wasn't so sure about Dee. At least Gloria's ranting had shed some light on Daniel and Dee's relationship for her.

As she started the engine, her thoughts went back to the attack on Henry. The intruder must have gone to Henry's house intent on thievery. It was the only thing that made sense to her. Henry had no enemies, and she couldn't conceive of anyone planning to hurt him. And it had something to do with Henry's new car. Last night she had been distracted by Henry's injury, but now she was certain of that connection. She carefully reviewed the scene in the garage.

If the burglar had intended to steal the car, he would have opened the big garage door, wouldn't he? But it had remained closed. He had come in the side door. And wouldn't he have opened the driver's door of the Buick, so he could get in or start the car? Mary didn't know much about hot-wiring cars, but she had a vague notion that if you didn't have a key, you had to do something either under the hood or under the dashboard on the driver's side to start it. But the intruder had opened the door on the passenger side of the Buick. Why?

The glove compartment, she thought. Maybe he was looking for something in there. She took out her phone and called Kim's number. After determining that Kim was at the hospital and that Henry's condition had not changed, Mary cleared her throat.

"Kim, I'm on my way home for supper. Is it all right if I stop at Henry's house and look at something?"

"No problem," Kim said.

Mary put her phone away and pulled out onto Jonquil Lane. It took only about five minutes to drive out to Bayshore Road. It was quarter past five, and she still had at least three hours of daylight. Even so, as she parked in the empty driveway and gazed out over the water, she wondered if she had been foolish to come out to this beautiful but secluded spot alone.

SIX

———◆◆◆———

Mary got out of her car in Henry's driveway and looked around carefully. She had to be sure no one saw what she was about to do. The neighbors' houses were not visible, now that the trees between them and Henry's place were leafed out.

She looked all along the driveway and the tree line, then down the path to the shore.

Mary caught her breath. Last night, Henry's small motorboat had been tied up at his dock below. Today it was nowhere in sight. She walked over to the top of the path that led down to the shore and stood at the top of the wooden steps.

The tide was about the same level it had been when she arrived for supper last night. But then, the boat had been clearly visible, tethered by its painter to one of the pilings at the end of the dock. The rope had been long enough to let the boat rise and fall with the tide. Even at tide's ebb, she thought she'd be able to see the boat from here. Certainly, the painter would be obvious, tied around the post—but there was nothing.

Who could have taken it? Because Mary was sure someone had. Henry would never be careless enough to tie up a boat in such a manner that it could come loose, at least not during fair weather. And last night had been calm.

Kim had come out here this morning. Mary tried to remember what time that was. Probably between ten and eleven, perhaps closer to eleven. It was after they had talked to Chief McIntosh at the hospital. She took out her phone.

"Hi, it's Mary," she said when Kim answered. "I'm at your father's, and I noticed something odd. Last night when I came, there was a small boat tied up at the dock. It's not there now. Do you know anything about that?"

"I saw it this morning," Kim said. "When I first went out there, I walked down to the dock. I didn't stay long, just wanted to look. But the boat was there then. I'm pretty sure it was Dad's little boat. I didn't notice when I left the house, though. I went straight to my car and drove away without even looking down there."

"Someone must have taken it between when you came out here and now," Mary said.

"I don't like that. Maybe someone was around while I was napping. Do you think we should tell the police?"

"Probably so," Mary said. "They could ask the neighbors if they know who took it, or if they saw anyone down near the shore today."

"I'll call the police station," Kim offered.

"All right. Do you know Officer Tilton? He was out here last night, and he was writing up the report of the initial investigation. You might want to ask for him."

"Thanks, Mary. I'll call right away."

Mary put her phone away and looked all around once more. When she was satisfied that she was unobserved, she went to the flower border beside the walkway. Several years ago, Misty had made a mosaic design in the mulch of her flower bed with crushed oyster shells. Other whole seashells were positioned in front of an old wooden lobster trap overgrown by blue flags and Egyptian mint. The previous fall, when Henry had planned a weeklong trip to visit Karen in Richmond, Virginia, he had shown Mary that under a brown auger shell speckled with white, on the right side of the geometric design, his spare house key lay nestled in a tiny plastic container.

Mary moved the shell aside and pried out the container, then put back the auger shell, in case someone came along while she was inside. Again, she glanced around before she went up the steps and unlocked the front door.

She went straight through the living room and into the kitchen, trusting her memory from Friday night. As she had thought, the keys to the Buick Century lay on the counter near the title to the car. She picked them up and set her purse on the counter. From deep in its depths, she pulled a small flashlight and then went to the door leading into the garage.

At the top of the steps, she turned on the overhead lights and paused for a moment, looking down at the floor where Henry had lain. Her heart ached, knowing how badly he was injured, and that he might be affected for some time. When he awoke, he might have pain, memory loss, and other health issues. Things like that shouldn't happen to people like Henry.

Carefully, Mary went down the steps and bent to examine them. As she had remembered, there was no blood on the wooden steps, no hair that she could see—nothing that could tell her what had happened. The doctors must be right—

Henry had been hit on his temple and fell backward, striking his head on the floor. As far as she knew, the police hadn't found a weapon. Had the thief carried a tool? Perhaps he had struck Henry with his fist.

She went around the car to the space between it and the Bel Air. She opened the passenger door to the Century and turned on her flashlight. For the next twenty minutes, she made a painstaking search of the interior of the car, not at all sure what exactly she was looking for. She shone the beam of the flashlight into every conceivable hiding place and felt inside them too. In the glove box, under the dashboard, under the seats, even under the pedals.

True, the police had already searched this car, but Mary had to do this for herself. The car was very clean, as she had expected. She checked the backseat area as well. If Chief McIntosh saw her hunched over the foot wells, would he be angry, or would he merely think she was foolish?

Satisfied at last that she had missed nothing in the passenger compartment, she opened the trunk. It was bare, except for the spare tire, jack, and tire iron. Again, she shone the light into every corner and ran her fingers over the carpeted floor of the trunk. The spare was bolted down, and she carefully twirled the wing nut that held it in place, until it came off and, with some effort, she was able to lift up the tire.

In the recess under the spare, she saw a tiny metallic glint, and she caught her breath. Closer inspection told her it was safe to pick up the object, but instead of metal, her fingers closed on what felt like paper.

She brought the little scrap out and held it close to her face, squinting at it. In her hand was what appeared to be a tag, less than an inch wide, made of light cardboard or poster board. The back was plain white, but the front had a black oval, embossed with gold edging and the word *Guthrie's* in gold script. Below the design was a white half-inch tab that would allow the tag to be inserted in a display.

She sighed. The only thing she had found for her pains was a little piece of trash. She supposed it wasn't anything to do with what happened to Henry, but you never knew. Instead of throwing it away, she let it fall back into the tire recess where she had found it and put the spare back in place over it. Gently, she closed the trunk and stood with the keys in her hand. Had the intruder really been after something in the car? If he had, then he must have found it and taken it away with him, because there was nothing here.

On the other hand, he might have been on a random search for small valuables, as Officer Tilton had suggested. Some people did leave CD players and GPS units in their cars—or even guns or small amounts of cash. Henry wouldn't, but did the thief know that?

In order to feel she'd made a thorough job of it, Mary went over to Henry's Bel Air and gave it the same meticulous search she'd given the Century. Of course, it wasn't quite as clean as the "new" car, though Henry kept his usual ride spotless. She found a little mud on one of the floor mats and a few pieces of lint on the upholstery. In the glove compartment were Henry's registration and insurance cards, along with a tire gauge, a folded handkerchief, and a few other miscellaneous items. She found nothing on the floor except for a dime under the floor mat. The trunk held a few more tools than the Century's, as well as an empty bait bucket and a pair of worn deck shoes.

Discouraged, Mary made sure both cars were closed up and the garage lights were off. She went back through the house, left the car keys on the counter, and retrieved her purse. A sweater of Kim's lay over one of the kitchen chairs, and half a pot of cold coffee sat on the counter, evidence of the twins' presence. Mary went outside and again reconnoitered before returning the house key to its hiding place.

She drove out onto Bayshore Road, thinking hard. Was there an obvious place she should have looked, but didn't? Nothing came to mind. She longed to go back to the hospital and be near Henry, but she didn't want to keep his daughters away from him. She supposed she ought to go home and eat supper with Betty. There would be time enough this evening to check on Henry. The twins would call her if there was any significant change in his condition.

As she approached town, she put on the blinker to prepare for the turn off Bayshore Road and glanced in the rearview mirror. How long had that dark car been behind her? As soon as she put the signal on, the other car's came on as well.

The car stayed a consistent distance behind her. Mary told herself she was silly to be suspicious. It was only because of what had happened to Henry, and the fact that she'd just been out to his empty house alone. She decided to prove the car wasn't following her. Instead of going straight home, she would take a little detour. At the last safe moment, she popped on her signal and turned onto Water Street, and then Main. She slowed down on Main Street and watched her rearview mirror.

See? she told herself. *You worry too much.*

And then the dark sedan rolled out of Water Street and onto Main, a block behind her.

Mary's heart lurched. Again she tried to calm her rioting pulse. *All right, so they were coming to Main Street. That's not unusual.*

But just to be sure, she decided one more detour was in order. She drove another block and swerved into the parking lot at the Ivy Bay police station. A few seconds later, the sedan rolled by. In the late sunlight, she wasn't sure if the car was black or dark blue, but that wouldn't matter if she could just—

She sighed as a pickup heading the other way blocked the sedan from her view. With the distance, the obstruction, and the fading light coming into play, she had only managed to make out *A7*, the first two characters of the license plate number. She got out of her car, squared her shoulders, and went into the white concrete-block police station.

She walked straight to the desk in the reception area and said to the officer on duty, "I'd like to speak to the chief or to one of the officers investigating the attack on Henry Woodrow."

"One moment, ma'am. Won't you have a seat?"

She nodded and walked to the chairs near the door to the inner parts of the police station. It was six o'clock, and she expected the chief to have left for the day, but McIntosh himself came to the door a moment later and beckoned her inside.

"Mrs. Fisher. Come on into my office."

Mary shook off her irritation at the way he had so easily claimed Chief McArthur's space as his own. That was what he was being paid for, and it was only temporary.

Chief McIntosh sat down behind McArthur's steel desk. The walnut top of it was almost bare, something she'd never seen when Chief Benjamin McArthur was in the office. She sat down in one of the two chairs facing it.

"How may I help you?" Chief McIntosh asked with a smile that didn't ease her anxiety one bit.

"I just came from Henry Woodrow's house, and I believe I was followed into town."

He sobered. "Why do you think that?"

"I noticed a dark car behind me shortly after I left the house on Bayshore Road. When I got into town, I made a couple of turns I don't usually make, and it stuck with me. I pulled in here, and the car passed slowly. I believe the driver was observing me."

"Can you describe him?"

"No." She frowned. "I think the windows were tinted, and anyway, I was concentrating on being able to identify the car."

"I see. Did you get the plate number?"

"It starts with *A7*," Mary said. "Another vehicle came along and blocked my view, so I couldn't get the whole thing."

He made what sounded like a low grunt.

"It was a black or dark blue four-door sedan," she said quickly.

"Well, be careful, Mrs. Fisher, and let us know if you see the vehicle again."

Mary eyed him for a moment. "Aren't you going to write down what I said?"

"About the plate number?"

"That's right."

"Hundreds of Massachusetts plates start with those two characters. Maybe thousands."

Mary clamped her lips shut to keep from blurting out her displeasure. After a moment, she managed in a civil tone, "I feel as though you're not taking me seriously, Chief."

McIntosh smiled and leaned back in his chair. "Not at all, Mrs. Fisher. I do believe a dark car was behind you as you drove into town, but just because the driver took the same route you did, does not mean he was following you. Now, if you could positively identify the car, we could go and speak to the owner. But you can't, and there's not much we can do. It would be a waste of man power to try to track this vehicle down."

"But it seemed to appear suddenly after I left Henry's house."

"Are you sure? Did it come out of a side road, or was it parked along Bayshore before it followed you?"

Mary looked down at her hands, clutching the strap of her purse. "I didn't see where it came from."

The chief nodded. "I can alert my men to watch for a dark sedan in Woodrow's neighborhood."

Mary leaned forward. "Are you aware that a short time ago, Henry's daughter called to tell the police her father's small motorboat is missing from the dock near his house?"

"Uh…" His blank look told Mary the word had not reached McIntosh, and she hurried on.

"It was there last evening when I went out to have dinner with Henry, and it was there this morning when his daughter Kim went out to the house. But it's gone now. Someone took it."

"Or it drifted away."

"Impossible."

McIntosh clamped his lips together and leaned back, looking at her pensively. "I'll have a man ask around the neighborhood to see if anyone's been seen at Woodrow's dock."

"That's a start," Mary said.

McIntosh's eyes narrowed. "I'll also have a patrol officer drive by the house now and then to see if anyone seems to be lurking out there. That's about all we can do at this point."

"But what if the person driving the car that followed me—or the person who took the boat—was the one who attacked Henry?"

McIntosh sighed. "I've come to the opinion that Mr. Woodrow's case was simply a homeowner confronting a would-be burglar and getting hurt for his pains. I see no reason why the burglar would return to the scene, especially if he knows we're watching it and that he'd be arrested for assault if we caught him loitering about the house."

Mary's dismay grew as he talked. "Surely you're not giving up on solving this case."

"No, we will certainly continue looking for leads as to who did it, but you shouldn't think that Mr. Woodrow was specifically targeted. I know he is your friend, but that doesn't mean—"

"But what about the open car door?" Mary asked. "Don't you think it's odd that the intruder was looking inside the car Henry had bought just hours earlier?"

McIntosh sighed and didn't meet her gaze. "The car's purchase is probably coincidental to the attack, Mrs. Fisher. We have to be careful not to make assumptions in a case like this."

"I see." Mary felt about as big as the fly buzzing against the screen on the window behind McIntosh. "Well, I do hope your men continue to patrol the neighborhood. Thank you for your time." She rose with as much dignity as she could muster.

As she went out into the parking lot, Mary tried not to let her spirits sink lower. Chief McIntosh might brush her aside and make light of Henry's case, but she would not let it go unsolved. Henry was one of Ivy Bay's upstanding citizens, and he deserved better treatment than this. She wasn't sure how she would do it, but as she turned her car homeward, she determined not to let the substitute police chief get in the way of justice.

SEVEN

※◆◆◆※

When Mary arrived home, Betty had chicken potpie ready, filling the kitchen with a warm, homey scent. Mary sank into her chair, grateful for her sister's care. Gus, who seemed to feel neglected, lingered under the table, winding around Mary's feet as she began to eat supper. She had stopped by the store on the way home to pick him up.

"I called the hospital to check on Henry about an hour ago," Betty said. "Karen told me you'd gone out to Henry's house."

"I did, but I didn't find anything."

"What were you looking for?"

"I'm not sure." Mary reached for her water glass. "I suppose I hoped I'd find something in that new car of his that would tell me why the burglar was there—what he was looking for. But that was overly optimistic. If there'd been anything like that, the police would have found it."

"I've wondered...," Betty said hesitantly, her fork halfway to her mouth. "I don't know this Daniel person that Henry bought the car from, but is it possible he'd left something in it and came to pick it up?"

"I don't see how," Mary said. "If it was Dan, I think he'd have gone to the front door, and if not, I don't think Henry would have yelled when he opened the garage door and saw him. He'd have said something like, 'Hey, Dan. What are you doing here?' And I certainly don't think his friend would have hit him. Of course, I don't know him either." She frowned. Henry hadn't said he knew Daniel York well, only that he'd met him through the Wheelers. The man might be a thug— but she didn't think so.

"You're probably right."

Mary looked up at Betty. "To be honest, though, he could be an ax murderer and I wouldn't know it. I went by his apartment this morning, hoping to meet him and get a feeling for what sort of person he is. But he wasn't home."

"All very unsatisfactory," Betty said. She took another bite of potpie and chewed it pensively.

"What did Karen say about Henry?" Mary asked. "Is there any change?"

"Nothing significant. The neurologist had been in to evaluate him, but there's really nothing new." Gus leaned against Mary's ankle, and she bent down to pet him. She wouldn't want to keep Henry's daughters from his side, but she knew she would feel a little easier if she saw him in person. And sometimes people who were there all the time didn't notice slight changes, but a person who had been away for a while might see a difference in the patient.

For the moment, she felt she had done all she could toward untangling the threads of the mysterious events surrounding Henry's purchase of the car and his injury. If she went to the hospital, maybe her mind would rest, and perhaps a new idea would come to her. Suddenly she felt more enthusiasm for her supper and began to eat in earnest.

She walked into the ICU about seven thirty. To her surprise, both Kim and Karen had chairs inside Henry's room. Had his condition worsened? When the twins saw her looking in through the glass, both rose and came out to speak to her.

"How is he?" Mary asked.

"The same," Kim said. "The neurologist said his reflexes are good. He expects him to wake up once the swelling in his brain goes down."

"Maybe soon," Karen said.

"Oh, that's a relief. I saw you both in there, and I thought maybe he'd had a turn for the worse."

Karen smiled. "Oh no. Dr. Teagarden said we could go in together, since we're his only children. I think the fact that we're twins and haven't been together for a while influenced his decision too. He saw that we needed time together, as well as with Dad."

"He did put a restriction on other visitors, though," Kim added.

Mary felt her spirits droop along with her shoulders. "I won't stay then."

"Not you," Kim said quickly. "We specifically told him to put you and Pastor Miles on the list of people allowed in."

"Since you're here," Karen said, "maybe you'd like to sit with Dad for a half hour or so while we go down to the cafeteria."

"You haven't had dinner?" Mary glanced at her watch. "Of course you should go! I'll be happy to stay with him."

"Thanks," Kim said. "We won't be long."

Mary watched them go out the door of the ICU unit and then entered Henry's glassed-in room. The curtains were drawn over the windows that overlooked the parking lot, and the overhead lights were off. Only the light from outside shining through the observation window, the monitor displays, and a television high on the wall opposite the bed lit the scene, but that was fine with Mary.

She sat down in the chair closest to Henry's head and reached for his hand. His face was still pale, and the bruise beside his left eye, reaching up his temple, was still a shocking deep purple. That might take a couple of weeks to fade. But his breathing seemed steady, and he looked peaceful as he lay there.

"Hi," she whispered, stroking the back of his hand. She was careful not to bump the oxygen clip attached to his index finger. "I admit I've been worried about you." She talked to him quietly for the next few minutes, telling him about the mundane parts of her day, but leaving out the parts about the missing boat and being followed from near his house to the police station.

"I really hoped I'd find something in that car," she said softly. "Some clue as to why that fellow was in the garage. But there didn't seem to be anything. Well, except a wadded-up program from the auto show. I gave that to Officer Tilton. It made me wonder if..."

As she spoke, her gaze drifted up to the television screen. The twins had probably had it on for the evening news, she surmised, but that was over now, and the sound was muted. At the moment, a car commercial was playing.

"...if someone from the car show had come out to the house." She froze. The man on the television screen, as if on cue, was someone who had been at the auto show—Bargain Bill.

Mary glanced around and saw the remote control on the bedside table. She grabbed it and fumbled with the buttons. The sound came on, too loud. Quickly she lowered it and glanced at Henry, but he slept on undisturbed.

"Folks, we've got the best bargains you'll find this side of Boston, and maybe even beyond. Come in today and take a test-drive. You'll be glad you did."

The ad ended and another came on, this one for an analgesic. Mary pushed the mute button and sat back in the chair, the remote dangling in her limp hand. Thanks to a burst of adrenaline when she saw Bargain Bill, her heart was thumping much faster than usual.

Bargain Bill had tried to buy Daniel York's cars yesterday, but failed. Was it possible he had gone to Henry's house later, hoping to strike a deal with him? And why did he want those cars so badly? Of course, the brassy showman always hoped to make a quick profit, but was there another reason he was interested in Daniel's vehicles? And how would that explain the open passenger door?

Mary sat slumped in the chair, thinking about it for several minutes while Henry's soft, even breathing continued.

At last she concluded that her ideas about Bargain Bill were far-fetched. People at the auto show had told her that Bill always went around and made low offers for other people's merchandise. He made his living by capitalizing on shrewd purchases. And Dan had turned down his offers. It didn't make a lot of sense to think Bill would go to Henry's after he'd bought the car from Dan.

And was the intruder really interested in the Buick, or had he picked the house as a random target as Chief

McIntosh assumed? If so, Mary thought, he must be either quite stupid or desperate to enter the garage so early in the evening, with people awake and lights on in the house. Maybe Chief McIntosh was right, and it was someone hoping to steal something valuable to sell for drug money. Maybe his need was so urgent he couldn't wait until the middle of the night.

A shadow blocked the light through the glass at the observation window, and she glanced up, expecting to see the nurse. Instead, she saw a man's silhouette. She squinted as she studied him. He was wearing a baseball cap, and she was sure it wasn't Pastor Miles. He didn't wear a cap, and if he did, he'd have removed it when he entered the hospital. The man was turning away. He didn't come to the door of Henry's room but headed straight out toward the main door of the ICU.

Mary jumped up and stepped quickly to the doorway and looked out. The big double door down the hall was closing. The ward clerk was returning to the main desk from the other side of the ward, and she smiled at Mary.

"May I help you, Mrs. Fisher?"

"There was a man just in here. Did you see him?"

The clerk frowned. "No. I had stepped over to room 3 to tell the nurse something. He couldn't have been in here long—I was only gone a minute."

Mary went back to Henry's bedside. She sat down and gazed at his peaceful face, but shivered involuntarily. What if that man was the attacker and he had come to learn Henry's condition?

The nurse breezed in. "Good evening." She looked at the monitors and made notes on her clipboard. She took

Henry's pulse manually and gazed down at him for a few seconds. "He seems to be doing fine." She smiled and left the room.

Her sunny attitude couldn't cheer Mary. What if the assailant had returned and wanted to hurt her friend again? Was Henry still in danger?

EIGHT

Mary sat uneasily in the dim room, listening to Henry's steady breathing but watching the doorway and the glass in the front wall. If the man showed up again, she would press the bell to summon the nurse, and then she would go to the door and ask him who he was and what he wanted.

Her plan didn't seem adequate, but she couldn't think of anything better. The clerk was alerted to watch for strangers who entered the ICU but didn't stop at the desk. Mary had turned off the television, so the room was in semidarkness now. She prayed silently, her hand clasped lightly around Henry's so that she would feel any change in his muscle tension.

About twenty minutes later, Kim and Karen returned, talking softly as they came to the door. Mary rose and stepped out into the reception area with them.

"Have a nice dinner?" she asked.

Karen smiled. "Yes. Thanks for giving us a break."

Kim held out a covered Styrofoam cup in a cardboard sleeve. "I brought you a cup of hot tea."

"Oh, thank you. That was very thoughtful of you." Mary accepted the gift with a smile. "I wanted to ask you..." She looked at them, so alike in features. They had the same golden-brown hair and ready smiles. She'd have known immediately they were twins, even though they were nearing forty years old and had lived separate lives for half that. Now both faces took on lines of anxiety as they picked up on her concern. Their eyes, green like Henry's, gazed at her intently. "You said a lot of visitors came in earlier."

"They sure did," Kim said.

Karen chuckled. "We're glad Dad has so many friends, but he does need to rest."

"The doctor didn't want all the well-wishers disturbing Dad," Kim added. "Mary, is something wrong?"

"What happens now when someone wants to see Henry?" Mary asked.

Kim glanced at her sister and said, "The desk clerk comes to the door and tells us. If we want to, we can go out and speak to the visitor in the waiting room."

Karen nodded. "We've done that several times."

"Did anyone try to come in here without stopping at the desk?"

The sisters looked at her blankly.

"I don't think so," Karen said after a moment. "Mary, what's going on?"

"A man was in here. Not in Henry's room, but here in the unit, looking into the room. The light changed, and I looked up and he was there." She stepped to the window, mimicking the man's pose. "He turned away, and I couldn't tell who it was. And he just walked out of the ICU, through those doors." She pointed to the main entrance to the ward. "I came to the door, but I was too late. He was gone."

"Maybe he was visiting another patient and just looked in out of curiosity," Kim said.

"Maybe," Mary said. She didn't want to worry the twins unnecessarily, but neither did she want Henry to be in danger if they could prevent it. "There's something else."

"Besides the boat being taken? What?" Karen asked, her face full of concern.

Mary glanced toward the nurses' station, but the clerk seemed busy with paperwork.

"Do you want to go into the waiting room for a minute?" Karen asked.

"No. I want one of us to be where we can see Henry all the time."

Kim's frown deepened. "Then let's go into his room. We can talk in there."

The three of them went in, and Kim stood over her father for a moment. "He looks fine for now. I mean, just like before."

"Yes, I don't think there's been any change," Mary said. "And the nurse came in twice while you were gone, but not when that man was here."

"Sit down," Karen said, pushing her gently toward the nearest chair. "Tell us what's troubling you."

Kim sat down too, and Karen leaned in close.

"When I left your father's house earlier this evening—about six o'clock—I thought someone was following me. This was right after I called you about the boat. I tried to lose them, but the car kept on behind me. So I went to the police station and told Chief McIntosh."

Both the women's jaws had dropped, and they stared as she related the incident.

"I'm glad you went to the police," Karen said.

Her sister nodded. "What if it was the person who hurt Dad?"

"That was my thought, of course," Mary said. "The police chief, however, didn't seem impressed. He thought I'd imagined it."

"But *you* didn't." Kim eyed her carefully.

Mary shook her head. "The driver stuck with me on the little detours I took. When I drove into the police station's parking lot, he went on by, and I didn't see him when I left and went home for supper."

"Do you think we should ask the police for a guard or something?" Kim asked.

"I don't think we have enough to convince them it's needed," Mary said. "Both the car and the man who came into the ICU could be totally unrelated to what happened to your dad. The boat too. Anyway, that's what the police would say."

"I suppose they could be ...." Karen brushed back her light brown hair, her face still tight with worry. "Maybe we could hire a private security guard."

Kim's brow furrowed. "Do you think we should?"

"I'd hold off on that," Mary said, thinking of the expense. "I did ask the desk clerk to be aware of anyone coming in who doesn't speak to her before coming toward this room."

"That's something," Karen said. "And the hospital does have security patrolling all the time."

"Has anyone come around Henry's house since you've been here?" Mary asked.

"Not that I know of," Kim said.

Karen shook her head. "I haven't even been out to his house yet. If they wanted to steal that new car Dad bought, they would come back, wouldn't they?"

"I don't know. The police patrols may have scared them off, or even just the encounter with Henry. The intruder doesn't want to be arrested for assault. But still, I think you need to be extremely careful when you're at the house. And if anything doesn't look right when you go out there, don't hesitate to call the police."

"Well, I for one don't think the police are doing nearly enough." Kim looked over at her father's still form, her green eyes misty.

"Mary, do you think Dad is in danger now, right here in this room?" Karen asked.

"I don't know." Mary slumped back in the chair. She hated being an alarmist. And yet, the memory of the shadowy stranger's silhouette made her shiver. "Let's just be extra cautious. If the nurses and ward clerks change shifts, tell them about our concerns."

The twins nodded, and Kim said, "And we won't leave him alone, even for a minute."

"I really can't imagine anyone wanting to hurt him." Karen's voice had a frightened squeak to it. Mary reached out and squeezed her hand.

"Neither can I. This is all very upsetting, and I do hope my imagination isn't adding to your stress."

Kim sat forward and hiked up her chin. "When Dad wakes up, maybe he'll be able to tell us who hit him."

"That's right," Karen said. "The doctor is hopeful that will be soon. Maybe we'll get some answers then."

Kim stood. "I'm going to ask the clerk if we can get another chair. There's room, don't you think?"

"I don't need to stay," Mary said.

"But we'd like you to, for as long as you want."

Mary gave in because the truth was that she *did* want to stay. The clerk brought in a folding chair that they could store out of the way against the wall when they weren't using it. The three women talked quietly. Kim caught Mary up on her family's doings, and Karen described her latest adventures in her job as a CPA. They asked Mary about the bookshop, and both promised to come in as soon as their father's condition was stable.

About quarter past nine, Henry let out a moan and turned his head to one side. Kim gasped, and Mary jumped up. They all hovered around the bed.

Karen took her father's hand. "Dad? Dad, can you hear me?"

Kim, on the other side, touched his left hand, careful not to disturb his IV lines. "Dad, we're here."

Mary waited for a minute, but Henry appeared to sleep on. Kim reached for the swab the nurse had left so they could moisten his mouth.

"Maybe we should tell the nurse," Karen said. "It wasn't much, though."

Mary looked out through the glass and saw Henry's nurse at the desk with the clerk. "I'll step out and tell her."

The nurse came in and examined Henry, upbeat but not too optimistic.

"Everything looks about the same, as far as his vitals go. It's not unusual for a comatose patient to make sounds now and then."

Karen sighed. "It startled us, is all."

"So you don't think he's starting to wake up?" Kim asked hopefully.

"I don't know. Both Dr. Teagarden and the neurologist expect him to regain consciousness soon, as you know. This may be significant, or not." She looked from one sister's anxious face to the other. "One of you is staying with him all night, correct?"

"Yes," Kim said. "I'll stay while Karen goes and gets some sleep, and she'll come back in the morning. I guess we'd better start swapping off."

The nurse nodded. "It could be a few more days. We just don't know."

After she had left the room, Mary stayed a short time, hoping for something more, but Henry didn't stir again. At last, she caught herself yawning and looked at her watch. "Oh dear, it's nearly ten. I'd better go home."

"I should go now too," Karen said.

"You're not afraid to go out to the house alone, are you?" Kim asked.

"No, but if there's the least little suspicious thing out there, I'm calling 911."

"It might be a good idea to let the police know you're going out there to sleep," Mary said. "Describe your rental car to them. If they see the lights on in the house, they'll know it's you, and they can have a patrol car swing by once or twice during the time you're there."

"Good idea."

A few minutes later, Karen and Mary left the hospital together and went out to their cars. They said good night in the parking lot, and Mary drove home. Gus met her at the door, demanding some attention, and she stooped to pat him.

"Yes, you can come on upstairs with me." A light came on in the hallway that led to Betty's room.

"Hi, it's me," Mary called.

Her sister came down the hall in her robe. "Hi."

"Did I wake you?" Mary asked.

"No, I was reading. How's Henry?"

"The same," Mary said.

"I'm sorry."

Mary frowned. "They keep telling us that's a good thing, and that he'll wake up in time, but it feels all wrong."

"I guess there's nothing else we can do but keep praying," Betty said. "Are you planning to go to church in the morning?"

"Yes, and I'd better turn in so I'll stay awake through the sermon. It's been a rather wearing day."

"I'm sure. Good night then." Betty went to her room, and Mary headed up the stairs with Gus bounding ahead of her. She prepared for bed, praying as she went through the motions of undressing, putting away her clothes, and brushing her teeth.

She slid beneath the covers and turned out the lamp. Gus curled up on the quilt beside her. Absently, she stroked his soft, gray fur. Praying was important, she knew, but it seemed so little. She wanted to do something physical, to help Henry by finding out who did this to him and why. Her mind raced with all that had happened in the last two days, seeking explanations. At last, she began reciting familiar Scripture verses for comfort and peace. She drifted off to sleep with "Never will I leave you; never will I forsake you" on her lips.

NINE

At church the next morning, Mary and Betty were mobbed between the services, when coffee was served. Dorothy was the first to reach Mary's side.

"How is he, Mary? I haven't had a chance to ask Pastor Miles yet this morning."

"About the same, I'm afraid," Mary told her.

Dorothy's gaze fell, and she frowned. "The poor man. I so hoped to hear good news this morning."

"We all did," Betty said, "but the doctors are optimistic."

"I called the hospital before we left home," Mary added. "The doctor hadn't been in yet, but Karen was there with Henry."

"Where are the girls staying?"

Dorothy was so hungry for information that Mary felt sorry for her. She took Dorothy's arm. "Let's sit down for a moment."

"Yes, and I'll get you both a coffee, if you'd like," Betty offered.

Mary thanked her and sat down with her friend. "Karen and Kim are staying at Henry's, taking turns being with him at the hospital."

Sherry Walinski and Heather Hastings came over with their cups in hand.

"Mary, is there any word on Henry?" Sherry asked.

"Not really. He's holding his own."

"I hope he gets better soon," Sherry said.

Heather nodded in sympathy. "We'll keep the prayer chain going for him."

"I'm hoping to go over after the worship service," Mary said. "If I hear anything new, I'll call the pastor and you, Dorothy."

Dorothy smiled sadly. She was a lead member of Mary's prayer group, and she also helped organize the prayer chain for urgent requests in the church. "Thank you."

Betty returned with their coffee, and Lynn Teagarden came with her.

"Hello, Mary," Lynn said, her face full of concern. "What an awful weekend you've had! How are you doing?"

"I'm well, thank you," Mary said. Lynn's husband was Henry's doctor, but she supposed he wouldn't share details of his patients' condition with Lynn. Even if he did, Lynn would never discuss it with others.

Sherry and Heather moved on, but other parishioners took their place. When they finally left the fellowship hall for the service, Betty patted Mary's arm.

"You'll need a nap this afternoon at this rate."

Mary smiled. "Maybe after we see Henry. I'll be all right."

As soon as church was over, they slipped out the side door and got into Betty's car. She drove directly to the hospital, and they went up to the ICU together. Kim saw them through the glass and got up to talk to them in the area near the nurses' desk.

"How is he?" Betty asked. "I won't go in, but I'm here for moral support."

Kim gave her a little hug. "Thanks, Betty. He's stirred some, but nothing more dramatic than when you were here last night, Mary."

"Is Karen resting?" Mary asked.

"Yes. She said she didn't sleep well last night, and I don't think she's caught up from her flight yet. Can you have jet lag, even if you land in the same time zone?"

"I think you can," Mary said with a chuckle.

"Travel is always tiring," Betty added.

"Add to that all this talk of prowlers and the possibility of the intruder going back to Dad's house..." Kim brushed her light brown hair back from her face. "Why don't you go in, Mary? Stay as long as you like."

"I'll just be a few minutes. Betty and I plan to have lunch together, but I thought I'd come back later, if you don't mind."

"Quit saying that. You're always welcome."

Mary was going to step away when Betty asked, "Have you heard any more from the police?"

Kim shook her head, her lips twisting in a grimace. "Not a word since yesterday. It doesn't seem as though they're doing much. At least, if they are, they aren't telling us."

"I'm sure they're looking for Daniel York," Mary said. "They wanted to ask him some questions about when your father bought the car from him. Other than that, I'm not sure they have many leads."

"I hope they're trying to find out something about that fellow who followed you," Kim said.

"So do I." Betty eyed Mary sharply. "I confess I'm starting to worry a little about *you*."

"It was probably nothing," Mary said. She hadn't mentioned the mysterious man who had come to the hospital room to Betty, and now she was glad. Her sister didn't need more to worry about. She hurried into Henry's room and sat in the chair Kim had vacated. Henry was turned slightly toward her, and he still looked too pale. She reached for his hand.

"Hello, Henry. It's me. I hope you're resting and healing." She sat still for a moment, calming herself. "We had a lovely service today. Pastor Miles spoke on God's mercy. Very thought provoking. And of course, everyone wanted to know how you are. Everybody's praying for you, Henry. I don't think there's one person in Ivy Bay who doesn't want you to get better fast." With the possible exception of the one who hit him and put him here, she thought. Again, she wondered about the mysterious man with the baseball cap who had peered in at Henry last night.

"Oh, and Pastor Miles said he'll be coming in later," she added.

As usual, Henry gave her no response. Mary talked on quietly, telling him more about the events at the church and snippets that friends had relayed to her.

"Jill Sanderson told me this morning that she's thinking of entering the ice-cream contest Blake and Tess are putting on. Apparently, Blake is already distributing flyers about it at the shop. I think it will become quite a community event. I certainly hope you're doing better by then. You won't want to miss it."

She stayed only about ten minutes, and then she went to the waiting room, where Betty and Kim were chatting.

"Mary, you didn't mention Dad's boat earlier," Kim said, rising. "I wanted to tell you I haven't heard any more about that either. I wonder if the police are trying to find it."

Mary frowned. "That also makes me wonder about the *Misty Horizon*. What if someone tries to take it?"

"Do you think they would?" Betty asked.

"I don't know," Mary said. "I didn't think anyone would take the little motorboat. In fact, I didn't think anyone would prowl around Henry's garage either. But if the person who took the boat knows Henry's in the hospital, what's to stop him from stealing his fishing boat too?"

Kim's brow wrinkled. "I don't like to think that, but you may be right. Now would be the perfect time to do it."

"Let's stop by the marina on the way home," Betty said.

"Good idea," Mary said. "If the *Misty Horizon* isn't at its usual mooring, we can call Lieutenant Peters at the Coast Guard station."

"You know someone there?" Kim asked.

Mary nodded. "He's helped me before. I think we should check on the boat, just to be sure all is as it should be."

"Thank you," Kim said.

They walked out to the reception area, and Kim hugged Mary and Betty before going into her father's room. The sisters went down to Betty's car.

On the short drive to the marina, Mary kept telling herself everything would be all right, but she couldn't help worrying.

When they arrived, she jumped out of the car. Betty followed her down to the nearest pier. Mary stared out at the dozens of boats moored in the harbor. The familiar lines of Henry's larger boat greeted her, and she sighed.

"There it is."

"Where?" Betty asked.

Mary pointed. "See it? White with navy trim."

"Oh yes." Betty sounded as relieved as Mary felt.

Mary scanned the other boats in the fleet. Several mooring spots were vacant, and at some of those, smaller boats bobbed. She spotted a fifteen-footer at one of the nearer berths and squinted at it.

"That looks like Henry's motorboat."

"The one that was taken?" Betty asked.

"Yes. I can't be sure, though. I don't know the registration number."

"We could write down the number on that one," Betty suggested.

"And then Kim or Karen could check it against Henry's registration for us," Mary said. She took out the small pad and pen she always carried. Between them, she and Betty managed to get all the digits down.

"Ready for lunch now?" Betty asked.

"As soon as I call Kim and give her this number." Mary made the call and then put her phone away. She smiled at Betty. "I'm starving. Let's go home."

Betty got behind the wheel again, and they were soon back at the house. They fixed lunch together and ate at the glass-topped table on the back deck. Mary was thankful for the peaceful setting, overlooking the ever-changing marsh.

They talked quietly, about Betty's garden and a book signing Mary hoped to set up at the shop.

After lunch, Betty headed to her room for a nap, but Mary fetched a notebook and returned to the back deck. It was time to organize all the information she had about Henry's injury and the clues she had examined while trying to figure out who did it. She wrote down what had happened so far—Henry's purchase of the car, the attack, the program she had found in the garage, her own search of the cars in Henry's garage, the suspicious car that had followed her, the missing boat, and the man who had come to the ICU.

The data she jotted down seemed depressingly small. She found herself focusing on Daniel York. He was the only person she knew of who had a definite connection to the car Henry had purchased, where the intruder seemed to have been lurking when Henry interrupted him. As far as she knew, the police hadn't talked to him yet, though she supposed Chief McIntosh wouldn't tell her if they had.

What did she know about Daniel York? Almost nothing, she admitted to herself. She did know that Henry had met him through the Ivy Bay Wheelers, the antique car club to which Henry had belonged for several years. She didn't have the impression that Henry knew him well, however. She didn't recall him ever mentioning Daniel's name before he purchased the Buick from him on Friday. If they were friends who saw each other outside the club meetings, surely she would have heard of this man.

She now knew that Daniel was divorced, and that he had only been married to Dee for about two years before they separated. In fact, if Gloria was to be believed,

Dee had recently left Daniel for another man. Dee's last name was Saxon now, not York, and Mary believed she was now Mrs. Erick Saxon, as she was photographed with him at the charity auction. Dee must have married the man for whom she had left Daniel as soon as she could do so legally.

Mary's one meeting with Dee had gone fairly smoothly. In fact, she had seemed quite gracious to Mary. She could easily have refused to give her Dan's new address, but she had supplied it, and she had even allowed Mary into the house while she got it. But both Gloria and Stan had reviled Dee. The club president had called her a gold digger and implied that she had ruined Daniel financially.

Of all the people who had given her information, Gloria seemed most approachable. But was she reliable? While she did seem to get emotional, Gloria was also a longtime neighbor of Dan York's, and Mary thought that counted for a lot. She probably knew Dan better than anyone else in town, since her husband had been a friend.

She went inside carrying her notebook. If there were more to learn about what led up to Henry's injury, she was determined to ferret it out.

Betty was in the kitchen, stirring something in a stainless-steel mixing bowl.

"I thought you were napping," Mary said. "Feeling better?"

"Yes, I am. I thought I'd bake some macaroons for my book club."

"That reminds me." Mary sat down at the table. "I need to come up with a new ice-cream flavor."

Betty glanced at the ingredients she had laid out on the counter. "Are you sure you're up to it? With all that's happened, maybe you should opt out."

"Making ice cream relaxes me," Mary said. "And anyway, I am holding out hope that Henry's better by then. Tess and Blake are going to hold a competition on the Fourth."

"I heard Jill mention it this morning." Betty smiled as she began spooning blobs of batter onto her cookie sheet. "That sounds like fun."

"It does, but I haven't had time to think about it. Since the voting is to be held on the Fourth, I'd like to do something patriotic but tasty."

"*Hmm.* Apple pie, corn on the cob, lobster, cranberry . . ."

"I don't think corn ice cream would go over very well. I do keep coming back to apple pie, though. Or cherry." Mary sat and chatted with Betty for a few more minutes. When the timer bell rang and Betty got up to remove the first tray of cookies from the oven, Mary said, "I've decided to go visit Daniel York's old neighbor again. Did I tell you about Gloria?"

"You mentioned her this morning in the car. Do you think she knows anything about Henry?"

"No. But I think she knows a lot about Daniel. Speaking of whom, I wonder if the police have caught up with him yet and talked to him." Mary glanced at the clock. "Maybe I'll go by his apartment first. He's the one I really want to talk to."

"Maybe you should go with a gift." Betty nodded toward the cookie sheet and set it on a hot pad. "These will only take a minute to set, and I can bag a few for you. Single men appreciate homemade goodies, you know."

"Great idea. Thanks, Bets." Mary got out a paper plate and plastic wrap, and soon she was on her way, with a covered plate of macaroons on the front seat beside her.

She drove into the apartment building's lot and rolled slowly toward Daniel's door. The reserved spot nearest his entrance was empty. She pulled into it and got out. As she'd anticipated, no one answered when she rang the doorbell. Had he stayed away all weekend? With a sigh, she went back to the car and drove to Jonquil Lane. Since Dan York wasn't home, Gloria might as well have the cookies.

She pulled into Gloria's driveway this time and parked, but she did look across the street when she got out of the car. The Saxons' house looked deserted. The window blinds were closed, and the garage doors were down.

Gloria opened her front door even before Mary had a chance to ring the bell. She smiled, and her glance went to the plate of macaroons in Mary's hand.

"Well, hello again."

"Hi." Mary returned her smile. "You were so nice to me yesterday I thought I'd drop by again and bring you some cookies."

"Thanks. Those look delicious. Would you like some tea?"

"I'd love it." Mary followed her into her sunny kitchen. While not as spacious or as finely decorated as Dee's, it was still a warm, inviting room. On one side of the counter, a book rack held an array of a dozen cookbooks. "Do you like to cook?" Mary asked.

Gloria shrugged. "It's okay. Not much fun, now that my husband's gone and the kids are grown."

"I know what you mean," Mary said.

"But I enjoy gardening more these days," Gloria added.

Mary took the chair Gloria indicated at the breakfast table, which sat in a niche with a bay window looking out on the backyard and a line of pine trees beyond. Gloria put a copper teakettle on the stove and sat down with her.

"Did you get hold of Daniel?" Gloria asked.

"Not yet. I don't suppose you've heard any more about him."

Gloria shook her head. "I never see him anymore, and Dee sure wouldn't tell me anything. Not that he's over there much these days, but she must have *some* contact with him."

"It seems so. She did give me his new address, but I think he must have gone out of town for the weekend."

"Too bad. How's your friend doing?"

"He's still in the hospital." Mary wasn't sure how much to divulge to Gloria. "I went over to the antique car show yesterday, hoping I'd run into Dan there, but apparently he only went on Friday."

"I thought the same thing," Gloria said. "He loves those old cars. I drove over to the fairgrounds myself yesterday morning, but he wasn't there."

"When was the last time you saw Daniel?" Mary asked.

"Oh, it's been weeks." Gloria jumped up to take the kettle off and fix their tea. A couple of minutes later, she rejoined Mary with their steaming mugs and took the wrap off the plate of cookies.

Mary sipped her tea. "So, you haven't seen much of Dan since the divorce?"

"No." Gloria frowned as she took one of the macaroons. "I admit, I miss him. He was a great neighbor. A great friend too." She met Mary's eyes almost defiantly. "What that woman did to him is despicable."

"I believe you said she and Daniel divorced about six months ago?"

"Yes, and Erick Saxon moved in with her as soon as Dan moved out. Within weeks after the divorce was final, she married Erick."

"Poor Dan," Mary murmured.

"I'll say." Gloria bit into her macaroon and chewed pensively for a moment. Her smile flashed. "These are great!"

"Thanks," Mary said. "My sister actually made them. I'll tell her you liked them." After a moment, she asked Gloria, "So, do you see the Saxons much?"

Gloria shrugged. "Not much. I mean I *see* them, but we don't talk much anymore." She popped the rest of the cookie into her mouth. After she had chewed and swallowed it, she added, "Seems like they're always either having people over, or they go out. I hardly ever see that they're both home in the evening unless they have company. And when they go out, Dee is always wearing some designer dress. And the jewelry— whew! All I can say is, Erick must make plenty, because I know she didn't have that much jewelry when Dan was around. He bought her a few things, but I don't think he could keep up with her appetite for expensive things, you know what I mean?"

"Maybe that's why they still live here," Mary suggested.

"Oh, you mean because she spends all of Erick's money on clothes and jewelry, so they can't afford a bigger house? You may have something there."

"You mentioned a ring," Mary said and took a sip of her tea.

"Oh yeah, that ring." Gloria made a face. "Dee showed it to me once, after Dan bought it for her."

"I thought you weren't friends?"

"Not really, but she liked to show off things. When she'd get something new, she'd yell across the street to me, if I was outside. She'd say, 'Hey, Gloria, want to see my new living room set?' Or something like that. That ring was the last thing she showed me. I don't think she's spoken a word to me since she threw Dan out."

"What sort of ring was it?" Mary asked.

"I've got to admit, it was gorgeous. It had this huge diamond."

"A big one, huh?" Mary set her cup down and tried to imagine the ring on Dee's finger.

"Yeah, and Dee said it was really old. I'm no expert, but it did look antique to me. Heavy gold setting with a lot of decoration on the band, and it had little rubies on each side. I remember thinking it must have been expensive. And Dee said now she needed a diamond-and-ruby necklace to go with it. She laughed about it, but I wondered if she pestered Dan to get her one."

"So this was definitely something she got from Daniel? It couldn't have been an engagement ring from her second husband?"

"Oh no. I had the impression that Dan just about emptied his savings to get it for her. And then, just a few weeks later, she tossed him out. I think..." Gloria paused and then shook her head. "Well, it doesn't matter what I think, does it?"

"Maybe not, but you're helping me get a picture of the relationships," Mary said.

Gloria eyed her keenly for a moment and then reached for another macaroon. "All right, I'll say it. I think she got Dan to buy her this expensive piece of jewelry and then dumped him. I think she knew already she was going to divorce him and marry Erick, and she wanted to leave the marriage with as many assets as she could. She succeeded too."

"And when was the ring stolen?" Mary asked.

"Just last week."

"Really!" So recently. For some reason, Mary had been under the impression that it had happened earlier. "Why do you suppose she suggested you as a suspect?"

"No idea, except that I'm broke. I thought for a while after Jonathan died that I might lose my house, but I'm past that now. I've got a job at the organic nursery. It's not a big income, but it's enough to take up the slack. But I would never start pilfering people's jewelry. The very idea that she would say so makes me furious."

"Do you know if the ring was insured?" Mary asked.

"No clue." Gloria sighed and reached toward the cookie plate, but drew her hand back. "I should quit now and save the rest of those for later. They're really good."

Mary tried to think of other things she should ask Gloria while she had the chance, but she wasn't sure where all of this would lead. She smiled. "I should get going."

"Nice talking to you." Gloria stood and walked with her toward the door. "I have to say, I liked this neighborhood a whole lot better before...well, in the old days. But I guess those days are over."

TEN

—◆◆—

Mary drove away thinking about the mystery of the stolen ring. Who would want to steal it? Any jewel thief, of course. Maybe the theft was incidental to what happened later with Henry. If Dee had flashed it around, a lot of people would know it was in her possession. Any unscrupulous person might target the Saxon house.

But a couple of particular people came to mind as she drove. First of all, there was Daniel York. If he and Dee had gone through a bitter divorce and he didn't think the assets were fairly divided, maybe he'd decided to even things up. Was it possible Dan had stolen the ring himself?

On the other hand, Dee Saxon might bear a close look. It wouldn't be the first time someone had pretended to have been burglarized and then claimed the insurance money. Her new husband, Erick, was also a contender.

The big question, in Mary's mind, was: If Daniel, Dee, or her husband took the ring, where was it now? If the Saxons had it, they would probably hide it in their house or in a secure place like a safe or a bank vault. Dee loved wearing her jewelry so much, it would be torture for her to leave it there for long, though. And Daniel...if he were the thief, Mary mused, he would probably have to wait a while before trying to sell the distinctive ring. Where would he put it to keep it safe until things cooled down?

The question of the ring's theft kept nagging at her. It seemed to have nothing to do with the attack on Henry, and yet the timing was almost too coincidental. Mary couldn't help feeling she should follow up on it. Maybe that would be a waste of time, but she couldn't get it out of her mind.

Not knowing where the police investigation on Henry's case was headed frustrated her terribly. She couldn't expect to get anything useful from Chief McIntosh, but maybe one of the patrolmen would be more helpful. Mary found herself driving toward the Ivy Bay police station. She wouldn't ask for a lot, just an assurance that they were still on the case.

When she entered the building, her nerves calmed a notch when she saw Officer Tilton standing at the front desk. Perfect. Only a couple of other people were in the lobby, and Mary stepped confidently up to the desk.

"Hi, Mrs. Fisher." Officer Tilton smiled at her, and Mary took that as another good sign.

She smiled back. "Good afternoon, Officer Tilton. I stopped by to see how the investigation is going into Henry Woodrow's assailant."

Tilton glanced around, as though making sure no other officers were within hearing range. "We're working hard on it. I can't really talk about leads."

Mary nodded sympathetically. "But I'm guessing you don't have anything solid as to who did it."

"Well..." He frowned. "I can't really say."

"It's all right," she said. "I did wonder if you heard about the car that followed me here from Henry's house yesterday evening."

"Yes, the chief did mention it to us." Officer Tilton seemed relieved to be able to talk about something not off limits.

"And Henry's stolen boat?"

"Yes, ma'am, I took the call."

Mary was beginning to wish she'd brought more cookies to leave at the police station. Maybe if she added a little information, Officer Tilton would loosen up a bit.

"I've been thinking a lot about the attack, of course," she said. "There are the obvious suspects, like Daniel York, because he owned that car before Henry—though I can't imagine why he would ever hit Henry. Have you been able to talk to him yet?"

"Sorry, I can't tell you that." Tilton stood looking down at her through half-closed eyes. He was nearly a foot taller than Mary, and it was hard to feel comfortable craning her neck to meet his gaze.

"That's all right, but I've also been thinking about other people. For instance, the people who were at the automobile show," she went on, watching his face and hoping he would give some indication that they were pursuing these threads. "Other vendors, and of course, customers. Maybe someone who wanted to buy that car but couldn't afford it."

"Do you know of anyone like that?" Officer Tilton asked.

"Well, no. I went out to the show yesterday before they closed up, and I did talk to some of the people, including Stan Auger, the club president. He implied that Daniel York needed money badly, and so he sold a total of three cars there on Friday. Did you know that?"

"Uh..."

"And there was another man there selling cars, the one they call Bargain Bill. You know who I mean?"

"Oh sure," Officer Tilton said. "He has the corny commercials."

Mary chuckled. "That's right. The couple who had the space next to Mr. York's told me that Bargain Bill had tried to buy Daniel York's cars early in the day, but he refused. I wonder how badly he wanted them. Maybe you should talk to him."

"*Hmm.*" Officer Tilton fished a small notebook and a pen from his pocket. "I'll make a note of that."

"Thank you," Mary said. "I don't really suspect him of hitting Henry, but he did express interest in that car on Friday. And I wondered if anyone had talked to the people who bought Mr. York's other two cars. It shouldn't be too hard to find out who they were, especially if you're in touch with Mr. York." She eyed him hopefully.

Officer Tilton wrote in the notebook for a few seconds, then looked down at her. "Thanks, Mrs. Fisher. I'll find out if anyone has looked into that."

"Oh good. And, one more thing." She smiled up at him. "I hope I'm not making a pest of myself, but this is very important to me. Henry is such a dear friend."

"Of course. I understand. Was there something else?"

"Yes, I've learned that Mr. York's ex-wife, Dee Saxon, had a valuable ring stolen recently—within the last week or so. Did she file a complaint on that?"

The door to the inner offices of the police station opened. Officer Tilton's face went stern again. "I'm sorry. I can't talk about that."

Mary sighed as another officer came out and took a seat near Officer Tilton and opened a loose-leaf binder on the desk.

"I just wondered," Mary said. "It seemed odd that two crimes were so closely connected to Mr. York in such a short time. Not that I think he attacked Henry—I don't. It just seemed strange."

Tilton nodded and came out from behind the desk, reaching out as though to take her arm and propel her along with him toward the door. "Coincidences do happen, you know."

"Oh yes, I know." Mary smiled and nodded. "Well, I'll leave you to it. Thank you very much, Officer Tilton."

She kept the smile on her face until she got outside, but inside she was far from encouraged. Probably Chief McIntosh was being strict with the men, and they were afraid of displeasing him. In the past, Chief McArthur certainly hadn't encouraged her to poke around his cases, but he had often accepted any information she brought to him. Sometimes he insisted she stay out of things, but it was usually for her protection. Now the police force as a whole seemed to think she was meddling. How much of that was McIntosh's influence?

She opened her car door and got in. She sat there thinking for several minutes, trying to come up with a new way to get some information. The police had to give out some information to the general public. After all, the *Ivy Bay Bugle* ran a column at least twice a week called "Police Log." If the officers were as tight-lipped as Tilton had been this afternoon, how did the newspaper staff get the data for their column?

Mary took out her cell phone and called her friend Johanna Montgomery at the *Bugle*.

"Well, hi, Mary. How can I help you today?"

The head reporter's cheerful greeting encouraged Mary, and she plunged right in. "I wondered if you could tell me about the police log," Mary said. "How do you get the information for that column?"

"I go over to the police station and look at their log. That's the book where they record all the calls that the officers respond to."

Mary laughed. "It's as easy as that?"

"Sure. You just go in and ask at the desk. They give you the logbook, and you look at it there. You can't take it with you, but you can sit down and make notes. That's what we do. We copy out anything that sounds interesting—but of course, we don't put anyone's name. And we usually skip the boring stuff like 'Barking dog reported on Hill Street.'"

"And anyone can walk in and do this?" Mary said, just to be sure.

"Absolutely. It's part of the public record. Sometimes I get leads for bigger stories that way. Are you thinking about reading the police log?"

"Yes, actually."

"Anything I might be interested in?" Johanna asked.

"Not yet. You know about Henry Woodrow being assaulted?"

"Yes, that was a shame. Have the police caught the guy who did it?"

"No. I want to check on something I heard about a person who's peripherally connected."

"Ooh, sounds interesting. Maybe I should go over this afternoon and ask for an update—although I've got to write up my article about the school board meeting. I'll put it on my list for tomorrow morning."

"Thanks, Johanna. Maybe they'll tell you more than they will me. It's good to know someone will be keeping the police on their toes."

"I'll tell them our readers want an update. The officers are usually pretty good about things like that, and I'm sure a lot of folks want to know what happened to Henry."

After ending the call, Mary picked up her purse and uttered a quick prayer for wisdom, then got out of her car and went back inside the police station. Officer Tilton was at the desk, but the patrolman who had joined him earlier was gone. Mary walked over and smiled when he looked up at her.

"Hello again. I would like to look at the police log, if I may."

Officer Tilton's eyes widened for a moment, but he nodded and stood up. "You can sit right over there, and I'll bring it to you." He pointed to a shelf on the side wall that could serve as a desk and had a straight chair in front of it.

Mary went over and sat down. She placed her purse on the shelf and took out her notepad and pen. She wondered if the officer would tell Chief McIntosh of her request, but he came around the counter almost at once, bringing a tall book that reminded her of a ledger.

"Here you go, ma'am." Officer Tilton laid it down, open to a page partially filled with handwritten notations. "These are the latest entries. If you can't read something, let me know."

"Thank you very much." She glanced at the pages to see what their system was. Apparently either the responding officers or the one on the desk wrote each entry by hand. Each gave the time, a thumbnail description of the call, and the address from which the complaint originated. The last entry was for that day. It read, *2:15 PM, 95 Maple Street, shoplifting.* Before that was *4:35 AM, 3102 Marsh Road, barking dog.* Mary laughed, wondering if Johanna had seen similar entries. On Saturday's page she found the brief notation of Kim Allen's call about the boat.

Mary turned back a couple of pages to the entries for the previous week. The complaints varied widely. Loud music, a missing toolbox, a raccoon in a trash can. At a couple of spots in the margin, she noticed a pencil notation of J.M. Johanna had left her mark at the spot where she had left off each time she checked the log.

It took only a few minutes to find what she sought. Ten days ago, officers had responded to 35 Jonquil Lane at 10:20 AM. Burglary, the note said. Mary copied the entry in her notebook. She read the entries before and after that incident for a couple of days, but found nothing else related to Jonquil Lane. She carried the open book back to the desk.

"I don't suppose I can get information on one of these incidents," she said.

"I'm not supposed to discuss it, unless you're directly connected to one of the complaints."

She had surmised as much, so she wasn't overly disappointed this time. "All right. I just wondered if you had solved this case." She pointed to the burglary entry. "This is when Dee Saxon reported her ring stolen. I wondered if the police had caught the thief yet."

Officer Tilton hesitated and then said, "That's an open case, ma'am. Sorry."

Mary nodded slowly. If they had caught the thief, the case would be closed, and he could acknowledge that. Therefore, she could conclude that the thief was still at large, and the ring had not been recovered.

She smiled at Officer Tilton. "Thank you. I understand about you not being able to discuss investigations. But I do wonder about the Saxons. Is it possible they reported her ring stolen in order to make a claim to their insurance company?" She couldn't quite figure out how, if the Saxons *had* committed insurance fraud, it had anything to do with Henry. But there was something strange about the timing of the stolen ring of Dan's ex-wife and the attack on Henry, who had bought his new car from Dan, so she'd look into the ring a bit more until the connection either fizzled or grew clearer.

"I...really can't talk about this, Mrs. Fisher. I mean, anything's possible. People have certainly done that before. But I can't speculate about this particular case."

"All right. Thanks a lot." Mary went out to her car slightly mollified, although she still had questions. Officer Tilton had acted correctly, she knew, but her life might be simpler if she could see the police report on the theft at the Saxons' house—not to mention the one on Henry's case.

ELEVEN

—◆◆◆—

As Mary pulled out of the police station's parking lot, her cell phone rang. She pulled into a nearby service station's parking lot to answer it.

"Mary? It's Karen. Kim asked me to call you and tell you I've found the registration to Dad's small motorboat."

"Oh, wonderful! Just a second." Mary took out the pad on which she had written the call letters of the boat she and Betty had seen at the marina. "Go ahead."

Karen read off a string of digits, and Mary followed along. "That's it. I'm going to call Lieutenant Peters and see if he can meet me at the dock. Thanks, Karen."

She placed her call and was happy to learn that Lieutenant Peters was available. She headed once more to the marina by the canal.

The lieutenant was waiting when she arrived and parked near the fish market. The white shirt of his crisp summer uniform stood out against the blues and grays of the marina. Another man, bearded and wearing a red-and-blue plaid shirt, stood beside him. Peters came to meet her as she walked down onto the pier.

"Mrs. Fisher! I think I have answers to your questions about Mr. Woodrow's boat."

"I'm so glad."

The lieutenant turned and beckoned to the other man to join them. "This is Larry Henshaw. He has a fishing boat yonder." Peters pointed to one of the boats moored a short distance out from shore.

"Mr. Henshaw," Mary said, nodding to him and searching her memory. "I think I've heard Henry Woodrow speak of you before."

The fisherman nodded. "I expect you have. Henry and I go way back. Been friends for fifty years."

"I'm pleased to meet you," Mary said.

Lieutenant Peters smiled at her. "Mr. Henshaw was just coming ashore when I got here—in the boat you described to me."

Mary caught a quick breath and looked down over the edge of the dock. Where a steep stairway came up, a small motorboat was tied. From above, it certainly looked like the same one she had seen at Henry's dock.

She looked from Lieutenant Peters to Mr. Henshaw and back, unsure what to say.

Mr. Henshaw stroked his beard. "Henry said I could use his boat for a few days. My son had an accident with mine last week and stove it up. I hope there's no problem, ma'am. I saw Henry Friday morning, and he said I could come out to his house anytime and get the boat, so I had Darren drive me out there yesterday. Henry wasn't home, so I just got in the boat and left. I figured he'd realize I was the one who took it."

"Oh, there's no problem," Mary said quickly. "In fact, I'm very relieved. I don't know if you're aware that Henry was injured Friday night and is in the hospital."

Mr. Henshaw's face darkened. "No! What happened?"

Quickly Mary gave him and Lieutenant Peters the gist of the story.

"Now, that's too bad," Mr. Henshaw said, frowning. "Poor old Henry!"

"I can see why you were concerned about the boat," Lieutenant Peters said.

"I'm sorry about the confusion," Mary told him. "Mr. Henshaw, we think someone went to Henry's house with theft in mind. Then the next day, his boat was gone. I didn't mean to accuse you falsely."

"Not a problem," the fisherman said. "And I'll take it back by the end of the week, soon's mine is seaworthy again. I sure am sorry to hear about his accident."

Mary didn't correct his misnomer, but she knew Henry's injury was no accident. She thanked the lieutenant and Mr. Henshaw and went back to her car. With two quick calls, she informed Karen and Officer Tilton that the boat had been found. But she was no closer to learning who had attacked Henry.

Mary couldn't shake the feeling that if she could just sit down with Daniel York, he might be able to fill in some of the blanks for her. As she drove away from the marina, she mulled over everything she knew about Dan. If he wasn't the one who hurt Henry, Mary couldn't help but think he would know something that would point her in the right direction.

She drove to his apartment building and hurried up the walk. It was nearly four o'clock. Surely he would come home today. He had a job, didn't he?

As before, no one answered when she rang the bell. Out of frustration, she knocked on the door, but that brought no better result. She glanced around. A dozen or more cars sat in nearby parking spots, but she saw no one watching her. She edged over to the window. The interior looked the same as it had before—messy. With a sigh, she went back to her car. Someone had to know where Dan was, but who?

She took out the program from the auto show and noticed Stan Auger's name. As president of the sponsoring organization, he had received recognition on the front of the program, and his telephone number was listed as well. Mary didn't hesitate to punch it in on her cell phone.

"Hello?" came Stan's voice, and she recognized it immediately.

"Hello. This is Mary Fisher. We met yesterday at the fairgrounds."

"Sure, I remember you."

"Mr. Auger, I've been trying to reach Daniel York, but he isn't at his apartment. From what I can tell, he must have gone away for the weekend. Do you know if he has a cell phone?"

"*Hmm*, if he does, I don't have the number," Stan said. "Sorry."

Mary pressed onward. "You mentioned to me yesterday that he had another piece of property, and I wondered if he could possibly have gone there."

"You may be right," Stan said. "It's a fishing cabin on some lake or other. I've heard him talk about it a few times, but I have no idea where it is."

"It's in Massachusetts, though?" Mary asked.

"Oh yes, I think so. I had the impression it wasn't very far away."

"Thank you," Mary said. "You've been a big help."

She checked her watch and wondered where she could get more information at four o'clock on a Sunday afternoon. On any weekday, she could go to the county clerk's office and ask for help. Probably Bea Winslow could tell her what properties Daniel York owned in two minutes flat. But not today. With a sigh, Mary tried to resign herself to waiting until Monday morning. The memory of the car following her and of the mysterious man at the hospital spurred her to action. If there was any way to find Dan York today, she'd be remiss not to try.

Who else would know the location of his cabin? Henry, maybe, but that didn't help. Perhaps some of the other members of the Ivy Bay Wheelers.

And Dee Saxon, she thought. So far, Mary had only managed to speak to Dee once, but maybe she could catch her at home again. She decided to phone instead of driving over to Jonquil Lane again.

Betty was reading in the living room when Mary walked in.

"Well, hi. I was wondering if you'd be home for supper." Betty laid her book aside. "I was thinking about making chicken soup."

"Let me do it," Mary said. "You sit still."

"I need to get up and move around anyway," Betty said.

"All right, you can help. I want to make a phone call first." Mary got the phone book and searched for Dee Saxon. "That's odd."

"What?" Betty asked.

"I'm not finding any Saxons under the Ivy Bay section of the phone book, and I know Dee Saxon lives on Jonquil Lane."

"Why is that name familiar?" Betty asked.

"It's the couple who were at the charity auction Friday night. Their picture was in the paper, remember? Mr. and Mrs. Erick Saxon."

"Oh, right. And you told me she used to be married to the man Henry got the car from, is that right?"

"You got it, but apparently the phone book people didn't. The Saxons must be unlisted."

"Maybe they only have cell phones," Betty said.

Mary nodded. "Or, wait a minute. Dee has been divorced from Daniel for less than a year. You don't suppose the phone is still in his name?" She quickly turned the pages to the *Y*s.

"It's been quite a while since we got a new phone book," Betty said.

"Got it!" Mary smiled at her. "Daniel York, 35 Jonquil Lane. Only Daniel doesn't live there anymore. With any luck, Dee hasn't bothered to change the phone number." She went to the kitchen phone and called the number.

"Hello?" a woman said brightly.

Betty was standing in the kitchen doorway, and Mary gave her a thumbs-up. Into the phone, she said, "Mrs. Saxon, this is Mary Fisher. We met yesterday morning, and you were kind enough to give me Daniel York's new address."

"Yes?" Dee's voice rose in suspicion.

"I'm sorry to bother you again, but I haven't been able to reach Mr. York yet, and it's very important."

"Oh? I hope your friend hasn't taken a turn for the worse."

"He's very ill, and I want to get word to Mr. York."

"Well, I have no idea where Dan is. I don't keep track of him."

"I'm sorry. I didn't mean to imply that. Do you know if he has a cell phone?"

"I don't think he does right now."

"I see," Mary said. "I was talking to another friend of his, and I was told that Mr. York has a fishing cabin. I thought perhaps he'd gone there for the weekend. I'd really like to speak to him today."

"I don't know. This seems a little invasive, Mrs. Fisher. How do I know Dan wants to talk to you?"

"I assure you I mean him no harm. It's just that my friend was with him part of the day on Friday, and—"

"Does this have something to do with the antique car show?" Dee asked. "Dan always went to those things."

Mary hesitated. Could it possibly hurt Henry if she was more open with Dee? She wasn't sure, but she decided to risk it.

"Yes, actually. They saw each other at the car show, and...well, Henry bought a car from Dan."

"I see."

After a moment's pause, Mary said, "There's nothing wrong with the car, I promise. But Henry was injured that evening, and, while I don't know Mr. York, I thought I should tell him. I know they were friends, and I thought Mr. York might be able to tell me something about how Henry was doing earlier, and if he needs anything else from him in regard to the car." She stopped talking. If she rattled on too long, Dee would probably hang up on her.

After a moment, Dee sighed. "It's at Federal Pond, on the other side of Myles Standish State Forest. Conifer Road, I think. He took me there once, and I hated it. Too rustic for me, so I let him have it when we split, along with his precious antique cars. What would I do with those? Now, if you'll excuse me..."

"Thank you," Mary said. "Thank you very much." By the time the words were out, Dee had clicked off.

"What did she say?" Betty asked.

Mary told her, and added, "It shouldn't take more than half an hour to drive out there."

"*Hmm*, that's if you knew exactly where it was. This Conifer Road could be ten miles long."

"But he's got to be right on the water if it's his fishing cabin," Mary said. "Let me see if my computer or my GPS can zero in on it."

"I'm going with you, you know."

Mary stopped and stared at her sister. "You are?"

"I can't let you go out there alone. We don't know for sure that this Dan York isn't the one who assaulted Henry. It's nearly five o'clock. You could be out there until dark. Forget the chicken soup! There's no way I'm staying here and wondering if you're all right."

Mary smiled. "Thank you. Let me see what I can find out."

Fifteen minutes later, armed with sweaters, mosquito repellant, flashlights, and a printout of directions to the lake, they climbed into Mary's car.

"What's in your tote?" she asked Betty.

"Sandwiches, cookies, and water bottles."

"Good idea. You always think of the practical things."

The drive went quickly, and they traveled through one of the area's least populated sections.

"I don't come over here often enough," Betty said with a sigh. "Are you planning to go back to the hospital tonight?"

Mary threw her a sidelong glance. "How would you feel about stopping there on the way home?"

"Sure, if it's not too late. I hope they've seen some improvement today."

"I know. It's what I pray for." Mary's voice broke. "Oh, Bets, what if he doesn't come out of it?"

Betty reached over and patted her arm. "Let's trust in the Lord for that. The doctors all agree the coma isn't permanent."

"Yes, but from what Dr. Teagarden and the neurologist said, it seems like he should have woken up by now."

"It's only been two days, Mar."

"You're right." Mary sighed. "It's hard to be patient."

They came to the turn for Conifer Road, and Mary glanced in her rearview mirror. One car was behind her, but quite a ways back. She made the turn onto the dirt road.

"According to my computer, this road is only a couple of miles long," she told Betty, "and the part near the lake is only the last half mile or so."

They drove through a wooded area, with the sun's late afternoon rays slanting down through the branches of the tall trees. Soon they passed a small cottage, and then another.

"Look!"

Betty pointed ahead, and Mary saw the silvery glitter of water between the tree trunks.

"We're here."

Betty looked toward the other side of the road. "There's an SUV at that cottage."

"Shall we stop and ask if they know Daniel?" Mary asked.

"Why not?"

Mary pulled in, and they got out and walked up to the cottage. A young woman in a swimsuit came to the door with a glass of iced tea in her hand.

"Oh, hi. Can I help you?"

"We're looking for a friend of ours with a cabin down here, but we're not sure which one it is. His name is Daniel York."

"*Hmm*, older fellow, glasses?"

"Yes," Mary said, though she wasn't sure about the glasses.

"I think he's just down the road two—no, three—places. There's a little sign on the tree out front that says York."

"Thank you." Mary and Betty got back in the car, and Mary drove slowly onward, down the gravel road.

"I hope we don't meet any cars," Betty said. "It's awfully narrow here."

The cottages were separated by several hundred feet of wooded land, but suddenly they came into a clearing, with light dancing on the lake's surface beyond. Four cabins stood fairly close together along the waterfront.

Mary squinted at the trees before each one.

"That one says Astin," Betty reported. "Keep going."

"York." Mary spotted the little wooden sign and pulled in beside an old green Volkswagen Beetle.

"Another of his antique cars?" Betty asked, eyeing the subcompact dubiously.

"It's probably all he's got left." Mary, suddenly a little nervous, shut off the motor and looked over at Betty. "Shall we?"

The yard flora consisted of pines and a few hardwood trees. A little grass grew on the path to the door, and under the trees, pine needles covered the ground. There were no flower beds or window boxes, as there were at some of the other cottages.

Rustic was a good word to describe the small cabin, Mary decided. It couldn't hold more than two or three rooms. The roof was covered with pine needles, and a little moss, unless she was mistaken. The front step sagged as she put her weight on it. She knocked on the door and waited. No one opened the door, and there was no sound from within. She knocked again and turned to Betty, who waited below the step.

"What do you think?" Betty asked.

A car rolled past the driveway, its wheels crunching on the gravel road. Mary caught her breath.

"What is it?" Betty whipped around to stare after the car as it passed the end of the drive.

"That car. It looks like the one that followed me last night."

TWELVE

---◆◆---

As the dark blue car slowly moved on beneath the pine trees lining the road, Mary focused on the rear license plate. Tree branches blocked it momentarily, but she caught another glimpse before it disappeared. They could still hear its wheels moving over the dry dirt lane.

"Two-four-seven," Mary muttered, rummaging in her purse.

"What can I do?" Betty asked.

Mary pulled out her little notebook and pen and thrust her handbag into Betty's hands. "Hold this." She scribbled the plate number on the first available sheet of paper, then drew a deep breath and wrote it again, more neatly.

"There! At least I've got the entire number now."

"The police can check on it," Betty said.

"If I can convince them it's a legitimate lead." Mary frowned. "They don't want to believe me about this, but it sure did look like the same car, and the first two characters were the same as what I gave them last night."

"The driver was gawking at us as he passed," Betty said.

"Really? I didn't notice. I was so determined to get the plate number I didn't even look at the driver. What did you see?"

"It was definitely a man, and I had the impression he was middle-aged, though I can't say for sure. He had on a hat of some kind. And the car—it's navy blue."

"Yes," Mary said. "I was sure of that this time." She wrote down the color and what Betty had said about the driver.

"Do you think Mr. York is here?" Betty asked. "If he's not, maybe we ought to get going. Some of the cottages are empty, and this is a fairly isolated place."

"He came here to fish. Let's at least take a look down near the dock before we go." Mary put her notebook and pen away. "Come on." She led the way around the side of the cabin.

"Oh, he's got a boat." She stopped and scowled at the empty trailer parked to the side of the building. "If he's out on the lake, we may never find him."

"He didn't pull a boat and trailer here with that VW Bug," Betty said.

"True. He probably brought the boat up here this spring and left it. I'll bet he had it in storage with his antique cars over the winter." That was another avenue she hadn't thought of—after Daniel had moved into the apartment six months ago, where had he kept his vehicles? If she couldn't find him, maybe she could follow up on that idea. He had to have stored those valuable antique cars someplace.

They rounded the cabin and saw that the ground fell away. A screened porch on the back of the cottage gave onto a path with a few steps built into the steepest parts and a handrail all the way down to the dock below. A small aluminum boat with an outboard motor was tied up at the dock.

"Looks like you were right," Betty said with satisfaction.

"Where is he?" Mary asked.

Betty pointed to the rocks to one side of the dock, where a man of about fifty was perched on a flat boulder about four feet above the lake's surface. He wore a canvas fishing hat, and in his hands he held a fishing rod.

Mary smiled. "Let's hope that's him."

As she and Betty made their way down the path, he cast his line out where a large oak tree overhung the placid water and began to reel it in. When she stepped onto the shore end of the dock, Mary called, "Hello."

He turned toward her, his mouth open in surprise. "Oh, hello there." He peered at them through his glasses.

"Mr. York?" Mary asked.

"Yes." His eyebrows shot up, and his gaze roved over them, as if he was trying to place them.

"I'm Mary Fisher, and this is my sister, Betty Emerson. We're good friends of Henry Woodrow's."

"Oh." His expression was even more baffled now, and Mary hastened to explain.

The breeze off the lake ruffled Mary's hair. She called, "I've been trying to find you to tell you that Henry was injured Friday evening, and he's in the hospital."

"Oh, shoot. I hope it wasn't the car..."

"No, not an auto accident," Mary said. "Could we talk for a few minutes?"

"Certainly." He reeled in his line and attached the hook to the reel so it wouldn't swing free. Carrying the rod, he climbed from his boulder to a smaller rock and down to the ground.

Mary left the dock and met him a few feet away from it. "I take it the police haven't contacted you yet?"

"Police? No. Why should they?"

Mary drew in a deep breath. "Henry was assaulted Friday night at his home. He had invited me over to see the car he bought from you. We were eating dinner, and someone entered his garage. We heard noises. Henry went out to see what was going on. It appears that the intruder hit him. He's been unconscious ever since."

Dan's jaw dropped. "That's terrible. Surely the police don't think I had anything to do with it. I've been here all weekend."

Mary shrugged. "I don't know what the police think. Since Henry is a friend of yours, I was sure you'd want to know about this."

"Well, yeah." Dan hesitated. "Did they catch the guy?"

"Not yet," Mary said. "It seems the thief was interested in the Buick. One of the doors was open when I found Henry lying on the garage floor. And you were one of the last people to see Henry before that incident. I'm sure the police will want to interview you."

He huffed out a big breath. "Wow. Poor Henry. I'm sorry that he's hurt, but I assure you, I'm not the one who did that." He eyed Mary sharply. "So, it had something to do with the Century?"

"No one knows for sure. The police may think the assailant was trying to steal the car. But I'm not so sure."

Dan stared at her, and Mary could have sworn his face went pale. Something was making Dan very uncomfortable.

His shoulders sagged, and his eyes seemed unfocused as he gazed out over the lake. Mary stepped toward him.

"Mr. York? Are you all right, sir?"

"I . . . yes."

His anxiety was evident in his tight mouth and now grayish skin. Mary looked at Betty.

"Perhaps we should sit down somewhere to discuss this," Betty said. "Can you make it to the house, Mr. York?"

"Yes. Come on up to the cabin, ladies. We can have a cold drink." He took a handkerchief from his pocket and wiped his forehead. He squared his shoulders as though determined to see this through and headed up the steep path.

Mary and Betty followed him up the trail and the steps. Mary kept as close behind him as she could without encountering the end of the fishing rod he carried over his shoulder. He had looked so shaken she was afraid he might stagger, but he made it to the top of the path without faltering. She looked back and saw that Betty was coming along slowly, hanging on to the railing and using it to help pull herself up the stairs.

"Are you okay?" Mary asked her. Betty was a trouper to climb all those steps with her arthritic knees.

Betty nodded and waved her on, so Mary turned to follow Dan. They entered the back screened porch of the cabin. He flipped on the lights and leaned his rod against the wall in a corner.

The inside walls of the cabin were unfinished, and the studs and board siding were clearly visible, as were the rafters above. It was a typical summer cottage, not winterized. A glance into the small kitchen beyond told Mary this was definitely a bachelor's domain. No flowers or decorations, no pretty dishes or kitchen towels. Everything was utilitarian.

Daniel paused in the doorway between the porch and kitchen. "So, a soda pop?"

"Thank you," Mary said, and Betty, just entering the screened porch, said, "That will be fine."

"All right then. Why don't you have a seat out here?" He gestured to the table on the porch and went inside.

Mary and Betty went to the plain pine table, and each sat down on one of the benches that flanked it, facing each other. The sun had set, but the screened porch was comfortably warm still. Mary looked out over the lake, comparing it to the bay view at Henry's house. Dan had found a lovely spot.

A moment later, Dan returned with three drink cans. He handed colas to Mary and Betty and sat down in the folding chair at the end of the table, his hand poised over the pop-top on his can.

Mary opened her can of cola. "Here," she said to Betty. "Swap with me." Betty switched cans for the open one, and Mary popped the tab on the second can. Betty shouldn't have to struggle with a flip-top with her arthritic hands.

Dan opened his can and took a deep swig of cola.

Mary took a sip from hers. The sweet drink was refreshingly cold.

"So, how bad is Henry injured?" Dan asked.

"It's pretty bad," Mary said. "A head injury. Henry is in a coma."

Dan shook his head. "I'm real sorry to hear that. Henry's a nice guy."

"The doctors think he'll recover, but he's in the intensive care unit at Ivy Bay Hospital. Mr. York, did you go to Henry's house Friday evening?"

"No, I told you. I went straight home when I left the car show, threw some clothes in a bag, got my fishing tackle, and came here. Things had gone really well, and I sold all three cars the first day of the show. It was a perfect opportunity to get in a quiet weekend of fishing."

"So you are planning to go back to Ivy Bay tonight?" Mary asked.

He nodded. "I have to work tomorrow."

Mary sipped her soda, mulling over what he had said. She was leaning toward believing his story, but she needed somehow to find out who was curious enough about Henry's new car to break into his garage, and who had followed her at least twice. Maybe someone from the automobile show was involved, after all. She leaned toward Daniel.

"Can you tell me how things went at the car show? I'm wondering if the attack on Henry really has something to do with his purchase of the car, or if it was a random break-in. Was anyone else interested in buying the Buick Century before Henry bought it?"

"Sure. Lots of people looked at it Friday morning." Dan shrugged. "It's a great car."

"Can you give me some names?"

"Most of them were people I don't know."

"Did you see anyone else talking to Henry at the car show?" she asked Dan.

He frowned for a moment, then shook his head. "No one in particular. Oh, the couple that had the display next to mine. I saw him chat with them for a minute or two. But everyone likes Henry. He probably made the rounds and talked to nearly all the exhibitors."

For once, Mary found herself wishing Henry wasn't quite so likable. She certainly couldn't question all the people who attended the car show. "What about Bargain Bill?"

Dan's eyebrows pulled together. "What about him?"

"I heard he tried to buy your cars on Friday."

"Oh well, that's nothing new. Bill goes around at every show first thing and offers the owners a low price. We all shake him off. But then he'll say something like, 'Well, if you don't sell it, come see me later.' But I didn't take his offers seriously."

"Why not?" Mary asked.

"He was offering less than half my asking price. I put a lot of work into restoring those cars. I wouldn't let them go for nothing. Bargain Bill is just a bag of hot air. He buys low and sells high. It's a fact of life that he'll never offer a fair price. And I needed to get a certain amount, among the three cars."

"I guess the storage fees aren't cheap," Mary said.

"Yeah, but it's more than that. If I didn't get my price for the cars, I might have had to sell this place, and I don't want to do that."

"It's a beautiful spot," Betty said.

Dan nodded. "If I could live here year-round, I would, but I can't. It's too far from my office, for one thing, and it's not winterized. But I love this place. So I sold the three cars to pay the legal fees from my divorce." He made a sour face and took another drink from his can.

"But that's behind you now," Mary said, watching his face.

"Oh yeah. I hope now I can get by on my salary. Although I haven't had a raise for three years. It's this economy, you know?"

"I do know. What is it you do?"

"I work for a title company." He gave a bitter chuckle. "I'm even driving that old VW Bug out front. Me. I can't imagine it. I always drive a nice car, but I'm reduced to this. I'll tell you, that marriage was the worst mistake of my life. I will *never* get married again." He took a long gulp from his can.

"Mr. York," Mary said, watching him closely, "I've actually met your ex-wife, Dee."

"You have?" His eyes widened, and his eyebrows shot up. "Are you a friend of hers?"

"No, not at all. I met her yesterday, when I was looking for you."

"Oh." He gazed at her uncertainly.

"Can you tell me about the ring you gave her?" Mary asked.

"The ring?" His mouth twitched. He tipped his can up to drain it, then set it down on the table. "What do you want to know?"

"I know you gave Dee a valuable ring before your divorce, and later it was stolen. You knew about the theft, didn't you?"

"She told me."

Mary faced Dan squarely. "Do you know anything more about that, Mr. York? I'm aware that Dee filed a police report, and they're investigating it."

"No. I only know what Dee told me. Why do you ask?"

Mary hesitated. "It's a loose end, and it seemed odd that another crime came up while I was looking into what happened to Henry. The ring that was stolen must have been valuable, or she wouldn't have reported it."

Dan sighed and slumped a little lower in his chair. "I don't know about the other stuff, but the ring was a present for our anniversary. The second one. Two years, that's all we were married. I wish I could say two happy years."

"What went wrong?" Mary asked gently.

"I don't know. As soon as we were married, it seemed like all the rules changed. No matter what I did for her, she was never happy. That ring—she said if I got her that ring, she'd be thrilled, and I believed her. I thought she'd at least calm down for a while. I used all my savings to buy it. But it was only a month or so later that she told me she wanted a divorce. She'd met somebody else. Who knows when that started? I sure don't."

"I'm sorry," Mary said. "I understand she got to keep her jewelry in the settlement."

"That wasn't fair." Dan looked down at his hands.

"I can see that the subject upsets you, but it may be important."

He met her gaze again, frowning. "I had just given it to her, and I bought it on the assumption that we would have more anniversaries together."

"I'm sorry you went through that," Mary said. "If you don't mind my asking, how much was it valued at?"

"Twenty grand. Worst investment I ever made, but at the time when we walked into Guthrie's, I figured it was worth it. *She* was worth it. Ha!"

Mary stared at him for a moment while her brain made connections.

THIRTEEN

G uthrie's?" Mary said softly.

Dan nodded. "That's the jewelry store where I bought it for her. It's in Boston."

"It's too bad you didn't get part of the money back," Betty said, eyeing him with sympathy.

"Yeah. The judge ruled that it was a gift, and he didn't count her jewelry in the split. I felt like *I'd* been robbed."

Mary said carefully, "I found a tag from Guthrie's in the trunk of Henry's car. I didn't see the significance then, but I should have known better. It was from the box that ring was in. The police will find that, I imagine." She didn't mention the fact that the police had already missed it once. She would tell them to look again.

Dan ran a hand through his already disheveled hair. "In the car? I...Look, I did *not* go to Henry's house Friday night. Like I said, I stopped at home and then came straight here after the car show. I'm sorry he got hurt, but I didn't have anything to do with that."

Mary studied his face, trying to sort out the truth. "What really happened to the ring, Mr. York?"

"I don't know." He picked up his can and shook it. "Excuse me."

As he got up and walked into the kitchen, Betty laid her hand on Mary's arm. "Do you think we should just tell him to go to the police?"

"I think we're close to something here," Mary said.

Dan came back carrying another can of cola. He stopped in the doorway and popped the top, then took a long swallow. He leveled his gaze at Mary.

"Like I said, I didn't see Henry after he left the car show. Period."

Mary sat back, thinking hard. She needed to find out what had put Henry in that bed in the intensive care unit. So far, she'd come up with two valuable objects connected to Daniel York—a car and a ring. Could she believe he was innocent? And where was the mysterious ring now? Both she and the police had searched the car and found nothing. Still, they weren't looking for a ring, which was a very small item. What if they'd missed it?

She shook her head. That jewelry store tag was even smaller, and she'd found it. The ring had been in the trunk of the car at some point, but by the time she found the tag, it was gone.

"How do you think the tag from Guthrie's got in the trunk of the car?" she asked.

"Probably after I bought the ring for Dee."

"You put it in the trunk after you bought it? Not on her finger?"

His gaze slid away from hers. "She wasn't with me when I picked it up. It was a surprise."

"You said she asked you to buy it for her."

"Right. But I didn't tell her I actually did. And when I picked it up, I put the bag in the trunk. I...I had to make another stop, and I wanted to make sure it was safe."

Mary considered that. She wasn't at all sure she believed him. "You have to go to the police as soon as you get back to Ivy Bay," she told Dan.

"I guess you're right."

"No guessing about it," Mary said. "You go."

"What if they arrest me? I didn't do anything."

"Just tell them the truth about everything," she said. "Don't try to hide anything. They may have already asked for a warrant to search your apartment."

His back stiffened. "Why?"

"Because you're missing. It looks bad, you know."

"I didn't intend for it to." Dan was beginning to sound a little sulky.

"Well, if you deliberately hide from them, you'll be considered a fugitive. I can't guarantee they won't arrest you, but you need to do the right thing."

"They think I attacked Henry?"

"As I said, I don't know what they think, but I do know they want to talk to you, and so far you haven't been available."

Dan sighed and looked around. "Okay, I'll pack up and go back tonight. I was going to anyway. I have to be at work at nine in the morning."

"Good. I'm going to hold you to that." Mary picked up her purse and looked at Betty. "Shall we head out?"

"Yes, I think so." Betty rose and followed her across the porch.

Mary opened the screen door. "Good-bye."

"Good-bye, Mr. York," Betty said with a quick smile.

The sisters walked out to Mary's car and got in. Mary turned the key and backed the car out onto the gravel road. "I sure hope he keeps his word and goes to the police tonight."

"He knows that you'll be checking up on him." Betty chuckled. "Do you think he was telling the truth?"

"I'm not sure. I think he was holding back something."

"It seemed that way to me too," Betty said. "I thought he might even be lying about that ring."

"He certainly knows more than he let on." Mary turned on the headlights because the dirt road was now shrouded in dusk. She headed for Ivy Bay, wishing she could feel more confident. Even though she believed Daniel's claim that he had not attacked Henry, she didn't feel much closer to finding the person who did it.

"Tell me about the jewelry store tag you found," Betty said as Mary drove toward home. "I didn't know anything about that. Were you bluffing?"

"No, I really found it, just like I said, but I didn't think it was important." Mary clenched her teeth for a moment. She was a little mad at herself for overlooking a promising clue. "I wish I knew if he's telling the truth about putting that ring in the trunk of the car when he bought it."

"He did seem a bit nervous when you pressed him about it," Betty said.

"Yes, and would you drive a pristine antique car like that into Boston? I know I wouldn't, with traffic the way it is in town."

"Too risky." Betty gave a firm nod. "Henry would certainly never take his Bel Air into the city."

"*Mm-hmm.* That struck me as very odd. But that tag should still be in the car. I'll have to go get it." She shot a glance at Betty. "Or maybe I should just tell the police about it and let them retrieve it."

"Do you think the police will do anything now?"

"I don't know," Mary said. "We didn't really find any evidence in Henry's case."

"But you did find Daniel York."

They rode in silence for a few miles, and then Mary said, "It's not much. But we also got the plate number off that suspicious car."

She took Betty to the house on Shore Drive and saw her inside. Gus came to meet them in the kitchen, meowing piteously.

"You poor thing," Mary said. "We've neglected you, haven't we?" She stooped to fluff his gray fur.

"You go on," Betty told her. "I'll take care of Mr. Gus."

"I want to spend a few minutes on the computer before I go to the hospital," Mary said. The hour was growing late, but their conversation with Dan York still bothered her.

She hurried up to her room and searched for the Ivy Bay Wheelers. The club had a Web site, and someone had posted photos of the weekend auto show. Stan Auger was credited with most of the pictures.

She scanned them quickly, looking for familiar faces. She found one of Dan York talking to a man she didn't know and leaning on the frame of an antique car that she guessed was one of the cars he had sold. She studied the photo carefully, but saw nothing out of the ordinary.

Another frame showed Henry from a distance, chatting with one of the vendors. Again, nothing struck a chord with Mary. Finally, near the bottom of the page, she found another picture of Dan. He was not the main subject of the photo, but was in the background, looking over his shoulder toward the camera. His face bore a strained expression, and his sideways stance allowed Mary to see that he had his hand shoved into his pocket.

She sat back in the chair and gazed at the picture, remembering how nervous Dan had seemed as she questioned him about his wife's jewelry.

A glance at the time told her she had better get over to the hospital if she was going. She gathered her things and called good-bye to Betty before she left the house.

Mary pulled into the hospital parking lot about ten minutes later and drove slowly toward the main entrance, watching for a vacant parking space. Soon she was getting off the elevator opposite the door to the ICU. Kim and Karen were both in Henry's room when she approached. They came out into the hall to meet her.

"No change, I'm afraid," Karen said, "but you can go in and see him. We'll go get some coffee."

Mary went in and sat down by Henry's bed. His pale face and stillness reminded her of how serious his condition was. What if Henry never woke up? All her efforts wouldn't make any difference.

That's not true, she told herself. The person who did this needs to be caught and punished, whether Henry ever knows about it or not.

She took his warm hand and stroked it. "Dear Henry. It's me, old chum. I hoped you'd be feeling better." Her voice cracked, and she swallowed back tears. "Oh, Henry, please come back to us!"

Was that selfish? She began to pray silently. *Lord, I'm not even sure what to pray anymore. Just, please, do what's best for Henry.*

Kim came in with two Styrofoam cups and handed her one.

"Thank you." The coffee smelled good, and Mary took a small swallow. Kim sat down beside her and patted Mary's shoulder.

"Have a busy day?"

"Yes. Betty and I found Mr. York."

"The man Dad bought the car from?"

"That's right."

"Karen will be right here," Kim said. "She stopped off at the restroom. You'll have to tell us all about it."

Soon Karen returned, and Mary began to unfold the tale of her trip with Betty to the lake. She told them about Dee Saxon's missing ring and finding the tag in the car that Henry had bought.

"That does seem odd," Karen said.

Kim sipped her coffee and then said, "What if he just plain lied to you?"

"I have considered that," Mary said. "But how would I prove it, if he won't admit it?"

"You don't think he hit Dad?" Karen said.

Mary realized her doubts had grown. "I didn't, but if he lied about other things, how do I know he wouldn't lie about that?"

Kim leaned toward her eagerly. "Maybe he *is* the one who hit Dad."

"He seemed genuinely shocked when I told him Henry was hurt," Mary said.

"Okay, so maybe it wasn't Mr. York," Karen said, "but what if his ex-wife's ring was in the car when Dad bought it?"

"That doesn't make sense," Kim said. "We know he didn't leave it in the car. He did give it to her."

"I mean, what if the ring was in the car again on the day of the automobile show?" Karen raised her eyebrows and looked at Mary.

"The little tag is proof that it was in there at least once," Mary conceded. "I do think it would be strange if the tag was lost in the trunk when the new ring was in its box inside a bag."

"Very strange," Kim said.

Mary said slowly, "If we discount Dan's story about the day he bought the ring, that means it was in the trunk at a different time. Possibly on Friday."

"But who would know it was in there?" Kim asked.

"Nobody but the person who put it there," Karen said.

"Maybe." Mary rubbed her forehead. "I wish I could look at those pictures from the car show again."

"I think it makes more sense if it was in the car on Friday," Karen said. "That would make Mr. York antsy when you came around talking about Henry and the car show."

"But where is it now?" Kim asked.

"I guess the person who hit Dad must have found the ring and taken it." Karen's face crumpled in bafflement.

Mary straightened. "Okay, let's just suppose for a minute that the ring *was* in the car that night. If the person who was in Henry's garage knew that, he'd have gone straight for the trunk of the car. That's if he didn't go to the front door first. I tend to think if it was Dan, he would have asked Henry if he could look in the car for something he'd forgotten."

"I suppose you're right," Kim said, leaning back in her chair, her eyes never leaving Henry's face as she tried to puzzle it out.

"But if some other burglar had been looking in the trunk and found it, wouldn't he have left as soon as he had it in his hand?" Mary looked to both of them for confirmation of her theory. "Why would he bother to open the car door?"

"That sounds right," Kim said. "Unless he hoped to find more loot in the passenger compartment."

Karen nodded. "But the thief must have known about the ring and was looking for it. I don't believe at all that this was a random burglary."

"Same here," Kim said.

Mary nodded. "Agreed, but I don't think he left your dad's house with the ring. I think he was still searching for it when your father opened the door from the kitchen and spoke to him."

"Then where is it?" Karen asked.

"That's a very good question." Mary sighed. "I guess I should tell the police all of this. I wish I had more answers first, but I can't hold back what could turn out to be evidence of the crime."

"Please don't go to them yet," Karen said.

Mary eyed her in surprise. "Why not?"

Karen looked at her sister, then said, "If that ring really was in the car when Dad bought it, the police might think he found it and kept it—or even worse, that he stole it from Dee Saxon in the first place."

"That's kind of wild," Kim said. "Do you really think the police would go that route?" Both sisters looked to Mary for reassurance.

"Well, they might think Henry found it," Mary said slowly, thinking through the implications. "If they didn't know Henry—and some of the officers don't—they might assume he would try to keep it for himself. We certainly don't want them considering your father as a thief or a burglary suspect."

"What if the thief had it in his hand when Dad went to the garage and saw him?" Karen asked.

Kim's face lit up. "Yeah. Maybe they wrangled over it, and that's when the tag fell out, and then he hit Dad."

Mary shook her head. "I'm afraid that won't work. The trunk wasn't open, remember? The tag was in the trunk, and it was closed, but the passenger door was open. I think I'd have heard the trunk shut."

They sat in silence for half a minute, all thinking about the scene in the garage.

"Maybe that ring doesn't have anything to do with it," Kim said at last.

"Maybe," Mary said. But inwardly, she believed it did. Dan York's guilty look had convinced her that the connection was there, if she could only find it.

She rose and reached for her purse. "Well, there's one thing I need to tell the police, anyway. Betty and I saw the car that followed me yesterday. This time, I got the license plate number. I'd better call and tell them now."

She went out into the hallway and made the call. The officer on the desk was very professional and efficient, but Mary wasn't at all sure that the information would be acted upon. She wondered whether she was wise to go with Karen's instinct and not tell the police what she had discovered about Dee's ring. She couldn't help feeling discouraged. In spite of the information Dan had given her, she was still a long way from solving the attack on Henry.

What next? she asked herself. Another look at Stan Auger's pictures. And a trip to Boston, maybe. Although it was quite a leap, Dee Saxon's ring seemed to be a factor in the assault on Henry. The link to the jewelry store seemed the strongest clue she had now. She might be able to learn more there.

She went back to Henry's room and sat down with Kim and Karen. "I'm thinking of driving up to Boston tomorrow and paying a visit to Guthrie's jewelry store. What do you think? Maybe I could learn more about the ring from them."

"You can't just call?" Kim asked.

"I doubt they'd tell me anything over the phone. But if I go there in person, they might give me some information. And if I can't make any progress, I guess I'd better tell the police everything and let them take it from there." She still wasn't happy with that option, but it seemed the only course left to her.

"What about your store?" Karen asked. "You won't have to close it, will you?"

"I have an assistant, Rebecca Mason. She can handle it alone. Maybe I'll just check in with her, before it gets too late." Mary stood and took out her phone again.

Rebecca assured Mary she would be fine at the shop, and that Ashley would be with her. When Mary went back to Henry's room, both the twins were leaning over Henry. Karen looked up at Mary, her face flushed.

"Dad moved his hand! Mary, he moved."

Mary hurried forward. "Did you call for the nurse?"

"Yes," Kim said. "I just pushed the button."

Henry stirred and moved his head to the side, moaning slightly.

The nurse strode into the room. "What's up?"

"He's stirring," Karen said. "He moved his hand, and he groaned a little."

She and Kim stepped back to let the nurse in to examine their father. Mary recognized Rhonda, who had been on duty Friday night when Henry was admitted. After taking Henry's pulse and eyeing him closely, Rhonda spoke to him.

"Henry, can you hear me?"

He lay still, and Rhonda consulted the monitors for the rest of his vital statistics.

"Ladies, his heartbeat is elevated. I'm going to ask the on-call doctor to come up and take a look."

"Thank you," Kim said.

Rhonda left the room. Mary, Kim, and Karen waited, hovering near the bed. Kim held Henry's hand, and Karen bent over him, talking softly. Mary stood on the other side and offered silent prayers. Was this the moment they'd waited for so anxiously?

The doctor who was on duty arrived within a few minutes and did a quick evaluation. He asked Kim and Karen to describe exactly what had occurred.

"I think I'll put in a call to Henry's neurologist," he said after they had told him all they knew. "This is the first time I've seen the patient, and it's good to have continuity in a case like this."

The doctor went out of the room toward the nurses' station. Mary stepped nearer the bed, and the twins moved closer on the other side. Karen took Henry's hand and massaged it with her fingers.

"Dad, you're so close. Can't you come back to us?"

Henry's eyelids fluttered open.

FOURTEEN

◆◆◆

Henry blinked and gazed up into Karen's face. Slowly, his green eyes moved, and he looked at Kim. He let out a puff of air and blinked again.

"Get the doctor," Kim cried.

Mary realized she had been holding her breath. She turned and scurried out toward the desk, where the on-call doctor was talking on the telephone.

"Doctor, please come quickly," Mary said. "He's opened his eyes. I think he's come back to us!"

The on-call doctor shot her a glance and said into the phone, "I'll get right back to you. Sounds like a major change here."

He hung up and crossed the waiting room, into Henry's room, with Rhonda on his heels. Mary followed and lingered in the doorway. Kim was supporting her father's shoulders and helping him take a sip of water through a straw.

"Well, now," the doctor said, stepping up to the bed. "Henry? How are you doing?"

Henry lay back, and Kim let him settle onto the pillow. He took a couple of shallow breaths, eyeing the doctor uncertainly. "Don't know," he said at last.

The doctor smiled. "Ladies, if you'll give us some privacy, I'll do an exam."

Mary and the twins went out, and the doctor pulled the curtain between the bed and the window.

"I can't believe it," Karen said, wiping a tear from her cheek. "I know they said he would wake up soon, but I guess my faith was pretty weak."

Kim hugged her. "I know, but it's happened."

"Praise God," Mary said. The twins drew her into their embrace.

"He asked for water," Kim told her. "That was the first thing he said."

They all stood listening and could hear the doctor asking Henry some basic questions—the type used to see if a person was disoriented: What season is it? Who is the president?

Henry answered him, but sounded confused and unsure of himself, and the doctor spoke again in soothing tones. "This is normal, Mr. Woodrow. Your injuries are healing, and it may take some time before you feel one hundred percent yourself again, but that's all part of the process."

A couple of minutes later, Rhonda came out and smiled at them. "Kim, Karen, you may go in now. The doctor is going to give new medical orders, and I'll call the neurologist back. He should be here within a half hour."

Mary waited just outside the room. Tears ran down her cheeks as she prayed, thanking God for this change.

In a surprisingly short time, the neurologist breezed through the door to the unit, wearing street clothes, and went straight to Henry's room. When the twins emerged a few minutes later, they both smiled, but tears glistened in their eyes.

"He's really better," Kim said, grasping Mary's hand. "He spoke to us again."

"I'm so glad." Mary couldn't hold back her grin.

"He knew us," Karen added. "I was so afraid he wouldn't, but he did. He called us by name. The only thing is, he had no idea what had happened to him. I told him he'd hit his head and that you could fill him in on the details later."

"The doctor says he should rest," Kim told her. I don't think they'll try to keep him awake much longer. He seems really tired, and he said his head ached."

"I'm sure it's hard on him mentally," Mary said. "Even though he's been comatose for a couple of days, he's probably fatigued. Healing takes a lot of energy."

"The nurse is going to give him something for the headache," Karen said, watching as Rhonda walked briskly into Henry's room again, holding a small plastic cup. "The neurologist told him it's all right to sleep if he wants to and they'll catch up in the morning. I sure hope Dad remembers things then." She yawned.

"You should go home and sleep." Kim poked her sister lightly as she stifled the yawn.

"Oh, excuse me," Karen said. "I *am* tired."

"You were up all last night," Kim reminded her. "Go to Dad's and sleep."

"I will, but not if there's a chance of speaking to him again. When I know he's sleeping, I'll go."

"We don't want him to feel as though we're all hovering and staring at him," Mary said.

Kim turned to her sister. "Why don't you go in first, and if he goes right to sleep, come and tell us. If he's awake and wants to talk, I'll come in too."

"And I'll just wait a while to see how it goes," Mary said. "It would probably be disconcerting for him to have too many people about, but I know he'll want you girls there if he's up to conversation."

"Don't go yet, Mary," Karen said.

She smiled. "I'll be here for a while."

To their disappointment, when the doctor had left and Karen went in to sit with her father, she soon returned.

"He drifted right off to sleep again. I'm sorry."

"Don't apologize," Kim said. "That's what the doctor says he needs."

"I know, but I was hoping he'd stay alert for a while."

"It's all right," Mary said. "Next time he awakens, he'll be stronger."

Mary left the hospital when Karen did. She'd gone in to see Henry one more time, but he didn't so much as flicker an eyelash while she was in the room. She was a little disappointed, but still thrilled that he had made such good progress. She'd seen his eyes, open and aware, when he gazed up at his daughters.

Tomorrow, she thought. I'll talk to him tomorrow.

Should she still go to Boston? The trip would be time consuming, but it might pay big dividends. She decided to stick by her plan, but to stop at the hospital before heading for the city. Maybe she would get to talk to Henry then. If he remembered the attack and could tell them about it, she would adjust her plans.

As Mary drove home, she thought some more about Dee Saxon and the burglary at her house. If she could find the burglar, would she also find Henry's assailant? The idea of another conversation with Dee made her uncomfortable, now that she knew more about her. Surely she could learn more about the woman without confronting her again.

Even though she arrived home quite late, Mary went online to search the *Ivy Bay Bugle*'s archives for photographs of Dee. She found a few, but none showed what she most wanted to see—the ill-fated ring. The most recent photo was the one from the charity auction. Prior to that, a picture of her and Erick appeared on the community page with their wedding announcement.

Next Mary decided to check a couple of social-networking sites, and it didn't take her long to find Dee's account on one of them. Dee, it seemed, loved to post pictures of herself, especially glamour shots. Mary scanned the newer posts and then clicked back into Dee's archives. About seven months back, she hit pay dirt.

"Look what my sweetie of a husband gave me for our anniversary," Dee crooned online. The item was accompanied by two photos, one of Dee wearing a large diamond ring as she stood talking to a man—not Dan York. The second was a close-up of her hand clutching a wineglass, and the ring was front and center.

Mary swallowed hard. The diamond was so large it would be vulgar, if not for the interesting setting. The ring looked old-fashioned, with a carved gold band and smaller rubies on each side of the massive diamond.

So, this was the ring someone wanted badly enough to make him inflict injury on Henry. Mary's anger bubbled. It was so unnecessary. Henry wouldn't stand in the way of someone that desperate.

She printed out the pictures. They might not help her find Henry's attacker, but she was determined to press on. When Henry was able, she would show him the photos and ask him if he had ever seen the ring. Maybe that would help him remember Friday night. And maybe it would lead them to his assailant.

FIFTEEN

❖

The next morning before breakfast, Mary looked up the address of Guthrie's jewelry store. The location should be easy to find. She went downstairs, dug out Saturday's newspaper, and opened it to the page carrying the photograph from the charity auction. Johanna Montgomery had taken the photo herself. Calling on her before setting out for Boston might be worth the trouble, Mary decided.

She ate breakfast with Betty and then drove to the bookshop, leaving Gus home for the day. When Rebecca arrived, they reviewed a few business matters. Then Mary walked over to the *Bugle* office.

Johanna was at her desk and greeted Mary warmly. "How's Henry doing?"

"Better. He was awake for a little while last night. We hope he's out of the woods. I'm headed over there next."

"I'm glad to hear that. Have any luck at the police station yesterday?"

"A little," Mary said. "Thanks for the tips you gave me on using their log."

"Anytime."

"Today I want to ask you about this." Mary held up the folded newspaper with Dee and Erick Saxon smiling out from the photo toward Johanna.

"Oh, the auction. I snapped a few pictures that night. We'll probably get some information soon on how much money they raised, and we'll run a short story on it. It wasn't held in Ivy Bay, but we try to cover nearby events that town residents are involved in."

"It seems several Ivy Bay residents were there that night. I know Eleanor Blakely was there."

Johanna smiled. "She was the one who called and asked if we would cover it."

"I wondered when you took the picture. I mean, what time?"

"Let's see…" Johanna leaned forward and flipped back a couple of pages on her desk diary. "I had the school board meeting first on Friday night. I was late getting to the auction, but our photographer was busy with sports events, so I told him I'd try to get over there and take my own pictures for that event. It wasn't mandatory that we run a picture, but we like to keep on the good side of all the civic organizations, and they had asked for coverage."

"I understand they were raising money for area fire departments," Mary said.

"Yes, Ivy Bay's included. It was a good cause. I think I got there about quarter to nine." Johanna looked up at Mary. "They took a short intermission, and people were milling around drinking wine and coffee. I probably took this about nine o'clock, or even a little later."

Mary nodded slowly. Betty had left the auction by then. The attack on Henry had come much earlier, closer to seven. She thought about it for a moment. She had left the bookshop at six, and gone home and then to Henry's. They had looked at the car and prepared dinner. Seven seemed about right, but her cell phone could tell her exactly when she called 911.

"Did you save the other pictures you took that night?" she asked.

Johanna pushed her chair back and rose. "Let's see. They're on the card in my camera. I usually delete the extras after a few days, but I'm pretty sure I still have those."

Johanna walked over to a file cabinet and took a camera case from on top of it. She opened the case and took out a small digital camera. "Let me bring them up." She turned on the camera and clicked a few buttons. "Here we go. Looks like I took eight or ten pictures at the auction. The first one is of the auctioneer. The rest are patrons." She placed the camera in Mary's hand. "Hit this button to go to the next one. If you get to one of a dog, that's the end of the auction. I took some earlier that day at a dog-agility fair."

"Thank you."

As Mary studied the small screen and viewed each picture, Johanna went back to her desk and opened a file folder. Most of the photos were of people Mary didn't recognize. One was of Eleanor. Mary squinted at it. She couldn't be sure because the image was so small, but Eleanor seemed to have her mouth open in a rather unflattering moment. She only found one picture of Dee Saxon—the one that had run in the paper.

"Why did you choose to run the one of the Saxons?" Mary asked.

Johanna shrugged. "It was a great picture. Mrs. Saxon is very photogenic, and, well, they're beautiful people, so to speak, and they live in Ivy Bay. I couldn't see running a photo in our paper of people who don't live here. For those reasons, of the shots I took, it was the best."

Mary gazed at the other pictures and nodded. Though they were fashionably garbed, none of the other auction patrons looked as glamorous or as happy as Dee. Her husband, Erick, was good-looking too, and had a dazzling smile for the camera. They did indeed look like a well-heeled couple willing to spend a lot for a good cause.

Finally she came to a picture of a black Labrador retriever wearing a red bandanna around its neck. Mary could have sworn the dog was grinning and preening for the camera. She smiled as she handed the camera back to Johanna.

"Thanks a lot."

"Learn anything useful?"

"Not really, but I wanted to make sure I wasn't missing anything." A sudden thought stopped her. She had gone over the Ivy Bay Wheelers' Web site again that morning without finding anything new, but the *Bugle* might be able to help her. "I guess you weren't the one who took pictures at the antique car show."

"No, our photographer did those on Friday. I'm not sure if he went back the second day or not—he may have been too busy."

"It's Friday I'm most interested in," Mary said.

"Hold on." Johanna left her for a moment and came back a short time later. "Roy said they're all on his computer, and he's forwarding the file from the car show to me right now." She sat down and clicked a few times with her mouse. "Okay, here we go. Why don't you sit down here and take a look? I need to make a phone call, but I can do it at another desk."

"Thanks." Mary took Johanna's chair and gazed at the first picture—one of Stan Auger standing by a sign for the Wheelers' annual show and smiling broadly. She clicked slowly through more than a dozen photographs, scouring each one for an image of either Dan York or Henry.

By the time she had looked at six pictures, she had decided the photographer went to the fairgrounds in the morning, arriving when the exhibitors were still setting up their displays. Henry, she knew, had gone later in the day. Still, there might be something she could use.

A picture of Dan talking to Julie Saunders caught her attention. It was a good picture of Mrs. Saunders, who had helped her husband run the booth next to Dan's. Dan seemed more relaxed than in the photo she'd seen on the car club's site, but still his posture looked a little stiff. His right hand, Mary realized, hovered near his pants pocket— the same pocket he'd had his hand in when Stan Auger snapped his picture.

"Why are you so protective of that pocket?" Mary said softly. Only one reason seemed logical—he was concerned about the contents. Sometimes she patted her pockets if she wanted to be sure her keys were there, but this seemed more than that. Something in Dan's pocket was very important.

Mary clicked through the rest of the photos in the file and stood. "Thanks, Johanna. I'm headed for Boston as soon as I've checked in on Henry."

"Boston?" Johanna's eyes widened.

Mary smiled. "I'll tell you if I find anything front-page worthy."

"You'd better." Johanna waved and grinned as Mary turned away.

———

Kim was in Henry's room when Mary arrived. She rose, stretching her arms and smiling sheepishly.

"Hi. I think I snoozed in my chair."

"Good," Mary said. She would have recommended more sleep away from the hospital, but she knew Kim and Karen didn't want to chance missing any of their father's lucid moments. "How is Henry?"

Kim's smile seemed more genuine now. "He woke up a while ago, and he talked to me for ten or fifteen minutes. They've sedated him because of the pain, but he's really back, Mary."

She squeezed Kim's arm. "I'm so glad. I hope the pain will go away, though."

"Every time he wakes up, he complains of a headache." Kim's eyes misted. "The doctor says it will get better, but Dad doesn't refuse the pain meds they offer him. He's not a complainer, so I figure it's severe."

"We'll have to keep praying about that."

"I told the pastor, and he's telling the prayer chain folks about the headache."

Mary sat down next to Kim and gazed at Henry, who was peacefully sleeping now. "What did he say when you were chatting? Was he able to get past the medical concerns?"

"Oh yes. I even asked him about Friday, and he remembered the car show."

Mary caught her breath. "That's wonderful news!"

"Yes, but I'm afraid he was hazy on anything after that. He didn't remember you going to his house that night, or the intruder in his garage. But one thing he was clear on was buying that Buick. He wanted to know if Karen and I had seen it yet."

Mary chuckled. "That sounds like Henry."

"Yes, personality-wise, he's fine," Kim said. "But the doctor said it may take a while for him to remember things that happened immediately before he got the injury." Kim shrugged. "I guess we'll take it as it comes."

"That's right," Mary told her. "It's all we can do."

"Karen called a little while ago," Kim said. "She was sorry she missed talking to Dad, but I assured her she'll get to chat with him later, while I'm sacked out. She said she slept straight through, and I'm glad."

Mary nodded. "She was exhausted last night." She leaned over and took Henry's hand, watching his face, but he didn't stir. "I won't stay long today. I'm going to drive to Boston and see if I can talk to the people at that jewelry store. I'm not sure how that ring of Mrs. Saxon's fits into all this, but I figure anything I can find out will bring us closer to knowing who did this."

"I wish Dad could remember," Kim said. "If he could just tell us who was in the garage that night!"

"The police don't know he's woken up yet, do they?"

Kim shook her head. "The neurologist wants to do an MRI later today. He said he doesn't think Dad's up to questioning by the police yet, and I think he's right. If Dad can't remember anything after the antique car show, what good will their questions do?"

Mary wished she could talk to Henry, but it sounded as though that opportunity wouldn't arise for several hours at least. She may as well be on her way and do the only thing she knew of that might be helpful to Henry.

"Let's pray together, Kim, and then I'll get going."

Kim took her hand. "Thanks, Mary."

On the way to Boston, Mary continually checked her mirrors as she drove. Was she being paranoid? Once she saw a dark car behind her, but as it pulled alongside in the neighboring lane and passed her, she realized it wasn't the one that had followed her and Betty. Though the color and model were similar, the license was different, and it had a distinctive bumper sticker she hadn't seen on the other car.

She told herself to relax and drove on, but she couldn't help wondering if the police had followed up on her report.

Her GPS took her to the block where she expected to find Guthrie's, but as she slowly drove the length of it, she couldn't spot the store. Frustrated, she went around the block and rolled down the street again. A parking spot opened unexpectedly, and she pulled into it and turned off the engine.

She double-checked the address she had written down for the store and looked for numbers on the nearby buildings. No Guthrie's.

She was only a few yards from a newsstand, so she walked over and bought a copy of the morning's *Globe*. As the vendor put her change in her outstretched hand, she asked, "Am I near Guthrie's?"

He grunted. "You're a couple of months too late."

"What do you mean?" Mary asked.

"It's gone. The place is closed." He leaned across his counter and pointed across the street and down a few buildings. "See that place where they're changing the signs?"

Mary looked and saw several workmen on scaffolding above a business's front entrance.

"That's a new outfit moving in," the vendor said. "Trendy clothes, I think."

"You mean Guthrie's has moved?" she asked.

"Moved? No, lady, they're out of business. Guess you don't read the paper much."

"Actually I do, but I don't live in the city, and I've never done business at Guthrie's before."

He snorted. "Well, the place was shut down two or three months back, and the owner was arrested."

SIXTEEN

◆◆◆

He was arrested? What for?" Mary asked.

"I don't remember," the newsstand vendor said. "Some kind of fraud, I think. It was in the papers at the time."

Other customers were lining up behind Mary, and the vendor was looking anxiously over her shoulder. Time to move on and not obstruct his business. She took her newspaper and walked slowly down the block to get a better look at the building across the street. She had asked the right person—that vendor probably had a great view of the proceedings when the police descended on Guthrie's. But what he had told her only raised more questions. How could she find out more?

She looked down at the paper in her hand. Her next stop would be the *Boston Globe*'s offices.

Back in the car, she perused the masthead for the address and set the GPS. To her relief, she didn't have to get onto any of the highways that crisscrossed the city in multiple levels. Fighting city traffic was not her favorite pastime.

The traffic was a bit dicey, but after twenty minutes of stop-and-go driving and only one angry driver's horn blaring at her as she changed lanes, Mary arrived at her destination and found a slot in a nearby parking garage.

The receptionist was helpful in directing her to the newspaper's morgue, where Mary could view past issues online or on microfilm. She soon had a news story before her describing the police raid on the jewelry store about two months earlier. The owner was arrested and charged with fencing stolen jewelry. Two employees were also implicated, and Guthrie's inventory was seized by the police. The store was closed the same day.

Mary searched for follow-up articles. Announcements were soon issued, saying that the store would not reopen. The investigating officer was quoted as saying there could be more than a million dollars' worth of stolen jewelry amid the confiscated inventory.

Mary made copies of the articles and searched for more. The owner's indictment rated a brief article. In the following day's paper, the police reported that they were working to restore stolen articles of jewelry to the rightful owners. Victims were directed to a liaison officer and told to take copies of their insurance claims with them and, if possible, photographs of their stolen jewelry.

About two weeks later, the *Globe* ran a story saying the police had so far restored about a hundred high-end items—more than $250,000 worth of jewelry—to its owners, but they still had nearly two thousand pieces in the evidence lockup. Some of Guthrie's inventory had been bought legitimately for resale, of course, and the reporter stated that it was not included in the figures quoted. The police had matched up legally purchased items with the company's business records. Soon afterward, Guthrie's accounting firm was also investigated.

Mary studied every scrap of information. A month after the store closed, police were still working on the stolen inventory. The value was higher than they had at first realized. Hundreds of items had been classified by the police investigators as pieces the owner bought "under the table." Many people had come forward, hoping to claim their missing jewelry, but a lot of them had been disappointed. The investigating officer was quoted as saying, "There's no way of telling how many stolen items Guthrie's sold before they were caught."

She sat back to think about how this related to Henry's case and Dee Saxon's ring. That ring may have been stolen and fenced at Guthrie's before Daniel York bought it from the store. Of course, it wasn't in the inventory that the police impounded, since Dan bought it several months before the store was closed. She wondered if there was any way she could find out if it was listed among the things the store purchased legally for sale. Thinking that Henry had been badly hurt— and possibly over the ring—she went back to her search, but she didn't find any more updates on the Guthrie's case. However, she decided to go back further in the archives and see what she could turn up on jewel thefts.

It was a long shot, she knew, but she went through the searchable files for the months before Dan bought the ring from Guthrie's showcase. After two hours of fruitless searching, her stomach began to rumble. She was tempted to give up and go home, but instead told herself sternly, "This is for Henry."

Finally she decided she had better get some lunch and call the hospital to check on Henry's condition. If nothing had changed, she could come back to the *Globe*'s morgue or try to contact the police liaison. She was about to close the file when a headline caught her eye: "Heirloom ring stolen from billionaire's wife."

It was enough to keep Mary on the trail. She opened the story eagerly and stared at the accompanying photo. A ring very much like Dee's was displayed in a velvet-lined box. She brought out her copies of the pictures from Dee's online site. Under close comparison, the stolen ring looked identical to Dee's. She settled back in the chair to read.

The ring had belonged to a woman named Starr Vandemire, wife of electronics mogul Brock Vandemire, who was worth billions. Mary had heard his name many times in connection with computer business items in the news. The ring and four other very valuable pieces of Starr's jewelry had been taken the previous winter, when their home safe was burglarized.

Starr Vandemire's background was almost as interesting as the tale of the burglary. She was the daughter of an Italian count, and she owned quite a few exquisite antique jewels. In the upper-crust Boston circles, she was known as a socialite and extraordinary hostess, and also as a world-class skeet shooter. The Vandemires had provided photos of the stolen pieces of jewelry to news reporters at the time of the theft, and of course they wanted them all back. Brock Vandemire was quoted as saying he would happily return the insurance company's money if the jewels were returned. He offered a reward and indicated he hoped the ring, in particular, would be found. It had been in Starr's family for more than three hundred years, he claimed, having been fashioned in the late sixteen hundreds for one of her ancestors.

Mary gazed at the pictures for a long time. She could imagine a noblewoman of the seventeenth century wearing that ring. Could this possibly be the one stolen from Dee Saxon's jewelry box? They certainly looked the same.

She copied the article and searched for follow-ups, but found none.

"Enough," she said out loud. She closed the file and shut down the monitor, gathered her things, and went outside. A coffee shop just down the block looked like a good prospect for a late lunch.

Walking toward it, Mary took out her phone and rang Karen. She hoped she'd picked the right sister and wasn't calling one who had gone to get some sleep.

"Mary!" Karen's voice rose in excitement. "He's so much better. Where are you? Are you coming in?"

"I'm in Boston, but I'm heading home soon. Should I come to the hospital?"

"Definitely. Dad wants to see you. They're going to do the MRI soon, but he may be done with that by the time you get here."

Mary checked her watch. "All right. I'll grab a sandwich and head out. I'll be an hour or maybe an hour and a half."

Mary's step had a new spring as she hurried toward the coffee shop. Henry was awake, and he wanted to see her.

SEVENTEEN

———◆◆◆———

The nurse at the desk in the ICU jumped up when Mary entered.

"Mrs. Fisher! I'm supposed to tell you that Henry's been moved. He'll be in room 322 after Imaging is done with him."

"That's good news," Mary said. Henry would be in a regular hospital room now, not the intensive care unit, and his MRI was under way. She walked out to the elevator and rode it up to the third floor.

Kim and Karen both waited in room 322, along with Pastor Miles. Kim jumped up to give her a hug.

"I'm so glad you're here. The nurses finally took Dad for the MRI, but he'll be back soon."

"Wonderful," Mary said.

"I hope he's not too tired to talk to you," Karen said. "He talked to us quite a bit before they took him."

"I sure hope we didn't wear him out," Kim added.

"He seemed in good spirits when he left here," Pastor Miles said with a smile.

"So tell us about Boston!" Kim pulled a chair forward for Mary.

"Yes, sit right there," Karen told her. "We want to know what you found out."

"Quite a lot, actually." Mary eased down into the padded chair. "It could mean nothing, or it could mean quite a lot. I've got pictures of an antique ring that was stolen last winter from a billionaire's wife, and I can't wait to show it to your father."

"A billionaire?" Pastor Miles's eyebrows shot up. "Something tells me there's a lot I don't know about."

Mary told them all about Mrs. Vandemire's ring and filled in the pastor on the details of Dee Saxon's loss. She took out the photographs of both rings and passed them to the twins.

"Okay, I know these are just printouts, and they're kind of grainy, but tell me that's not the same ring."

The others bent over the pictures for a moment.

"It sure looks like it," Kim said.

"I agree." Pastor Miles looked up at her and smiled. "I'd say you've done some excellent investigative work. What happens now?"

"I don't know," Mary confessed. "I'm hoping Henry can help us out a little."

"Me too," Karen said, "but I'm not sure this will help him any. He doesn't remember taking the car home or anything after that."

"There was something I wanted to be sure and tell you," Kim said, eyeing her sister anxiously. "Remember that man who came in an hour or so ago?"

"That's right," Karen said. "Tell Mary about him."

Her interest piqued, Mary turned her full attention to Kim.

"When the nurse took Dad for the MRI, we helped one of the aides move his stuff up here," Kim said. "The nurses were still making up the bed for him when a man came to the door."

Karen nodded. "We both saw him."

"So did I," Pastor Miles said. "I thought maybe he was looking for another patient."

"Did he speak to you?" Mary asked the women.

"No, but he looked in and just kind of scanned the room," Karen said. "I was about to ask if we could help him, but he left."

"What did he look like?" Mary asked.

"*Hmm*," Kim said, frowning. "He wasn't very tall. Well, not as tall as Dad or the pastor." She cast a glance at Pastor Miles.

"Middle-aged," Karen said. "Maybe in his forties. And he had on a lightweight jacket. Blue, I think. Or black."

"What about his hair?" Mary prodded. "Any hat?"

"No hat," Kim said quickly. "He had brown hair, but thinning. No beard or mustache."

"I agree with that description," the pastor said. "I'd put his height at about five feet nine. He had a dark complexion— or a good tan. And he wasn't fat, but I wouldn't think he'd missed many meals."

Mary nodded, wishing she had gotten a look at the driver who had followed her. If the man they described had been wearing a baseball cap, she'd have been pretty certain he was the same man, but this might all be coincidence. "Could you recognize him again?"

"I think so," Kim said, and Pastor Miles nodded.

"Yeah," Karen added. "We got a good look at his face. And of course I thought of the man you saw the other night and wondered if he was the same person."

Pastor Miles smiled apologetically. "I didn't realize there had been an earlier incident. When Kim and Karen told me about it, I hurried out into the hallway to see if I could catch up with him, but he was just getting on the elevator, and I couldn't get there fast enough."

"It may be totally unrelated," Mary said, but she felt that there was a connection, and that this man was the same one she'd seen in the ICU, and possibly the one who had followed her car.

A slight commotion at the door drew their gazes. A nurse and an aide were wheeling a gurney into the room.

"The star of the show is back," the aide called cheerfully.

They all stood and moved out of the way. Pastor Miles quickly shifted the chairs to allow the women space to work.

"Hey, Dad," Karen said brightly.

Henry, lying on the gurney, lifted one hand in an abbreviated wave. Mary's gaze caught his, and he grinned.

"Hello, stranger."

"Hi," Mary said, melting a little inside. She had wondered if she would ever see that special smile again.

The nurse and the aide transferred Henry to his new bed and hooked up the monitors. Then they left the room, and the others gathered around Henry.

"How are you feeling, Dad?" Kim asked.

"Not too bad. I think I fell asleep in the machine." He looked over at Mary, smiled, and reached toward her. She took his hand and squeezed it gently, then let go. He turned back to his daughters. "I wish they'd let me out of here."

"Now, Dad," Karen said sternly, "you know what the doctors said. They want to observe you one more day before they make any decisions. You had quite a knock on the head."

"Well, the nurse told me that the police chief is coming in to talk to me later." Henry frowned. "She didn't say Chief McArthur, though. It was a different name."

"Chief McIntosh?" Mary asked.

Henry nodded. "I think that was it. Where's Chief McArthur?"

"He's on vacation. McIntosh is his temporary replacement." And we'll all be glad when Chief McArthur is back, she thought.

"Huh. Well, the girls told me that somebody hit me over the head, and I believe it—I've had a headache ever since I woke up. But I don't know how it happened. I just know I'm in the hospital and my head hurts."

"It was at your house," Mary said. "On Friday evening. You had invited me over for dinner—and to see the new car that you'd bought at the antique auto show."

Henry sighed. "That's right. I remember that part. I went over to the show and wound up buying a '55 Buick Century from Dan York."

Kim laughed in delight. "No problem with that part of your memory, Dad! Do you remember asking Mary to dinner?"

"Afraid not." Henry's eyebrows lowered, and he looked troubled.

"We should have known you'd remember the details about the car," Karen said.

"You called me at the shop and invited me," Mary prompted. "I could tell you were happy about your purchase, but you didn't want to tell me much over the phone. You wanted to keep it a surprise."

Kim nodded. "Mary told us you cooked scallops that night. You must have bought them at the market that day."

"Maybe." Henry's eyes sought Mary's.

"I remember you telling me you'd stopped at Sweet Susan's for the rolls, but we don't have to talk about it now," Mary said. She didn't want to upset him or make him feel that he needed to work at remembering. The doctors seemed to think that it would come back naturally if he relaxed and let his brain rest.

"Mary," Kim said, "is this a good time to tell Dad about the ring?"

"Ring?" Henry stared blankly at her. "What ring?"

"There was a ring that belonged to Daniel York's ex-wife," Mary said hesitantly. "Betty and I went to Dan's lakeside cabin and talked to him last night. We both felt he was holding out on us, especially when I asked him about his ex-wife's stolen ring. Now I'm wondering if her ring might possibly have been in the car when he sold it to you."

"What—" Henry broke off as a man entered the room.

Mary turned and looked up at the tall, somber man. Chief McIntosh. He wore a conservative gray suit with a white shirt and a blue-and-silver-striped tie. He nodded at the three women and the pastor, then focused on Henry.

"Mr. Woodrow, glad to see you looking better. I'm Police Chief McIntosh, standing in for Chief McArthur. How do you feel this afternoon?" As he spoke, he walked forward and stood by the bed.

"Well, my head still aches, but other than that, pretty good, I guess." Henry's green eyes swept over the chief in appraisal. "What can I do for you?"

"Should we wait outside?" Pastor Miles asked, standing.

McIntosh glanced around at them. "It is a little crowded in here."

"Let the girls stay," Henry said.

Mary was glad he had done so. She didn't want him to face McIntosh's questions alone, especially when Henry still seemed a little confused about recent events.

She and the pastor stepped out into the hallway.

"Perhaps I should go," Pastor Miles said softly.

Mary gazed up at him, her heart uneasy. "I wish you'd stay a little longer. This man has a way of putting people on edge, and Henry may need some reassurance when he's finished."

"In that case, I'd be happy to stay."

"Thank you." Mary sighed. "Do you think I should tell the chief everything I've learned about the ring?"

"That would probably be best," Pastor Miles said. "It might help them in their investigation of who attacked Henry. Is there any reason why you wouldn't tell him?"

"Not really." She smiled ruefully. "Just that he's not Chief McArthur, I guess."

"You don't trust him?"

"I don't think it's that." Mary tried to analyze her ambivalent feelings toward Chief McIntosh. "I'm not very comfortable with him. It's probably just a personality thing. But you're right—I shouldn't let that stand in the way of giving him information that could help them. The twins were afraid that the police would suspect Henry of stealing that ring—"

"Why would they think that?" Pastor Miles frowned. "Henry's as honest as the day is long."

"I know that, and you know that, but does Chief McIntosh know that?"

"I guess Kim and Karen feel the same way about the new chief as you do."

Mary shrugged. "Chief McIntosh wouldn't get any awards for good public relations."

"I see."

"But you're right. I know you're right. And with what I learned in Boston this morning..."

At that moment, Chief McIntosh came out of Henry's room. He would have walked past them with only a nod, but Mary jumped toward him.

"Excuse me, Chief, there's something I need to talk to you about. It concerns Henry and the car he bought Friday."

"Oh?"

"Yes, you see, I spoke to Daniel York last night—"

"You what?"

Mary hesitated. Chief McIntosh seemed more than just surprised. His jaw clenched, and unless she was imagining it, he was angry.

"I...My sister and I drove to his cabin and talked to him."

Chief McIntosh's eyes narrowed, but he said nothing.

"He said he would go home last night, and that he would talk to you." Chief McIntosh said nothing, and Mary went on. "Anyway, one thing we talked about was a ring that his ex-wife, Dee Saxon, had reported stolen. When I looked inside the trunk of the car that he sold to Henry, I found a tag from a jewelry store in Boston. Mr. York admitted to me that the store was the one where he bought the ring last winter. I left the tag in there—your men can probably find it, if you want to see it. Anyway, I decided to go to the jewelry store in Boston today, but when I got up there this morning, I learned the store had been closed. The owner was arrested about two months ago for trafficking in stolen jewelry."

Chief McIntosh continued to stare at her. Mary decided it was a good time to stop talking.

"Indeed? And what was the name of the store?" the frowning chief asked.

"Guthrie's." She gave him the address. "I printed out some newspaper articles that tell about it being shut down and the Boston police confiscating the inventory. They've been trying to return stolen items to the rightful owners."

"You're saying this ring of Mrs. Saxon's may have been stolen?"

"Yes."

"But we knew it was stolen from her home."

"That was afterward," Mary said. "I'm suggesting the ring was stolen twice. Once from Starr Vandemire, and the second time from—"

"Who did you say?"

"Starr Vandemire. She's married to Brock Vandemire, the electronics billionaire."

"Yes, I know who he is. I was just…" Chief McIntosh's brow furrowed even more than before. "Go on."

"I have pictures in my purse. It's in there." Mary pointed toward the door of Henry's room.

Chief McIntosh drew in a breath and squared his shoulders. "Show me."

"Of course." Mary hurried into the room.

"What's going on?" Kim whispered.

"I told Chief McIntosh about the ring, and he wants to see the pictures."

She took the printouts from her bag and rejoined him in the hallway.

Pastor Miles was smiling at the chief and saying, "... Grace Church. We'd love to have you come." Mary smothered a chuckle. She highly doubted Chief McIntosh would show up for services at her church, but trust Pastor Miles to graciously invite every newcomer to Ivy Bay. On the other hand, maybe she was being a tad judgmental. She tried to swallow her frustration toward the chief as she held out the papers.

"This one is of Dee Saxon wearing the ring. I found it on one of her online accounts. And this picture is the one the Vandemires gave the *Boston Globe* when they were reporting the theft of the ring last winter."

The chief studied the papers thoughtfully. "And you think whoever stole it fenced it at this Guthrie's jewelry store?"

"It's a theory," Mary said. "Daniel York bought the ring for his wife there a few months later. I'm guessing they didn't display it for sale right away, but waited until the publicity died down about the theft from the Vandemires. Maybe they didn't display it at all, but waited for a customer willing to spend a lot of money, and then brought it out just for them."

"But you're not sure that is the same ring," Chief McIntosh said flatly.

"No, but they look rather like the same ring. And if we could find it—"

His eyes darkened at the word *we*, and Mary quickly amended her words.

"If your men could solve this case and find Dee Saxon's ring, then maybe you could also solve the Vandemire case." That would be a boost to McIntosh's reputation, and she counted on him liking the idea of being the one to solve an older and larger case. Even though Mary didn't personally care about the other case, she hoped that connecting the two would spur the chief to find Henry's assailant.

"Mrs. Fisher, I'm asking you again—no, I'm *telling* you— to stay out of this case. Let my officers do their work. If you go around investigating on your own, asking questions and so on, you may tip off our suspects before we have a chance to talk to them. Do you understand?"

"Yes, sir." Mary felt her cheeks heat.

"And I don't want you broadcasting this possible connection to the Vandemire case either. Do I make myself clear?"

"Y-yes."

"Good. Just let us handle it. Now, has Mr. Woodrow seen these pictures?"

"No, not yet. When you walked in, I had just told him about my talk with Mr. York, and I mentioned the ring, but he didn't seem to know what I was talking about. I was going to show these to him."

"I'll do that." He turned without waiting for permission and walked back into Henry's room.

Mary let out her breath.

"Are you all right?" Pastor Miles asked.

"I think so. A little rattled, but otherwise fine. Thanks for staying here."

"I don't mind. And I can see what you mean about his bedside manner. You've given him a lot of new information, and it could be very useful to him, whether he admits it or not, so cheer up." Pastor Miles patted her shoulder.

Mary smiled at him. "Thanks." It had seemed as though Chief McIntosh took her research—all right, her interference—personally. More personally than an objective police officer should, anyway. She walked over to the doorway, and the pastor went with her. They didn't enter but listened as the chief continued to question Henry about Dee Saxon's ring.

"So you don't know anything about the seller of the car's connection to a stolen diamond ring?"

"No, I don't know a thing about it. Mary said something a minute ago, but Dan didn't mention anything to me about it at the car show. At least I don't think he did. We're not that good friends, and it's not the kind of thing he and I would have discussed. But you know, my memory is on the fritz right now."

"So I've been told," McIntosh said. "I have a couple of pictures here that I'd like you to look at, if you don't mind."

"Sure," Henry said. "Kimmy, will you raise my bed up a little?"

Kim leaned over and pushed one of the buttons on the bed rail, and the head end of Henry's bed rose slowly until he was sitting up fairly straight.

"That's good," he said.

Kim helped him situate his pillow to his liking and then resumed her seat. Chief McIntosh handed Henry the pictures.

"Take your time," Chief McIntosh said as Henry studied them. "Have you ever seen a ring that looks like either of these?"

"I don't think so," Henry said. "Is this the same ring in both pictures?"

McIntosh glanced at Mary and said, "We're not sure. But the one in your right hand is the one that was stolen from Mrs. Saxon—that is, York's former wife."

"*Hmm.* Well, I don't think I ever met her." Henry frowned and gazed at the prints for a long moment. He shook his head. "I don't know, Chief. This is all news to me."

"All right." McIntosh took the pictures back and stood for a few seconds, looking pensively down at Henry. Mary wondered if he suspected Henry of lying, and maybe of hiding the ring for Dan. Or maybe he even thought Henry had found it in the car and hidden it to keep for himself.

She turned away from the doorway.

"How are you doing?" Pastor Miles whispered.

"All right. Just letting my imagination run away with me."

Chief McIntosh came out into the hallway. He held up Mary's printouts. "I'd like to hang on to these."

"Of course. And the Web sites where I found them are printed at the bottom of each sheet."

"Right. Now, I meant what I said, Mrs. Fisher. Leave this to the police."

"Yes, sir. I'll remember that."

"Nice to meet you, Chief McIntosh," the pastor said.

McIntosh nodded and strode toward the elevator.

EIGHTEEN

------- ◆◆ -------

Mary exhaled and looked at the pastor. "Come on. Let's go see what Henry thinks of him."

When they entered the room, Kim and Karen were trying to soothe their father.

"Dad, that's his job," Karen said.

"He didn't mean anything by it," Kim added, stroking Henry's hand.

"He's treating me like a criminal," Henry said, sinking back onto his pillow. "If I could just remember what happened!"

Pastor Miles stepped forward. "Don't let the chief distress you, Henry. I imagine he's feeling a bit frustrated now. His people have been investigating for three days, and I don't think they've found much. He was probably hoping you could tie things up for him. But it's all right that you can't. The Lord knows all about it."

"That's true," Henry said grudgingly. "But a diamond ring? I ask you, if I had found something like that in the car, would I have kept it?"

"No," Kim and Karen said together.

"Of course I wouldn't. And I'd have shown it to Mary that night. She'd have known about it."

"I think you're right," Mary said. "That would have been something very odd, and you would have told me, either first thing or while we were getting our dinner ready." Of course, she reasoned to herself, he might not have gotten around to it yet. They were only partway through eating their dinner when they were interrupted. She supposed it was possible it had slipped Henry's mind while they talked about the new car. Maybe she should go back and search his whole house, just to be sure.

"Would you mind if we had prayer together?" Pastor Miles asked, looking at his watch. "I don't want to run off, but I promised Trevor I'd play catch with him this afternoon."

"I'd like it if you prayed," Henry said. "Pray that I'll remember who hit me."

Pastor Miles smiled, but then sobered. "I do hope it comes back to you, Henry. I know it's not a pleasant thing to think about, but I hope you regain those hours you've lost. But God's timing is perfect, and it will happen in good time."

He began to pray, and Mary bowed her head. Her anxiety eased as she listened to the pastor's comforting words, and soon it was overshadowed by her thankfulness. God had blessed them all by allowing Henry to get better. The pastor spoke their gratitude, and when he finished, they all murmured, "Amen."

"Henry, if you're still here tomorrow, I'll stop in again," Pastor Miles said, shaking Henry's hand.

"Thanks for coming," Henry said. "I hope to be in church next Sunday."

"We'll see about that," Kim said sternly.

"I hope you're able, Henry, but only if the doctor says it's okay." Pastor Miles said good-bye to all of them and left the room.

"Sit down, Mary," Kim said, pulling a chair over for her.

"Thanks." Mary sank onto the seat. "You know, it occurs to me that Chief McIntosh hasn't spoken to Dan York yet. Otherwise, he'd have known more about the ring and not been so upset when I said I'd found Dan at his cabin."

"I'll bet you're right," Karen said. "That would make him upset with you—you've shown up his men."

"I don't know about that, but it really wasn't that hard to find Mr. York, once I put my mind to it." Mary looked over toward Henry and discovered he was watching her with a smile on his face. "What?" she asked.

Henry shrugged. "I don't know what was going on in his mind, but I don't like that guy. If you can figure this thing out faster than he and the whole Ivy Bay Police Department can, then I say good for you, Mary."

"Thanks. I know Chief McIntosh told me to stay out of it, but I'm a little put out myself right now. Daniel York said he'd go home last night and talk to the police. If he didn't do that, maybe he needs another push."

"Do you think he stayed at his cabin?" Kim asked.

Mary shook her head. "He said he had to work today. Now, if I just knew where he worked . . . . "

"It's some office in Middleboro," Henry said. "A real estate agency, I think. No, that's not right. A title company, that's it."

Kim had her smartphone out and was tapping away. "What's the name of it, Dad?"

"I don't know. Something Harper, I think."

"Craig, Knowland, and Harper?" Kim asked, her eyes on her screen.

"That sounds right." Henry closed his eyes, and Mary realized how worn out he looked. The skin beneath his eyes was dark, and his face was pale.

"We should let you sleep." She stood up. "Middleboro isn't that far. I think I'll drive over there and see if Dan went to work today."

Henry opened his eyes and smiled wanly. "Sometime we're going to have a good, long talk."

"That will be lovely," Mary said. "Now, you get some rest."

She said good-bye to the twins and promised to check in with them later and then hurried out to the elevator. As she left it on the ground floor and walked toward the hospital entrance, her phone rang.

"Hi," Rebecca said. "I thought you'd want to know Tess Bailey was in. She and Blake have worked out the basics for the ice-cream contest."

"Oh, I nearly forgot." Mary squinted at the bright sunlight outside and walked quickly toward her car. "What do I need to know?"

"They're printing up posters and will advertise it in the *Bugle*. Anyone can enter a flavor and take their recipe in to Bailey's. If there are too many, they'll decide which ones are the best for the taste-off in the park on July Fourth."

"That sounds good," Mary said.

"Tess and Blake have ideas about how to regulate it," Rebecca went on. "Probably best to narrow it down to a few flavors, if they want to offer them for sale. Oh, and they've come up with a theme—American Flavor. They asked if they could bring us flyers to put in our customers' bags, and I said sure. I told her you'd probably come by and talk to them as soon as Henry was out of the woods."

"Thanks." Mary unlocked her car and slid in. "I'm sorry I've left you alone so much."

"It's okay," Rebecca assured her. "Ashley's with me this afternoon. Dorothy Johnson called and volunteered to come in and help tomorrow."

"How sweet of her," Mary said. "I expect I'll be there all morning at least—unless something comes up with Henry, of course. Right now, I'm going to go and interview someone connected to the case."

"Do whatever you can to help Henry. We're fine here at the store. And we've sold a good number of books today. We had quite a crowd of tourists come in around noon."

"Wonderful. And I'll try not to neglect you so much tomorrow."

Mary signed off and drove to Middleboro. On the way, she thought a little bit about all-American ice-cream flavors. Apple pie? That one appealed to her. Chips of buttery crust, maybe, and flavorful apples with just a tiny tang. Cinnamon, too, and a dash of nutmeg. A semi roared past her, and she decided she'd better concentrate on the road. Summer traffic on Cape Cod could be tricky.

By the time she arrived at Daniel's office, it was nearly four o'clock. She spotted his green VW in the parking lot and went in. The receptionist directed her to his cubicle. Dan sat behind his desk, facing a side wall. He hunched over a computer keyboard, typing rapidly, with pauses to consult some papers beside him.

He looked up as Mary approached, and his eyebrows shot up. "Hello."

"Hi. Remember me?"

"Of course, Mrs. . . . uh, Fisher, wasn't it?"

"Yes, Mary Fisher. I'm here because I saw the police chief this afternoon, and he didn't seem to know anything about where you were."

Dan swallowed hard and looked past her, as though afraid someone else in the office would hear their conversation.

"I got home late," he said.

"You promised."

He looked away. "I was scared. I admit it. After you left the cabin, some guy came and demanded to know where Dee's ring was."

Mary's heart clenched. Was the stranger who confronted Dan the same man who had followed her? "Who?" she asked.

"I'd never seen him before. He didn't seem to believe me when I said I didn't know where it was." Dan gulped and met her gaze. "He threatened me."

"How? What did he say?"

Dan dropped his voice to a whisper. "That I'd regret it if I didn't cough up the ring. I was scared out of my wits. I don't have it, but I wished I did then. He was a nasty customer."

His pleading eyes convinced Mary. She stepped closer to him.

"Mr. York, I don't think you realize how important this is. I gave Chief McIntosh pictures of that ring today. The police will be talking to you, one way or another, and it will look a lot better if you come forward. Especially since this stranger confronted you at the cabin. He could be the same man who hurt Henry. Tell the police!"

"Okay." He grabbed a tissue from a box on the desk and wiped a bead of sweat from his forehead. "I get out of work at five. I'll go straight to the police station."

"Can't you go now?"

"I don't want my boss to know about this."

She sighed. She didn't like to think she had led some unsavory character to Daniel, but she had to consider the possibility.

"There's another thing," he said, glancing toward the outer office.

Mary leaned in closer. "What?"

"After he left, I packed up in a hurry. I got out to the car, and I realized it had been searched. I drove home, and my apartment had been tossed."

"Tossed?"

"Ransacked. You know. Someone trashed it."

"You think the same person did that?" Mary remembered looking in the window and thinking how messy Dan's living room was. Maybe he wasn't the one who had left it that way.

"I don't know who else would. But if he's looking for that ring, I honestly don't have it. At first I wondered if the police had been to my place, but I don't think they would make such a mess. Would they?"

"I doubt it," Mary said, but she wasn't certain.

"Well, now you know why I was afraid to do anything last night. I figured either they'd arrest me, or that man would show up again and do something worse."

"So you chickened out."

He looked away. "I prefer to think I procrastinated. But now I'm thinking, which is worse—being arrested, or maybe being beat up by a thug?"

"Good point," Mary said. "I think you should leave work now and go to the police." She looked pointedly at the clock, which showed ten minutes past four.

Dan's shoulders slumped. "You're right. I'll do it." He turned back to his keyboard and clicked a few keys.

"Do I need to go with you?" Mary asked.

"No, no. I'm going."

"All right then, I'll leave you."

"Hey, do you think that guy who threatened me is the same one who hurt Henry?" Dan asked.

Mary shivered. She had been thinking the same thing. "It could very well be. You need to give the police a good description, so they can find out who he is."

Daniel nodded.

Mary turned away and walked past the other cubicles, toward the entrance. No one seemed to notice her, not even the receptionist, who was on the phone when Mary passed. She went out to the parking lot and froze with her key ring in her hand. A squad car was pulling into the lot.

She hesitated and decided her best course was to leave. No sense letting McIntosh or his men find her there. She got into her car and eased it out the far end of the parking lot as two uniformed officers headed for the entrance of the building.

She hadn't planned to go back to the hospital until after supper, but she found herself pointing the car in that direction. The cars in the parking lot had thinned out, and she found a spot near the main entrance. As she put the transmission in park, the doors opened and a nurse came out, pushing a woman in a wheelchair. Beside them walked a man who carried a flower arrangement and a large plastic bag, like a hotel laundry bag.

Mary caught her breath. Whenever a person was admitted to the hospital, his clothing and personal items were put into a bag like that and given to the family or stored in the patient's room. Where was the bag with Henry's things?

She went in and hurried to the elevator. When she got to Henry's room, the twins were still there. Henry was dozing, and Mary tiptoed in.

"Hi," Kim said with a smile. "I didn't expect to see you until later."

"I didn't think I was coming back yet either, but I'm glad I did." Mary bent down, and the twins leaned toward her. "Where are your father's things? The clothes and other things he had on him when he came here?"

Karen looked at Kim. "I don't know. Do you?"

Kim nodded. "They had them in a bag at the ICU, and when they moved him to this room, they gave it to me. I stuck it in that cupboard over there and figured I'd take it home tonight." She pointed to a tall, narrow door on the wall near the bathroom.

"May I?" Mary asked.

"Of course," Kim said.

Mary walked to the cupboard and opened the door. Inside was a narrow closet space with a couple of hooks and two shelves. At the bottom was a bulging plastic bag. She carried it over to one of the armchairs.

"This may be nothing," she said to the twins, "but I saw someone carrying one of these bags out of the hospital, and it occurred to me that if Henry did find something in the car, he could have had it on him that night and just not gotten around to telling me about it yet."

Karen's jaw dropped.

"It's worth a look," Kim said.

Mary carefully dumped out the contents onto the seat of the armchair.

At the bottom of the bag was a pair of brown deck shoes, which landed on top of the pile. Mary recognized them as the pair Henry had worn on Friday evening. She picked them up, ran a hand into each one to be sure nothing small was caught inside, and then handed them to Karen.

"One pair of shoes," Mary said.

"Check." Karen set them aside on another chair.

Mary picked up the khaki pants. The brown leather belt still ran through the belt loops. She reached into every pocket and pulled out a few coins, a pocketknife, a small lead item she recognized as a sinker for a fishing line, and Henry's wallet. She passed all of them except the wallet to Karen.

Glancing over at the bed, she whispered, "Think he'd mind if we looked in this? I just want to see if there's anything odd in there."

Kim hesitated and then reached for it. "Let me." She opened the wallet to a plastic window. Henry's driver's license showed through. Kim scanned the contents of the bill pocket.

"Forty-two dollars," she whispered. In the other pockets, she found Henry's commercial fishing license, two credit cards, and his insurance card, as well as pictures of his grandchildren.

"Seems normal to me," Karen said.

Kim nodded soberly. "Nothing odd here."

"Good." Mary picked up the print shirt. The breast pocket was empty, and she passed it to Karen.

Lying in the seat of the armchair were two more items: Henry's watch and a small, square box.

NINETEEN

◆

K im let out a little gasp.

"That looks like a jewelry box," Karen said.

Mary nodded. "A very small jewelry box." She picked it up. The outside of the little square box was made of a velvety, light blue material. A catch that looked like a tiny pearl button was mounted on one side.

"What are you girls up to?"

They all turned around to find Henry eyeing them curiously.

Mary thrust the ring box into Kim's hand.

"We were going through your clothes, Dad," Kim said. "I was going to take them home this evening, okay?"

"No, not unless you bring me something clean to wear tomorrow when they discharge me."

"Oh, I will." Kim looked at Mary, and she nodded firmly. "Uh, Dad?"

"What?" He blinked at her and focused on her hand.

Kim walked over and held out the little box. "This was in your bag of clothes. Do you know what it is?"

Henry frowned. "No, I—Oh yeah." His face brightened. "That was in the—" He broke off and looked at Mary.

For a moment, she feared the memory had slipped away again.

"Henry?" she said gently. "Do you recognize that box?"

He struggled to sit up. Karen scurried around to the other side of the bed and pushed the button to raise the head end of the mattress. When he was comfortable, Henry reached toward the box Kim held.

"Let me see it."

Kim placed it in his hand. Henry studied the box for a few seconds and then sprang the catch. It popped open, and he gazed at its contents.

Mary and the twins moved closer. Twinkling up at them from the box in Henry's hand was Dee Saxon's antique gold-and-diamond ring. The little rubies glinted on each side of the setting, and the burnished gold, cleverly carved, gave an impression of solid luxury.

"Oh yeah," Henry said softly.

"What, Dad? You remember this?" Karen bent close, and Henry met her gaze, frowning.

"I think so." He looked back at the ring, his mouth tightening. After a few seconds, he nodded. "I found it in the trunk of the Century, after I got it home. It was under the spare tire. I don't even know why I was looking in there . . . . "

"It's all right," Mary said. "The point is, you did find it and apparently put it in your pocket. It must have fallen out in the bag of clothing when the nurses packed up your things."

Henry looked up at her, his green eyes troubled. "I tried to call Dan as soon as I found it, but there was no answer. Then I remembered he'd said he was going fishing."

Mary nodded. "You're doing great, Henry. What else?"

"I thought I'd show you the ring that night. I guess I forgot about it while we were getting dinner. But I was going to call Dan later too. It looked valuable, and I figured Dan would know, since it was in his car."

"He paid twenty thousand dollars for it," Mary said, "but from the clippings I found in Boston, I'd say it may be worth even more. If this really is Mrs. Vandemire's stolen ring, that is."

"Wow. So this is the ring in those pictures the chief stuck under my nose." Henry glanced around the arc of their faces. "I honestly didn't remember a thing about it until just now."

"Of course you didn't," Karen said. "We know you were telling the truth."

Henry glanced up at her. "Thanks. So, what do we do now?"

They all looked at each other.

"We have to take it to the police," Mary said.

"Not so fast," Kim said. "Let's all sit down and think this over. I know it has to go to the police, but we need to think about how we're going to do it. We don't want them accusing Dad of anything."

"I'm not sure I want to talk to Chief McIntosh again," Karen said. "He's not very friendly, and I thought he was outright rude to Dad and Mary."

"Well, we have to get it to him," Mary said. "I admit I'm not crazy about taking it over to him, but I don't want to ask him to send someone here for it either."

Kim nodded emphatically. "Dad's had enough today, without having to deal with the police again."

"I have an idea." Karen looked at Mary hesitantly. "The pastor said that if there was anything we needed, to call him."

"You're thinking he might have some advice on how to deal with this?" Kim asked.

"No, I'm thinking that if he has time, he might go with Mary to the police station. Then we'll be assured the chief won't bully her."

"Aw, come on," Henry said. "Mary's not easily bullied."

"Thank you," Mary said. "And I'm not. But I wouldn't mind having a man with me—and a man I know I can trust. Thanks for thinking of it, Karen. I'll give Pastor Miles a call."

She went out into the hallway and made the call. Pastor Miles answered the phone right away and agreed readily to go with her.

"I'll stop by the hospital in ten minutes and pick you up," he said.

"Thank you. I'll go downstairs and meet you out front." Mary put her phone away and went to tell Henry and the twins. "We're going in his car," she told them. "When he brings me back, I'll come up here and tell you how it went."

"Thanks for going to all this trouble, Mary," Kim said, giving her a squeeze.

Henry caught her gaze and nodded. "Chin up, girl. You can do this."

That put a smile on Mary's face as she hurried to the elevator with the ring box nestled in her purse. She could do this for Henry—piece of cake.

Pastor Miles drove up only moments after she'd reached the sidewalk outside the hospital. She opened the passenger door and hopped in.

"Thanks so much for doing this. Seems like we're using up your day off."

"I'd just dropped Trevor off at his house when you called. I don't mind doing this," the pastor said, and Mary knew he meant it.

———

Mary was a little nervous as the pastor drove to the police station. She couldn't help it—the prospect of another meeting with Chief McIntosh made her stomach roil. When they were shown into his office, the chief half rose from his chair and nodded.

"Mrs. Fisher, Pastor Miles. Won't you sit down?"

Mary perched on the edge of one of the chairs. How many times had she sat in this office discussing a case with Chief McArthur? She'd never felt this anxiety when he was the one sitting across the desk from her.

She cleared her throat. "Thank you for seeing me again, Chief."

"I have to say I'm a bit surprised. I told you, Mrs. Fisher, the police can handle this case. You need to just ease up and let us do our job."

"Yes, sir, but something came up, and the Woodrow family and I all agreed that you needed to have this new evidence as soon as possible."

"New evidence?" Chief McIntosh's expression was so stony she shivered.

"Yes. It's this." She took the ring box from her purse and set it on the gleaming walnut desktop.

He stared at it for a moment, then snatched it up and opened it.

"Aha. I take it this is Mrs. Saxon's ring?"

"I believe it is, sir." Mary shifted in her chair. "You see, it was in the bag with Henry Woodrow's clothing at the hospital. None of us realized it until today—well after you were gone. When Henry saw it, he remembered finding it in the car he'd bought. He said he tried to call Mr. York that day—Friday, that is—but he couldn't get hold of him. He had no idea that it belonged to Mr. York's ex-wife."

"I see." Chief McIntosh opened a desk drawer and took out some papers, which Mary could see were the printed photographs she had given him earlier. He turned to the computer on his desk and made a few clicks with the mouse. Mary was at the wrong angle to tell what he was looking at, but he studied the screen for a few moments and then picked up the ring in its box and looked at it intently.

Mary glanced at Pastor Miles. He smiled at her, and she took some reassurance and comfort from his calm, solid presence.

Chief McIntosh picked up the receiver on his desk phone and pressed a button. "Send an officer in, please." He put the phone down.

A moment later, a uniformed man came into the room. Mary was relieved to see that it was Officer Reed, the one who had taken her statement on Friday. He glanced at her and nodded, but walked straight to the desk.

"Could you please call Mrs. Saxon and ask her to come down here?" Chief McIntosh asked him.

"Yes, sir."

"If she's reluctant to come, tell her that I'd like her to identify a piece of recovered jewelry."

Reed nodded and left the room.

Mary said nothing, but she couldn't help staring at the chief and wondering what would happen next.

Chief McIntosh gave her a somewhat condescending smile. "I was going to interview her again anyway, in light of my recent conversation with Mr. York. We need confirmation from her on a few things, and I also planned to show her the photographs of the ring. Now it seems I can show her the real thing."

Mary exhaled. It wasn't a thank-you, but at least he had acknowledged her efforts and let her know that he was using the information she had brought him to find more answers. That made her feel better about him. Pastor Miles reached over and patted her shoulder lightly, and she smiled at him.

Turning back to face McIntosh, she dared to pose a question. "What will you do with the ring if it is Mrs. Saxon's?"

Chief McIntosh eyed her coolly. "I'd appreciate it if you'd wait in the lobby, Mrs. Fisher. Pastor Miles."

Mary determined to remain as expressionless as McIntosh did. She rose and walked out with the pastor. Several people were in the lobby, talking to the officers at the desk or waiting in line. Mary and Pastor Miles found seats on a bench.

After a few minutes, Mary leaned close to the pastor and said, "I wonder what we're waiting for. I do hope I'm not taking too much of your time, but I suspect I am."

"I try to relax on Mondays, and I'm sort of enjoying this." The pastor winked at her. "It gives me a new perspective on what your life is like, Mary."

Officer Tilton came from behind the desk. "Hello, Mrs. Fisher. The chief asked me to take an amended statement from you. I understand you brought in a new piece of evidence in the Woodrow case."

"That's right."

He glanced around the lobby, which was still fairly busy. "Let's go into the interview room, if you don't mind."

"Not at all." Mary stood and asked, "May the pastor come too?" She didn't need his moral support when dealing with Officer Tilton, but she had the feeling he'd like to observe one of his congregants giving an official police statement.

"Sure, I don't see why not."

They followed him into a spartan room with a table and four chairs. A camera was mounted high in one corner, and one wall was curtained. Mary knew from past visits that it covered one-way glass, from behind which officers could observe if they wished.

Officer Tilton sat down opposite her and the pastor and flashed his boyish smile. "All right. What do we have today? Tell me about this ring and how you found it." He opened his notebook and sat ready to take down her explanation. When Mary had finished, he asked a few questions, made more notes, and then stood. "You can go out to the lobby now. If you'll wait just a few minutes, please, I'll have this typed up, and you can review and sign it before you leave."

When they were in the hallway again, Pastor Miles grinned at her. "Just like on TV."

"Well, sort of," Mary said. "I think real police work is a lot more boring than what we see on television."

Ahead of them, the door leading into the lobby opened, and Officer Reed came into the hallway with Dee Saxon. Dee's face was drawn, and her makeup couldn't hide the stress lines. She wore white capri pants, a faux-fur jacket, and very high heels. Her long jet earrings swayed as she strode into the hall.

"Where is my ring? You have it here, in the building?"

"We have *a* ring, ma'am," Officer Reed said, his face deadpan. "We'd like you to look at it and tell us if it's yours."

"And I can take it home?" Dee paused and turned to stare at him, demanding an answer.

"I didn't say that, ma'am. It may be evidence in another case."

"Well, if it's my ring, I want it back!"

Reed's eyebrows twitched, but he only said, "Come this way, ma'am. Chief McIntosh will speak to you."

Mary and the pastor had hesitated, and now they moved against the wall to let the pair pass. Dee's eyes all but sparked as she threw them a haughty glance.

"Mrs. Saxon," Mary said with a tight smile.

"Oh, hello. Uh...Mrs. Fisher, isn't it?"

"Yes." Mary walked on.

Behind her, Dee resumed badgering Officer Reed. "My husband bought me that ring, and I want it. Now."

Mary reached the door, and Pastor Miles pushed it open and held it for her. She walked out into the lobby. A woman and a sullen teenage girl had claimed their previous bench, but two chairs had opened up across the room, and Mary and the pastor went to them and sat down.

"So that's Dee Saxon," the pastor said.

Mary nodded. She wondered what he would say about the woman, but after perhaps fifteen seconds, he only shook his head and said, "Well."

In a surprisingly short time, Tilton returned with a clipboard. Mary read the typed statement carefully. It seemed accurate, and she signed at the bottom.

"Thanks," Officer Tilton said with a smile. "Sorry you had to wait."

"That's it?" the pastor asked.

"You can go."

"Thank you," Mary said. "Everyone's been very gracious today. I hope you find out soon who attacked Henry Woodrow."

"We're working on it, ma'am. We've got some good leads now. Thanks for your part."

"I'm happy I could help."

As they headed for the exit, Mary heard muffled yelling from deep within the building. She managed to keep a straight face and not look back.

In the parking lot, Pastor Miles opened the car door for Mary and smiled wryly at her. "That was quite an experience. Are you all right?"

"Yes, thanks. I'll try not to bother you again today."

"No problem."

He dropped her off in front of the hospital entrance. The daylight was fading, and Mary looked at her watch. It was past the time when she and Betty usually ate supper, and the sandwich she'd eaten in Boston was a distant memory. She got in her car and headed for home. She could return after supper and tell Henry and the twins about her trip to the police station.

Betty was eager to hear how her day went, and Mary told her the details while they ate.

"Sounds like you've made a lot of progress," Betty said, "if not in the direction you'd hoped."

Mary sighed. "I'm glad we found the ring, but we still don't know who hit Henry. I'm afraid I won't be satisfied until that riddle is solved."

After the meal, she went to her laptop to catch up on e-mail. On a whim, she returned to the Ivy Bay Wheelers' Web site. The photos of Dan York had convinced her that he was hiding something from her, and now she knew it was Dee's ring. But why had he been so nervous that day?

When the page came up on her screen, she was surprised to see that more pictures had been loaded. "Photos of the show by Julie Saunders," she read.

Eagerly, Mary scanned the new pictures. Had Julie captured something Stan Auger had missed? As she scrolled down the page, one view caught her attention, and she stopped.

"Now, there's a familiar face!" Mary took a photo of the picture with her smartphone and looked at her watch. She was eager to share her new discovery with Henry, so she grabbed her purse and went out.

At the hospital, she hurried inside and caught the elevator up to Henry's floor. Karen had gone home to rest, but Kim greeted her cordially. Henry had been dozing, but he opened his eyes at the sound of their voices.

"Well, hi. How did it go?"

"Not badly, all things considered." Henry wanted to know what happened at the police station, so Mary held off on her other news. She sat down and told him about the change in

McIntosh's attitude after she produced the ring. "And he had an officer call Mrs. Saxon immediately so she could come and identify it."

"Good," Kim said.

Henry eyed her cautiously. "They don't think I stole it, do they?"

"No, I don't think so."

"Well, that's something," Henry said.

"After I talked to the chief, I had to give a new statement, and then they had to type it up so I could sign it." Mary gave a little chuckle. "While I was waiting for that, Dee Saxon came in, and she wasn't happy. The officer escorting her implied that she wouldn't be able to take the ring home with her, and she was furious."

"I expect they'll keep it until they tie up loose ends with the Boston police," Kim said.

Mary nodded. "They'll want to have the Vandemires see it and tell them if it's the same ring that was stolen from them last year. That could take some time."

"And if it *is* their ring, Mrs. Saxon will never get it back," Kim said.

She reached for her bag, about to pull up the cell phone photo, when Henry held out a hand, as though reaching for something. Mary looked sharply at his face. He was frowning, his eyes not focused on anything in the room.

"Henry?" She bent closer to him.

He turned his head and looked into her eyes. "Mary. I remember."

"You do?"

He grasped her hand and squeezed it tight. "I do. I remember Friday night, in the garage. And the guy who hit me."

TWENTY

◆◆◆

Mary sank into a chair, still holding Henry's hand. "That's wonderful. Are you sure?"

Henry nodded, still frowning. "I didn't recognize him that night, but I would now. I don't know his name." He looked up at her. "I may have seen him someplace else, I'm just not sure. Maybe you'd better call the cops now, in case I forget again."

"Are you ready to talk to them again?" Kim's face was drawn as she gazed at her father. She shot Mary a glance. "What do you think?"

"If he feels up to it."

"I do," Henry said.

"All right." Mary smiled ruefully. "I'm not sure the police will be happy to hear from me again so soon."

"I'll call them, if you want," Kim said. "I don't mind. Not for this."

"Thank you." Mary gave her the nonemergency number, and Kim went out into the hallway.

"You don't need to stay," Henry said. "Unless you want to." He had an almost puppy-dog look, and Mary's heart melted. Henry was usually so confident and self-reliant. This injury had shaken him more than he might realize.

"I don't mind staying."

His soft smile told her she'd made the right choice. He squeezed her hand. "Thanks. I admit I hoped you'd say that."

Mary's heartbeat quickened as she debated on what to do next. Finally she leaned closer to him and said, "Henry, I think I know who it was—the man who attacked you."

"You do?"

"Yes. And I have proof that he was at the car show. He could have followed you or learned who you were and where you lived after you left."

"Who is it?" Henry asked.

"I'm not sure I should say—not with you just now remembering what he looks like. Maybe we should wait until the police get here and see if your memory matches up with what I think. I don't want them thinking I planted the suggestion in your mind."

"All right." Henry reached for her with his other hand as well, and Mary placed her hand in his.

"God is so good," she whispered.

"He sure is." Henry closed his eyes for a moment. "Thanks for everything you've been doing. The girls told me that even when you weren't here, you were out there working for me."

"I couldn't do anything else."

Kim came back in, and Henry sat up a little straighter. "Are they coming?"

"Yes. They'll be here soon."

Mary's phone beeped, and she checked her messages. Tess Bailey had texted her: "Meet tomorrow about taste-off?"

Mary smiled. Tess and Blake weren't going to let her forget about that. She texted back, "OK. Will call u in morning."

In only a few minutes, Chief McIntosh himself arrived with Officer Reed. The two greeted them and stood over Henry. Mary joined Kim in a corner.

Mary wished the younger officer had come alone. That would be less intimidating for Henry, and for her and Kim as well.

"So, you think you would recognize the man who attacked you if you saw him again?" Chief McIntosh asked Henry.

"Yes, I'm pretty sure I could. I saw him, plain as day."

"But you don't know his name."

"That's right," Henry said.

The chief turned and frowned at Mary and Kim. "Perhaps you ladies could give us a few minutes with Mr. Woodrow."

"No, let them stay," Henry said firmly, before either of them could speak.

Chief McIntosh's lips pressed into a thin line. He didn't say anything, but turned back toward the bed, and Mary took that as assent. Kim looked at her anxiously, and Mary patted her shoulder and stood her ground. Henry wanted them here, and they were staying.

Chief McIntosh pulled a chair over and sat down. "Could you describe him, please? Officer Reed will write down your description."

Reed stood at the chief's shoulder, his notebook and pen ready. "Just tell me what happened, sir, and what you remember about him."

"He had dark hair, and he was fairly tall—"

"How tall?" Officer Reed asked.

Henry frowned. "When I opened the garage door, I saw him bent over, looking inside the new car. He had a flashlight, and he stood up and stared at me. He was probably five feet ten or so. See, I was standing in the doorway, and there are a couple of steps going down into the garage, so I was looking down at him, but when I spoke, he stood up straight, and judging from how he looked standing beside the car, I'd say he was at least five feet ten, but probably not as tall as I am."

Officer Reed scribbled away.

Chief McIntosh said, "How old do you think he was?"

"*Hmm*, maybe fifty or fifty-five. He wasn't gray, but his face looked middle-aged. Wrinkles, I guess." Henry smiled. "Maybe he covers his gray."

"Weight?" McIntosh said without cracking a smile.

"Average. Not thin, not plump. Probably works out a little to stay fit."

"Why do you say that?"

"I don't know." Henry's eyes narrowed. "I just got the impression that he was in pretty good shape for his age."

Mary smiled to herself. Henry was describing the man she suspected with precision.

"He came around the back of the car, and I jumped down to get between him and the door. I wasn't going to let him get away without knowing what he wanted. And then he hit me. I guess..." Henry looked bleakly at Officer Reed. "I guess I flew back, toward the steps. I'm not really sure. That must be when I hit my head on the concrete floor. At least that's what Doc Teagarden thinks."

"Did he strike you with his hand, or with something else?" Officer Reed asked.

Henry brightened. "The flashlight. It was a long silver one, the kind that takes four or five batteries, and he swung it pretty hard."

Mary winced, amazed that Henry hadn't suffered any fractures.

"I dodged, but I was too late, and he got me anyway." Henry ran his fingertips over his bruised cheek. "I guess he didn't hit me as hard as he might have. Oh, and he had dark hair. Did I say that? Not sure about the eyes, but I'm guessing brown. He would probably be called a handsome man."

"Any facial hair?" Officer Reed asked as he wrote.

"No."

"Scars?"

Henry frowned. "None I could see."

Officer Reed paused with his pen above his notebook. "Tattoos?"

"Not that I saw."

"Do you remember anything about the shape of his face?" Chief McIntosh asked.

"Kind of a square chin, I'd say. Nose wasn't overly large, but a good, strong nose." Henry shrugged. "That's about it, I guess. No dimples or moles or anything like that."

"All right, we're going to show you some faces." Chief McIntosh stood and nodded to Officer Reed. The younger man sat down and held up a three-ring binder.

"I've put several pictures in this notebook, Mr. Woodrow. Some of them are connected to this case or to you in some way. I'd like you to look at them and see if you think any of them was the man who attacked you."

Mary's excitement grew. Did they have a photo in there of the man she thought was guilty?

Officer Reed opened the binder so that two plastic-covered pages showed, facing each other. He placed it in Henry's hands. Mary and Kim edged forward. Mary could see that each of the two pages held six photographs in plastic pockets, but she couldn't tell who they were from where she stood.

Henry surveyed them quickly, and a smile touched his lips. He pointed at one.

"That's Dan York. It wasn't him."

"Look at each one carefully, please," Chief McIntosh said.

Henry nodded and focused on the pictures soberly. "*Hmm.* This one looks like that fellow on the TV commercials. You know, the cut-rate car salesman? Bargain Bill, that's what they call him."

"Is he the one?" Officer Reed asked.

"No, I'm just saying. And he *was* at the car show." Henry turned back to the task. "There's Oscar Littlefield," he muttered.

Mary smiled. Oscar had a fishing boat at the marina, so of course Henry knew him. For a moment she wondered what Oscar was doing in the mug book. Then she remembered that he'd been briefly arrested the previous year for exceeding the fish limits and had paid a stiff fine.

Suddenly Henry's face lit up. "That's him." He pointed to one of the faces on the second page.

"Are you sure?" Officer Reed asked.

"Well, it's not a good likeness."

"It's from his driver's license," the officer said.

Henry laughed. "Well, that explains it, eh? Yeah, that's him. Who is he?"

Officer Reed looked up at Chief McIntosh, as if for a cue.

"It's Erick Saxon," the chief said.

"Should we pick him up?" Officer Reed asked.

Chief McIntosh frowned. "The man has an alibi. He and his wife attended a charity event on Friday evening."

Mary's pulse picked up a notch. "Excuse me, Chief. I know something about that charity auction that you might find interesting."

Chief McIntosh turned slowly and eyed her severely. "Of course you do. Well, out with it."

She stepped closer to the bed and looked down at the array of photos in the binder Henry held. She spotted the picture of Erick Saxon and pointed to it. "I've never met Mr. Saxon, but I recognize this photo because I've seen several others recently."

Chief McIntosh's jaw twitched, but he didn't say anything, so she went on.

"When I was looking for pictures of Dee wearing the ring, I saw pictures of her new husband on her social-media page. And there was a picture of them both in Saturday's paper, taken at the auction."

"I'm aware of that photo," the chief said.

Mary nodded. "This evening, I was looking at the Web site of the Ivy Bay Wheelers. Some of the members have posted photographs there from last weekend's car show."

"And?" McIntosh seemed to be getting impatient.

Mary took the photo she had printed from her bag. "A woman named Julie Saunders posted this picture today. She took it while Henry and Dan were looking over the car Dan sold Henry. If you look closely, you'll see that Erick Saxon was at the car show on Friday. He's on the extreme right of that picture, and in this shot, he seems to be watching Dan and Henry."

"Erick was at the car show?" Henry asked.

Mary nodded. "He sure was. Earlier, I saw other pictures of Friday's auto show taken by both Johanna Montgomery and Stan Auger. In those pictures, Dan seemed to always be touching his pocket."

Henry nodded.

"In one, he was looking over his shoulder," Mary added.

"He did seem nervous that day," Henry said.

Officer Reed was taking notes. "What are you saying, Mrs. Fisher?"

"It's a connection," Mary said. "Erick Saxon saw Henry and Dan make their transaction for the car. I think Dan observed him and was afraid of Erick. Dan had the ring on him that day, and he was afraid Erick would confront him. Dan told me he didn't have it, but I think he did. And at some point, he hid the ring in the car so that if Erick approached him, he wouldn't find it. But if Erick was suspicious, he could easily have asked other people at the car show who Henry was and where he lived. That evening, he went to Henry's house to see if he could find the ring in the car."

"But Mr. Saxon has an alibi for Friday evening," Chief McIntosh said. "He was at the charity auction."

"Was he at that time?" Mary asked. "I spoke to Johanna Montgomery at the *Bugle* office. She did the story on the auction and took the picture that was in the *Bugle* herself. She said it was nearly nine o'clock when she took it."

"That's more than two hours after the attack," Officer Reed said.

Mary nodded. "And that's not all. My sister, Betty Emerson, was at the event earlier. She left when I called her and told her about Henry's injury. She told me she saw Dee Saxon there, but she couldn't remember seeing her with a man. She also saw the photo in the *Bugle*, and she didn't recognize Erick Saxon. So if that auction is Mr. Saxon's alibi, maybe you could look more closely at what time he arrived there."

Everyone was silent while Chief McIntosh breathed in and out twice. At last he managed a strained smile and said, "Thank you, Mrs. Fisher. We'll take it from here. Reed!"

Officer Reed took the binder from Henry and stood. Chief McIntosh nodded at Henry and strode out the door. Officer Reed looked around at them for a second, his mouth slightly open.

"Uh, good-bye, folks. Thank you! Glad you're feeling better, Mr. Woodrow." He hurried away after McIntosh.

Kim walked over to the chair the policeman had vacated and slumped down in it. "Well!"

"I agree," Henry said, and they all laughed.

Mary brought another chair over and sat down on the other side of the bed. She couldn't help but notice how Henry's eyelids drooped. "Tired?"

"A little. Funny, I never used to get worn out just looking at a picture album."

"Ten minutes with Chief McIntosh wrings me out like a dishrag," Kim said with a sigh.

"Same here," Mary said.

"So why do you suppose they hit on Saxon and had his photo in the book?" Henry asked.

"I suppose because the ring belonged to his wife and was stolen from his home."

"But if they went to the police..."

"Yes," Kim said. "If they knew where it was, why did they even report it?"

Mary said, "Dee definitely wanted the replacement value. And they reported the theft several days before the car show. Maybe it took them that long to settle on Dan as their main suspect for the theft. By then, I think Erick was convinced Dan had the ring and was determined to get it back."

Kim's cell rang, and she fumbled to get it from her leather purse. "Oh, hi!" Her features lit up, and she mouthed "Karen" to Mary and Henry. "Yeah, McIntosh and one of his men were just here. Wait until you hear!" Kim listened for a moment and then said, "Sure. That'd be great." She looked over at her father. "Dad, Karen's coming in, and she's stopping for some takeout food. You want anything special?"

Henry shook his head and winced.

"Dad says nothing for him," Kim said into the phone. "We'll be here. I'll probably go home and sleep after we eat."

When she had put the phone away, Mary said, "I'd better get going myself. It's been a very long day, although a satisfying one."

"You accomplished a lot today," Kim agreed. "Thanks, Mary."

Henry reached over and squeezed her hand. "Ditto from me. I know you've done a lot more than I know about. You're a good scout, Mary."

TWENTY-ONE

———◆◆◆———

Tuesday morning, the sky was overcast and a fine mist filtered down. The bookshop was filled with customers, and Mary spent a great deal of time on her feet, guiding people to books they would enjoy and ringing up their purchases. Rebecca had done well without her the previous day, but tasks had piled up, and Mary knew she had a lot of paperwork to deal with.

When the crowd thinned out a little, Rebecca took over behind the counter and located books for people while Mary caught up on financial records, shelving, and marking order forms for restocking.

At last she felt things were under control. She couldn't resist making a brief online visit to the *Boston Globe*'s archives. The stolen ring kept flitting into her mind, and she wondered if they could make a positive connection between Dee's ring and Starr Vandemire's heirloom.

She reread the account of the theft from the Vandemires' luxurious home, but she couldn't find any new details. The police department's spokeswoman had given out limited information about the investigation.

Several of Mary's friends came in, including Pastor Miles, and Mary left her computer to speak to him.

"How's Henry doing?" he asked, and then, eyeing Mary keenly, he said, "Perhaps I should ask first how *you're* doing."

"Me? I'm fine. A good night's sleep did wonders."

"Yes, you look well. And Henry?"

"He was fine when I left last night, and I spoke to Karen this morning. They want to keep him one more day, just to monitor him. The MRI looked good, but because of the concussion, they want him to go slowly."

"That's probably wise," Pastor Miles said.

"Did you hear that after our trip to the police station, Henry remembered more about Friday night?"

"No. Is his memory complete now?"

"We think so. He identified his attacker." Mary leaned closer and whispered, "Mr. Saxon."

Pastor Miles nodded gravely as more customers entered. "That makes sense, from what you've told me. I'll try to drop by the hospital later."

Lynn Teagarden and Amy Stebble, both members of Mary's prayer group, came into the shop a few minutes later.

Amy's face lit up when she spotted Mary behind the counter. "Mary, how's Henry?"

"He's much better, thank you. He'll probably go home tomorrow."

"That's great," Amy said.

Lynn, who was taller and thinner than Amy, smiled in contentment. "I'm so glad. Gary hasn't told me much. He's been so busy I haven't seen much of him the last couple of days."

"Does this mean you'll be able to join us for prayer group this week?" Amy asked.

"I plan to be there," Mary said.

"Good. We've all been in touch by phone and praying for Henry," Lynn said. "The pastor said Henry's daughters are here, and we couldn't visit because they had him in the ICU."

"They moved him to a regular room yesterday," Mary said. "Still, he's mostly there to rest, but I'll bet he'd like a visit later in the week at home."

"We could take him some cookies." Amy looked up at Lynn for confirmation.

"Good idea," Lynn said.

"Are you enjoying your summer off from school, Amy?" Mary asked. Amy was the elementary school principal, and she often spent her time away from the office reading and studying.

"I'm preparing for next term," Amy admitted. "But I wondered if the special order I placed last week was in, and I want a new mystery for my downtime."

"Same here," Lynn said. "I had trouble sleeping last night, so I finished the novel I was reading. Now I need something new."

Mary happily showed her friends the latest releases. She retrieved the book Amy had ordered and chatted with them for a few more minutes, until several other people came in.

By noon, she was ready for her lunch meeting with Tess Bailey, but she let Rebecca take her lunch hour first, and Dorothy arrived while Rebecca was out. Her face was full of concern when she saw Mary at the counter.

"Oh, Mary!" Dorothy hurried across the store to her. "How is he doing?"

Mary didn't need to ask whom she meant. "He's much better, Dorothy. The doctor will release him tomorrow if everything goes well. Kim is going to stay with him a few days after he goes home, just to make sure he's up to speed."

"Do you think he'll want company then?"

"I'm sure he'd be pleased to see you."

Dorothy smiled. "I'll call the house tomorrow afternoon and see if he's there."

Mary almost advised that Dorothy should give Henry a day or two to recover at home first, but she had a feeling they had done well to keep her away from the hospital this long.

At one, when Rebecca came back with Ashley along, Mary hurried out and down Main Street toward the Black & White Diner. Her stomach was rumbling, and she knew exactly what she would order.

Tess was headed toward the diner as well, and they met on the sidewalk in front of the door.

"Well, hi," Tess said with a laugh that sent her auburn hair shimmering.

"Hi," Mary said. "I don't know about you, but I'm famished."

"Me too. I made myself not eat anything since breakfast so I'd enjoy this to the max."

Mary chuckled and opened the diner's door, holding it for Tess. "That must be hard when you're making ice cream."

"It's tempting," Tess admitted. "I made strawberry swirl and moose tracks this morning, and those little chocolate candies for the moose tracks usually get to me, but today I stood firm."

"Great!" Mary sat down at a booth near the front windows, and Tess slid in opposite her.

Nicole Hancock came over to take their order.

"I'll have a BLT," Mary said. "I've been hankering for it all morning."

Tess looked up from the menu. "Oh, that sounds good, but I think I'll have the chicken salad. It's something I never make at home, for some reason." She laughed. "Probably because it's so good here, and mine would never match up."

"Thanks, ladies." Nicole took away the menus and brought them each a glass of water.

Tess settled back in the booth. "I'm so glad Henry's out of the woods now."

"Me too," Mary said. "It's been a hectic four days."

"How long are his daughters staying?"

"I'm not sure. I think Karen has to go home soon because of her job. Since Henry's so much better, she'll probably leave soon after he's settled at home. But Kim spoke of staying a few days longer, just to make sure he does all right on his own."

"He gave them a real scare."

"All of us," Mary admitted.

"You probably haven't had much time to think about ice cream. I hope we didn't pressure you too much on it."

"Actually, I have done a little ruminating on the subject," Mary said in a teasing voice.

Tess's face lit up. "Great, because Blake is getting really excited about the taste-off. I've got flyers for you." She passed Mary a bag.

"Thanks." Mary took one out and looked at it. "Very nice. I like the flags and fireworks."

"Appropriate to the day," Tess said with a smile. "Blake's had posters made, and he's already put an ad in the *Bugle*.

We're putting out flyers all over town. We're rushing to get this done because Blake says we'll need all the entries at least a week in advance. That way we can stock up on all the ingredients for making the winners' flavors."

"You're going to make all the flavors people enter?" Mary asked. "What if there are a hundred of them?"

"We've decided to have the entrants bring in a homemade sample for us to try. We'll narrow it down to no more than a dozen."

Mary nodded. "Good, but that's still a lot of new flavors."

Tess wrinkled her nose. "You're right. Maybe not that many. We'll see how it goes."

"Well, you're the one who'll be making it all the day before the Fourth," Mary said. "Don't make it too hard on yourself."

Nicole brought their sandwich plates and set them down with a smile. "I heard you talking about the ice-cream contest. My mom is thinking of entering."

"Fantastic," Tess said. "Deena would come up with something yummy, I'm sure."

"Oh yes, her cooking is wonderful," Mary said with a chuckle. "Which is why we're here. She really should enter."

"I'll tell her," Nicole said. "Anything else I can get you ladies?"

"No, thanks," Mary said. "It looks delicious. But, say, Nicole, why don't *you* enter the contest?"

"Me?" Nicole's eyes flared.

"Sure," Tess said. "Why not?"

"How about a bacon ice cream?" Nicole said.

"Bacon is a very important food in American history," Tess said with a laugh.

"Yes, and this place is known for its amazing bacon," Mary added, though she couldn't quite imagine it in ice cream.

"I'll think about it," Nicole said. "Enjoy!"

After a pause for Tess to ask the blessing and take a few bites of her meal, Mary turned the conversation back to the ice-cream event.

"I like Blake's theme. American Flavor is perfect."

"Yes, and I'm glad that's settled. We went round and round with it. We're going to rent a big red-white-and-blue awning to put up in the park, just in case it rains, and Blake wants to deck out the shop in bunting and all that. He has his heart set on patriotic hoopla."

"That's appropriate," Mary said. "Will you sell ice cream in the park all day?"

"We'll probably start right after the parade ends. And we want to keep the store open too, because a lot of tourists will be browsing downtown for antiques and art."

"And books," Mary said. "Maybe I should keep the bookshop open." She made a mental note to discuss it with Rebecca, though she had been planning to close for the day.

"Blake's really putting a lot of effort into this," Tess said. "Instead of introducing the July flavor of the month on the first, like we usually do, we'll put it off until the Fourth, when the winner is announced. And be forewarned, he's planning on a lot of hype for this."

"I figured that out." Mary picked up the remaining half of her sandwich. "There'll be a large crowd on the Fourth. This could be big for Bailey's."

"It sure could. We could get a lot of orders for packed ice cream, and that could carry beyond the season. It would be nice to sell more ice cream during the off-season."

Mary and Tess chatted while they finished their meal.

"So, what's your idea for a flavor?" Tess asked as Nicole brought them coffee and slices of her mom's coconut cream pie.

Mary smiled. "I was thinking apple pie ice cream."

"What's more American?" Tess grinned.

"Right. Maybe a new twist on the classic. My brain—or maybe it's my stomach—keeps shouting, 'Sweet, spicy apple pie!' Maybe I could make up something like pie filling and swirl it into the ice cream, with little flakes of buttery crust."

Tess's eyes widened. "Ooh, I love it already, and I haven't even tasted it! No one else has mentioned an apple pie flavor to me yet."

When she and Tess had finished their talk, Mary waved good-bye and set out for the hospital. She was determined to stay only a short while, and she hoped she could get a parking spot close to the entrance.

Before she turned into the lot at the hospital, she glanced in her rearview mirror. A spurt of adrenaline made it suddenly hard to breathe. The car that had followed her and Betty was coming down the street behind her.

Mary parked and sat in her car, her heart pounding. This was the one loose end concerning the assault on Henry.

Lord, show me what to do!

She waited, and sure enough, the dark blue sedan rolled into the lot and passed the end of the row where she had parked. With judicious use of her mirrors, Mary was able to follow its progress as the car wound through the rows of vehicles and came to rest in a slot two rows almost directly behind her.

She waited a few more seconds, but the driver didn't open his door.

Now what? If she didn't get out, he would find that odd. But she couldn't just walk into the hospital knowing he was sitting there.

"I guess now would be a good time to call the police," she said softly. She took out her phone. Officer Tilton was on the desk, and he took her call.

"I'm sure it's the car that followed me into town the other day, and the same one that followed my sister and me to Daniel York's cabin. I saw the license plate, and I'm positive."

"We'll send a unit right over," Officer Tilton said.

"Thank you." Mary put her phone away, relieved to know the police were on the way. Still, it went against her nature to walk off and leave that man sitting there in his car. More than anything else at that moment, she wanted to know why he was following her.

Finally, she made her decision. It couldn't take more than another minute or two for the officers to arrive. She got out of her car and strode through the ranks of parked vehicles to where the dark sedan sat.

The man in the driver's seat seemed to be avoiding eye contact. Mary walked right up to his window and tapped on it.

He looked up at her with an expression she interpreted as mild surprise and chagrin. The fleeting thought that she might have put herself in danger flashed through her mind. What if he pulled out a gun?

He lowered the window partway.

"Yes?"

"Why are you following me?" Mary asked.

TWENTY-TWO

◆◆◆

Following you?"

The man's attempt at innocence didn't cut any ice with Mary.

"You followed me from Bayshore Road to the police station Saturday, and on Sunday you followed me all the way to Federal Pond and confronted Daniel York in his cabin after I left. And here you are today."

His jaw clenched for a moment, and then he let out a sigh. "All right, you burned me. I'm investigating a matter—"

"Investigating? Are you a police officer?" Mary had never considered that he might be an undercover policeman. Surely Chief McIntosh would have told her if that were so.

"No," he said. "I'm a private investigator."

"Oh." Mary frowned. "May I see your identification, please?"

He unbuckled his seat belt and twisted to take his wallet from his pocket.

"Here."

Mary studied the credentials he showed her. The license appeared to be genuine, but she wasn't sure she'd know if it was forged.

"You're Joseph Melvin?"

"That's right."

"Who hired you to follow me?" Mary asked.

"Follow you? Nobody. I mean, my client hired me to look into a certain matter, and...well, my search has led me to Henry Woodrow. I decided the best way to find out when he'll be released from the hospital so I can talk to him is to keep an eye on you."

"Henry?" She stared at him. "Who on earth would want to investigate Henry?"

"I'm sorry, but I can't reveal my client's name. But I assure you I meant you no harm. I'm sorry if I frightened you."

Mary thought about that for a moment. Just because he didn't bear her any ill will, didn't mean Mr. Melvin didn't want to harm Henry. "All right, but I've told the police you were following me."

"Oh, great. Just what I need."

"What do you mean?"

"McIntosh."

She frowned. "You know Chief McIntosh?"

"I know Detective Sergeant McIntosh. We had a run-in over another case a few months back. I'm not his favorite person. And now I find he's down here on temporary assignment—"

"Detective sergeant?" Mary asked.

"Yeah, that's his title in Boston. They loaned him out as acting chief here for a few weeks. I've been trying to fly under his radar."

"I see." Mary handed his wallet back. "Well, consider yourself grounded. I reported you on Saturday, and I'm sure he knows by now that you're in town, Mr. Melvin. In fact"—

she glanced toward the street, where a patrol car was just turning in to the hospital parking lot, and smiled—"one of his men is here now. You may not have to reveal your business to me, but you'd better prepare yourself to explain what you're doing to them."

Mary waved to the officer in the patrol car. It drove closer and parked behind Melvin's vehicle, effectively blocking his exit.

Officer Reed climbed out of the car. "Hello, Mrs. Fisher. Everything all right?"

On the way up the elevator a few minutes later, Mary decided not to tell Henry about the private investigator yet. No use upsetting him until the police had sorted out Melvin's reasons for shadowing her and wanting to talk to Henry. No sense alarming his daughters either, before she knew the full story.

Henry had eaten his lunch when she arrived at his room. Karen was reading him the clues to the crossword in the Boston paper, and Henry was supplying the answers for her to fill in. Mary smiled at them as she walked in.

"You look like a happy pair."

"We are," Henry said. "The doctor has promised to release me tomorrow."

"Terrific!"

"I told him I'm fine and I should go today, but he—"

"Dad, we've been through this," Karen said. "One more night to make sure everything's good."

"Yeah, yeah." Henry scowled, but he didn't look too upset.

"Kim and I will stay the night with him tomorrow," Karen said, "and I'll fly home the next day if all goes as planned."

"If," Henry said with disdain. "All *will* be peachy tomorrow."

Karen smiled. "I believe you, Dad, but I'm not booking my flight yet."

Mary sat down and set her purse on the floor. "So, is your headache gone?"

"Pretty much," Henry said.

Karen made a face at him. "You still need the painkillers."

"Well, yeah." He shrugged. "It's gone if I keep taking the meds."

"I understand," Mary said. "I'm glad Kim will stay a few days."

Henry nodded. "She says she can stay until Saturday morning. Then she needs to get home and get the kids ready for camp."

"How exciting!" Mary told him about Blake and Tess's plan to hold an ice-cream-flavor contest. She was just getting to her plans for her apple pie–flavored creation when the doorway darkened and Chief McIntosh walked in.

He looked first toward the bed. "Good afternoon, Mr. Woodrow. Feeling better?"

"Yes, sir, I am. I plan to go home tomorrow."

"That's good." McIntosh nodded at Karen and Mary. "Mrs. Fisher, I wanted to tell you and Mr. Woodrow that we're closing the case on the assault."

"You got the guy who hit me?" Henry asked.

Chief McIntosh nodded and stepped closer to him. "Erick Saxon is in custody for the assault. He says he didn't mean to hurt you, but in light of how serious your injury was, we plan to prosecute him."

"Well, if he didn't mean it," Henry said, looking toward Karen and Mary.

"Now, Dad," Karen said firmly, "he nearly killed you. You have to press charges."

"We will anyway," Chief McIntosh said. "The state, that is. In a case like this, you don't have much choice, Mr. Woodrow."

Karen patted her father's arm. "He's just too kindhearted sometimes, Chief."

"He did come into my garage intending to take something," Henry said.

"Yes, he did, so we have quite a string of charges for him to face in court." The chief smiled, and the transformation in his face jolted Mary. He might actually be a handsome man if he weren't so grim all the time. "You've helped in a couple of other cases too, Woodrow. And Mrs. Fisher."

"The stolen ring," Mary said.

"Yes. Daniel York confessed to stealing it from Mrs. Saxon."

"Good. That was the only explanation I could think of that made sense. At the car show, he was nervous, and he kept checking his pocket. I figured he must have had the ring with him, though I can't imagine why."

"He said he planned to take it to the bank and put it in his safe-deposit box that morning," Chief McIntosh said. "He felt the divorce settlement was unfair and he should have gotten the ring back. After things cooled down, he figured he could take it somewhere away from Cape Cod and sell it. However, he was running late getting all his antique automobiles to the show, so he didn't have time to go to the bank. That left him with the ring in his pocket."

Henry nodded. "So what happens to Dan now?"

"We're charging York in connection with the theft of the ring." Chief McIntosh's brow furrowed. "However, now there's some question as to whether Mrs. Saxon had a legal right to it in the first place. You were correct about that too, Mrs. Fisher. It was the same ring that was stolen from Mrs. Vandemire last year. Apparently the thief who took it from her mansion in Boston fenced it at Guthrie's, and they resold it to Mr. York. Boston PD is sending two men down here to fetch it today. They hope to return it to the Vandemires."

Henry's face puckered. "What I'm still not clear on is, how did Erick Saxon know the ring was in the Buick? Somehow, he must have seen Dan put it in the car."

Chief McIntosh shrugged. "He said he wasn't sure, but he went to the car show hoping to confront Dan York. He did notice that when York saw him, he seemed awfully nervous. And while York was talking to you, he kept putting his hand in his pocket. That made Saxon think he might have something valuable concealed there."

"I noticed Dan was a little distracted," Henry said. "Couldn't figure it out. I guess I'm not very observant or I'd have spotted the guy. He didn't come and talk to Dan while I was there."

"No, he waited around while you took the test-drive. Then, after you left, he went over and asked York point-blank where the ring was. York said he had no idea, and he supposed Dee had it." Chief McIntosh shook his head. "Saxon wasn't having any of that. He told him, 'Come on, you know you've got it on you.' But York turned out his pockets and laughed at him."

"Laughed at him?" Karen said. "That doesn't seem very wise."

"No, it wasn't," the chief said. "It made Saxon more sure than ever that York had the ring. And he figured that while Mr. Woodrow and York took the test-drive, York had hidden the ring inside the car."

"And then Henry bought it and drove off in it," Mary said with a chuckle.

"You led him on a chase, Dad," Karen said.

"Guess I did." Henry let out a deep sigh. "Chief, I assure you it wasn't my intention to cause any trouble. I had no idea that thing was in the car when I drove home from the show."

McIntosh hesitated, then shrugged. "As it turned out, it's just as well. If you hadn't driven off with it, Saxon would probably have found a way to turn that car inside out at the antique auto show, and maybe there would have been some violence between him and York. As it was, you were the one who suffered at his hands. But before he went to your place, he went to York's apartment and ransacked it, to make sure he didn't have the ring hidden there."

"Mr. Saxon went to all that trouble, and now he and his wife won't get to keep the ring," Mary mused. "There's poetic justice, I think. But Henry had found the ring by the time Mr. Saxon got to his house, and he had it right there in his pocket when Mr. Saxon struck him."

"I think I like that part best," Karen said. She leaned over to kiss her father's cheek. "You saved the fabulous jewels,

Dad, and the thief didn't have the presence of mind to check your pockets."

"What did he do when he failed to get the ring at Henry's?" Mary asked.

"His story is that he figured York took the ring with him and skipped town after he sold the cars. He didn't expect him to come back to Ivy Bay so soon."

"I guess they helped incriminate each other," Karen said. "Did the Boston police ever catch the thief who stole the ring from the Vandemires?"

"No, and it's been nine months. They're a little embarrassed about the whole jewelry ring business. They closed down Guthrie's, but apparently several thieves were selling stolen goods there, and only a couple of them have been caught. But the trials are coming up soon, and they hope some of the people from the jewelry store will give up some more names beforehand, to cut deals."

"Well, that all makes sense to me, I guess." Henry ran a hand through his hair and touched his temple gingerly. "I wonder if the nurse could give me another dose of that headache medicine."

"I'll go out to the desk and ask," Karen said.

Mary looked at her watch. "And I must get back to the bookshop. Henry, I'm so pleased that you're able to go home soon."

"If we don't see you first, Kim and I will give you a call tomorrow when he's settled," Karen said. "Come by the house, if you want."

"I'm sure Henry will want to rest," Mary said, at which Henry made a face but didn't protest. "I'll talk to you soon," she told Karen. "Good-bye."

Chief McIntosh went out into the hall with her and fell into step beside her. "There's one more thing, Mrs. Fisher. I wasn't sure how much you'd want me to say in front of Mr. Woodrow and his daughter."

Mary stopped beside a linen bin in the hallway and looked up at him. "What is it?"

"That fellow who was tailing you—Joseph Melvin."

"Officer Reed was very prompt and professional in answering my call," Mary said.

"Yes, well, I guess you know Melvin is a licensed investigator."

"He told me that much, but he wouldn't say anything about who hired him. He did say he wanted to talk to Henry."

Chief McIntosh nodded. "He wasn't after Mr. Woodrow, though. He says he meant him no harm. He only wanted to question him about the ring."

Mary frowned. "The Saxons hired him to find it?"

"No. Brock Vandemire. He was angry with the Boston PD for not catching the thief who stole his wife's jewelry. That ring is a treasure in her family, and it's worth a lot more even than Daniel York paid for it. So Vandemire hired this PI to try to find it."

"But *I* never had the ring. Well, except for the few minutes it took to get it from the hospital to you at the police station."

"Melvin didn't know that. He'd learned that the ring came on the market through Guthrie's, but it was too late. They'd already sold it. He put some pressure on the people from Guthrie's, and one way or another he found out the store had sold the ring to York. Melvin was trying to find York and get the ring back, but by the time he arrived in Ivy Bay, it had been stolen again. Apparently, he saw you snooping around at York's apartment building and realized you were connected to this somehow. Then he followed you out to Woodrow's."

"When I went back to search the car," Mary said.

McIntosh nodded. "From then on, he kept an eye on you."

"I led him right to Dan York's cabin on Sunday."

"Unfortunately, yes."

"I'm sorry about that. At least he didn't hurt Dan."

Chief McIntosh nodded. "Since York didn't have the ring, Melvin couldn't get it from him. I told Melvin that the police have the ring now, and that we're in contact with the Boston PD about it. He wasn't too happy to hear that—I'm guessing because he didn't get to play the hero and collect a big bonus from Vandemire for finding it. I told him to back off and go back to where he came from."

"Good for you." Mary chuckled. "He said he knew you in Boston."

Chief McIntosh's eyebrows drew together in a frown. "We've met before. Melvin walks a thin line sometimes in the methods he uses in his investigations."

"He scared Dan out of his wits when he showed up at the cabin," Mary said.

"Yeah, York wanted to press charges. Said Melvin had threatened him. But Melvin denies it, and it's one man's word against another's. Always hard to get a conviction in a case like that. But I decided it was worth taking Melvin in for questioning. We'll get all the details from him, but we'll probably have to let him go. From what Officer Reed told me, he probably hasn't done anything illegal, unless we can make the criminal threatening stick."

"He didn't by any chance have a baseball cap in his car when you detained him, did he?"

McIntosh eyed her shrewdly. "He did."

She smiled. "I saw him once here, looking into Henry's room, but I wasn't sure it was the same man."

"I'll have Officer Reed ask him about that. I imagine he came in to get a firsthand look at Woodrow and see if he was conscious. Probably hoped to ask him if he knew where the ring was."

Mary held out her hand. "Thank you so much, Chief McIntosh. I'm glad to know you and your men are doing such a good job."

He clasped her hand for a moment and released it. "No problem, Mrs. Fisher. I don't recommend citizens getting involved in criminal cases. It can get you into all kinds of unhealthy situations. But I have to admit the tips you gave us did help on this one."

"That's good to know."

Mary drove back to the bookshop basking in the chief's praise, mild as it was. Her estimation of McIntosh's efficiency had ratcheted up a notch, and he seemed to be thawing the tiniest bit around the edges of his personality. The ring was recovered, the mysterious car following her was explained, and Henry was going home from the hospital. Now all she had to do was experiment with her ideas for the apple pie ice cream. The competition would be fierce.

TWENTY-THREE

On Thursday evening, Mary was cleaning up the kitchen when Betty came home from her book club meeting. She was glad she'd gotten all the pans washed and put away before her sister saw what a mess she had made.

"What are you up to?" Betty asked.

"I've been working on my new ice-cream recipe."

"Ah. Is it perfected yet?" Betty unbuttoned her light jacket.

"You can be the judge of that," Mary said with a smile. "There are three batches in the freezer."

"Three?" Betty stared at her. "You know I'm always willing to taste your creations, but that's an awful lot of ice cream."

"I wasn't sure exactly which spices to use or how much filling to swirl into the ice cream, so I tried some variations." Mary headed toward the freezer.

"I can't wait, but I doubt we can eat it all. Maybe you should give some away."

Mary stopped and turned around. "Kim Allen is still at Henry's. Her husband is bringing the boys down tomorrow. We can give them some and get their opinions too."

"I'm sure the boys would appreciate it," Betty said.

"Yes, Brody and Max will be good testers. Not to mention Kim and Greg, and of course, Henry."

When Mary came back with the ice cream, Betty had hung up her jacket and set out bowls and spoons on the table. Mary put the containers on the counter and opened the first one. "This was my first attempt. It's good, but I decided I should add some cloves. Just a touch. Try it and see what you think. Then I'll give you the one that has the cloves."

"All right, but don't give me much. Eleanor served refreshments tonight, so I'll only taste these recipes, not indulge in a whole bowl."

Mary got her a glass of water, and they sat down at the table together. Mary had already tasted each batch, but she took a little of the one she liked best. Betty took her time sampling each one and considering the texture and combination of flavors.

"Really good," she said after swallowing the first one.

"Just wait." Mary smiled and watched as Betty took a sip of water and scooped up a spoonful of the second option.

"You're right. This is better. It's very subtle, but I can taste the change."

"And now you need to try the one with the crust chunks."

"Crust? Oh, Mary!" Betty rolled her eyes. "I can smell the calories. You used butter in the crust, didn't you?"

"I sure did, and I sweetened it a little."

Betty took an experimental spoonful. She closed her eyes, and a dreamy look came over her face. When she had swallowed, she sighed. "This is the one. It's as good as Mom's apple pie with ice cream on top. I mean it."

Mary laughed in delight. "That's the taste I was aiming for. Now, if we could only make the pie filling part hot."

"I don't think that's possible, but you've captured it. And you'd better get all of this out of the house tomorrow. If you don't give it away, I'll keep wanting more. It's positively decadent."

"Never fear. Tess needs my recipe and sample soon, so I'll pack her a serving of that last one and take the rest to Henry and Kim."

Satisfied, Mary gathered the containers on a tray and took them back to the freezer. She might not win, but she'd created a strong contender, she was sure, and that was all that mattered.

———

Sitting beside Henry in the '55 Buick Century just over a week later, Mary pulled off her scarf and let the wind whip her short curls. The drive along Bayshore Road thrilled her. A few puffy clouds scudded over the harbor, but the sun bathed everything in golden light and sparkled on the water, brushing the small blue-gray waves with highlights of gold. A small flock of terns glided overhead and landed on the narrow beach.

Mary had gone into town that morning with Betty, to watch the parade and witness the opening of the taste-off at the booth Blake and Tess had set up in the park. Other vendors were hawking treats too—hot dogs, cotton candy, soft drinks, fried clams, and onion rings, among others. Mary had gone against her better judgment and snacked at the various booths in lieu of lunch. Her dessert was a small portion of two of her competitors' ice cream.

Now she and Henry were headed back for the closing ceremony, when the awards would be presented. All the contest entrants had been asked to be on hand at four o'clock.

As they neared town, they passed the bog, where the cranberries were swelling. Mary inhaled deeply. That scent of salt water, lush vegetation, and the perfume of pine needles always made her feel alive. She smiled over at Henry as he shifted to a lower gear.

"We couldn't have picked a better day to take a spin in the car," she said. "It certainly rides smoothly."

"Thanks. I'm sure Tess and Blake are pleased with the weather." Henry winked at her as he eased up to a stop sign.

"I'm just glad Bailey's made all the ice cream for today, not me." Mary settled back in the comfortable seat. The Buick might be nearly sixty years old, but it still felt like a luxury car. She ran her fingers over the leather dash. "I could get used to this ride."

Henry laughed and headed them toward Albert Paddington Park. "I should have gone to town this morning for the parade."

"Now, you know Dr. Teagarden told you to take it easy for a couple of weeks. One major outing a day is enough."

"Still, I haven't missed the parade in years. I can't remember when."

"Betty and I walked downtown to see it. It was wonderful. All the floats, and the marching band, and of course, the fire trucks. Blake and the girls were doing a lot of business when we left."

Henry nodded. "Good. I hope it's a big moneymaker for them. I guess it's best that I stayed home this morning. Hate to admit it, but I still get tuckered pretty easily."

"You're wise not to jump back into things too quickly," Mary said.

"They set up near the gazebo, right?"

"Yes, and that's where the award ceremony will be. Blake built a big booth for Bailey's, all decked out in flags and bunting. People can taste any or all of the eight flavors."

"Eight! How will I ever choose?" Henry moaned.

"Tess said Blake and the girls have been practicing making dishes with a tiny scoop of each, for people who want to run the gamut."

"Tempting."

Cars lined the street for blocks on either side of the park.

"Blake's got a small parking area over there reserved for the contestants," Mary said, pointing.

"Oh, good." Henry followed her direction, and soon they found the reserved spots, where Officer Tilton was directing traffic and assisting with the parking crunch.

"Hey, Mr. Woodrow," he called, waving to them. "Mrs. Fisher, I think you're the last entrant to arrive, except for Todd Milton."

"Todd entered the contest?" Henry asked.

Officer Tilton nodded. "He sure did. Everyone in town seems to want to give Mrs. Fisher a run for the title of best ice-cream maker."

"I hope they brought their A game, because she's hard to beat." Henry got out of the car and came around to open the door for Mary. Officer Tilton walked over and gave her a conspiratorial smile.

"Tell the truth now, Mrs. Fisher. Did you name your Frosty McIntosh Pie ice cream after the temporary chief and his frosty attitude?"

Mary felt her cheeks redden. "Well, I did use McIntosh apples."

Henry laughed. "I wondered as much myself, but I wasn't going to say anything."

Tilton's smile grew. "All the fellows at the station were talking about it this morning. We think you nailed it."

"I guess that wasn't very discreet of me," Mary said. "I hope the chief doesn't take offense."

"Oh, he won't hear about it," Officer Tilton said. "He left two days ago."

"You mean—"

Officer Tilton nodded with obvious contentment. "Yup. The real chief's back."

Mary sighed. This was shaping up into a lovely day. She took Henry's arm.

"Thanks for telling me that. The morale must be high at the police station."

"It sure is. I must say, McIntosh looked happier when he left than he did the whole time he was here."

"Do you think he was glad to leave Ivy Bay?" Henry asked.

"Not so much that as having the Vandemire case solved, along with yours. See, McIntosh was one of the original investigators when Mrs. Vandemire's jewelry was stolen. I think it gave him quite a shock, Mrs. Fisher, when you turned up those pictures of it and Mrs. Saxon's ring and pointed out how similar they were. They still haven't caught the thief who stole it from the Vandemire home, but at least now they've gotten that antique ring back. McIntosh was very pleased about that. He should have sent you two an engraved thank-you note."

Mary laughed. "Well, Henry's the one who found it for him."

"A lot of good that does, when you don't remember what you've found," Henry said.

Officer Tilton chuckled. "Glad you're feeling better now, sir. Have a nice time today." He turned to speak to a driver seeking a parking spot.

"Do you know what the other ice-cream flavors are?" Henry asked.

"Yes, but I haven't tasted them all," Mary said. "When I took my test batch over the other day, Cynthia Jones had just brought in a blueberry-ginger sample. It looked delicious. And this morning, I stopped in to see how Tess was coming with the creaming. She was horribly busy, of course, but I saw that she was working on something very chocolate, and she said it was Megan Winslow's flavor."

"Sounds good," Henry said, patting his stomach.

"It is. Betty and I both tried it this morning."

"Nice to see a young person get involved in something like this." Henry steered her around a cluster of chatting tourists.

"Megan's very creative," Mary said. "I tried one of the others this morning too—Mason Willoughby's. Very interesting, and different. I can hardly wait to taste some more of the finished products. They have a list hanging up at the booth."

They walked at a leisurely pace along one of the stone paths, greeting people along the way.

"Looks like everyone in town and all the tourists within striking distance are here," Henry said.

"Hey, Henry! How are you?" Jerry Avakian, the owner of Meeting House Print and Copy, walked over to meet them. His wife, Patricia, followed in Jerry's wake. Both carried dishes of ice cream.

"I'm doing all right, thanks," Henry said.

"Hi, Mary," Patricia said with a smile.

"This stuff is great," Jerry said, holding up his ice-cream dish. "I got the sampler."

"I just got yours and the blueberry one, Mary," Patricia told her. "They're both really good."

"Thanks," Mary said. "I admit I'm anxious to taste more of the competition's."

She and Henry walked on to the ice-cream booth. At least ten customers stood in line, and they fell in at the end of the queue. Across the top of the booth's front, a big plastic banner shouted American Flavor Ice Cream Taste-Off, Sponsored by Bailey's Ice Cream. On each side of the booth, large posters listed the eight competitors and their flavors.

Henry stood gazing at the list for a long moment before he said, "Wow!"

Mary smiled, surveying the roster. The ice creams were listed in alphabetical order, with their creators' names beside them:

Blueberry Ginger—Cynthia Jones
Cherry Pie Dream—Deena Hancock
Cranberry Almond Truffle—Mason Willoughby
Frosty McIntosh Pie—Mary Fisher
Hershey Bar Max—Todd Milton
Pumpkin Spice—Jill Sanderson
Ultimate S'more—Megan Winslow
Watermelon Mint Sherbet—Jayne Tucker

"That's quite a list," Mary admitted. She noted that Nicole's bacon flavor hadn't made the final cut.

They worked their way up to the counter, where Blake and his two daughters were dipping out the merchandise.

"Hi, Mrs. Fisher, Mr. Woodrow." Jamie grinned at them and held up an ice-cream scoop. With her gleaming auburn hair pulled back in French braids and her glistening green eyes, Mary thought she could be taking Hollywood by storm, instead of here in Ivy Bay serving ice cream.

"Hey, Henry," Blake called, handing two dishes of ice cream down to another customer. "How are you, man?"

"I'm good," Henry said. "Did anyone screen these to make sure they taste as good as they sound?"

Blake laughed and rubbed his tummy. "Oh yeah. Several times."

Jamie nodded sagely. "Twenty-one people turned in recipes for the contest, but Mom said we could only do eight in one day and do it well, so we had to narrow it down."

"That's what the sample batches we took in were for," Mary told Henry.

Paige Bailey, Jamie's sister, paused in her work of opening a new carton of ice cream. "You betcha," she said with a grin. "The Bailey family had the sweetest tasting party ever. These eight are the crème de la crème."

"And she means that literally," Jamie added. "Have you made up your minds what you want?"

"I'll have the sampler, I guess," Henry said.

Mary sighed. "I had the blueberry and s'more earlier. I'd like to try the cranberry now. Oh, and I have to see what Todd's Hershey Bar Max is like."

"I'm thinking it will be good," Henry said. "Todd has good taste."

Mary hid a smile. "Well, he does own the Beacon Inn, and I've eaten there a couple of times. I've never had anything I didn't like at his place."

"It tastes exactly like a Hershey bar," Jamie said. "The only difference is, it's cold and creamy."

"Oh, the watermelon sherbet sounds so good. And I haven't tasted Deena's cherry yet. Or Jill's pumpkin spice. This is a real dilemma."

Mary decided to limit herself to three, including Jill's Pumpkin Spice with her first two selections. Blake quickly put Mary's scoops in a plastic dish, while Jamie worked on Henry's sampler. "Here you go, Mary."

She reached to take it from Blake. "What seems to be the most popular so far?"

"You need to ask?" Blake glanced around as though gauging who was listening and leaned toward her over the counter. "Your apple pie and Megan's s'more are going fast, and so is Deena Hancock's cherry pie."

Mary nodded. "Makes sense. Everyone loves chocolate, and Deena's a great cook. Everyone who loves her food at the diner is probably supporting her."

"And how. This is shaping up to be a record-selling day for us. Tess is over at the store now, making more of your flavor and Megan's. We're on our last tub of s'more, and it's getting low."

Mary smiled. "Thanks, Blake."

Henry reached for the dish Jamie held out for him. "Thank you, young lady."

"Enjoy," Jamie called as they walked away.

Ivy Bay residents mingled with summer tourists in small groups about the park. Henry looked around. "Want to get a spot near the gazebo?"

"Good idea," Mary said. "The barbershop quartet is going to perform in about twenty minutes."

They strolled between flowering shrubs and other vendor booths and were surprised to see two people get up off a bench just as they approached the gazebo.

"Well, what do you know? We get seats." Henry steered her toward it. "I do have a couple of folding chairs in the trunk of the car. Maybe I should get them, so someone else can use the bench."

"Let's wait until you've at least eaten your ice cream," Mary said.

They settled on the bench and enjoyed the frozen confections, perhaps paying more attention than usual to the subtleties of each flavor. Mary had to admit Todd's tasted wonderful, but it wasn't the prettiest of the offerings, so she wondered if it would garner many votes.

"Hey, Henry!"

Mary looked up and almost dropped her spoon. Dan York, Stan Auger, and a woman were ambling toward them.

Henry stood. "Hey, Dan. Rita, Stan, how are you?"

Mary set her dish aside and stood next to Henry. "Hello, Mr. York. Mr. Auger."

Stan smiled. "Hi, Mrs. Fisher. Call me Stan. This is my wife, Rita."

Henry turned and set his nearly empty ice-cream dish on the bench. He extended his hand to Dan. "It's great to see you."

They shook hands, and Dan said, "You too."

Henry, always forthright, said, "I hope you don't mind if I mention it, but I saw in the paper that you've been to court."

Dan nodded. "I'm on probation. I'm really sorry about what happened to you, Henry."

"Wasn't your fault," Henry said.

"Well, if I hadn't put Dee's ring in the Century, Erick never would have gone to your house looking for it. He really did a number on you. I should have just given it to him."

Henry shrugged. "I'm fine now. Really. I'm glad they didn't lock you up."

"Well, not for long," Dan said. "I spent one night in the slammer, just until my indictment. The judge was easy on me, I guess, but because I didn't have a record, he gave me probation and community service. He also seemed to take into consideration that it was my former house I broke into. The funny part was that Dee didn't get to keep the ring after all."

Henry nodded. "I guess that rich lady's going to get it back. You just never know, do you?"

"I'll say." Dan grimaced. "I doubt I'll ever see any of the money I paid for it, though. And Dee would like to see me in jail, I'll tell you. But it's Erick who's locked up now."

"Yeah, they told me I'll have to testify when he goes to trial." Henry didn't like to think about that part, Mary knew. He frowned, and he still looked too thin and a little tired. Even though his bruise had faded until it was barely noticeable, she thought perhaps he wasn't as fully recovered as he'd thought.

"My lawyer said Erick will probably get a suspended sentence," Dan said. "Or maybe he'll serve a few months and have the rest suspended."

"That's not much, for hurting Henry," Mary said.

Henry shrugged. "He didn't really want to hurt me. It was a spur-of-the-moment thing, not a premeditated attack."

"I suppose so," Mary said, but she still wasn't happy about it.

Stan Auger had stood by with his wife, following their conversation with glittering eyes. "I can't believe all this was going on in the middle of the Wheelers' show and I didn't know anything about it."

"Well, I wasn't broadcasting my part in it," Dan said sheepishly. "I know it was wrong of me to go back to the house and take the ring. I was too mad to think straight at the time."

Stan laughed. "I guess the judge straightened you out on that."

"You got that right. And I almost lost my job over it."

"Oh no," Mary said.

"Things are smoothed out there now," Dan told her, "but my boss wasn't happy about it. He's agreed to keep me on, but I'm sort of on probation there too. If I do any more stupid things, I'm out on my ear."

"So just keep working hard, like you always did," Henry said.

"That's right," Stan added. "You never had any trouble at work before, right?"

"Right."

They chatted for a moment about the fine weather, and Stan brought the conversation around to the ice-cream taste-off.

"You made the apple pie flavor?" Rita Auger said to Mary. "Oh, it's *so* good. I love it!"

"Thank you." Mary smiled. "I didn't actually make what they're serving today, but it's my recipe, and I made the original test batch for the contest. Tess Bailey made all the ice cream they're serving today, so they'd know it was all done in an approved, commercial kitchen."

"They all taste good," Stan said. "I'm kind of leaning toward the Cherry Pie Dream, though."

"What's that cranberry one about?" Dan asked. "I didn't care for that."

Mary smiled. "That's Mason Willoughby's. He owns the art gallery."

"Oh, that explains it." Dan rolled his eyes.

"Actually, I thought it was quite good," Mary said. "Not your usual combination."

"The white chocolate bits saved it, I thought," Stan put in.

Rita laid her hand on his arm. "But it's so pretty. I think Mr. Willoughby was going for artistic effect, as well as flavor."

"You may be right," Mary said. She could imagine Mason in his kitchen, making batch after batch until he got it just right, or at least brought it to what he considered perfection. Mason was meticulous in whatever he did.

"Looks like the barbershop quartet's getting ready to sing," Henry noted. He glanced around at the crowd. "I'd better go get our chairs. Stan, you folks can have our bench."

"I'll help you get them," Dan offered. He and Henry walked quickly toward the parking area.

Mary picked up her dish. "I'd better finish this before it melts."

"By all means. That was quite an episode Henry went through," Stan said, shaking his head.

"Yes, and I'm sorry for Dan's part in it," Rita added. "At least he wasn't the one who hurt Henry."

Stan added, "Henry's such a great guy. I can't imagine him being assaulted in his own home. Guess you never know these days."

"We're all glad he came through it so well," Mary murmured.

Stan nodded emphatically. "He looks great now. You'd never know what happened."

The barbershop quartet, in their red jackets and straw boater hats, took their places on the gazebo steps, and the crowd thickened. Henry and Dan came back with the folding chairs and set them up. As the first strains of "Sweet Adeline" floated across the park, Mary settled back beside Henry with a sigh to enjoy the harmony. This was a perfect summer day on Cape Cod.

When the concert ended, Selectman Randy Overholt climbed the steps.

"Hey, folks, wasn't that great? I know you want to hear the results of the ice-cream taste-off. Blake Bailey is here to give us the winners."

As Blake made his way to the arched opening of the gazebo, Mary noticed Tess and Jamie standing to one side, watching. Paige hurried over to join them, still wearing her apron.

Blake grinned from ear to ear as he faced the crowd. "Thanks, everybody, for being so supportive of our American Flavor Ice Cream Taste-Off. We've been dipping and selling all day, and we ran plumb out of three of the eight flavors. Of course, some of you came back for thirds. You know who you are."

Someone in the crowd shouted, "Woo! Yeah!"

Blake laughed. "We'll keep the booth open until sunset, and there's still plenty of ice cream, but the voting is now closed. I know you're all dying to hear which flavor won the competition."

"That's right," called a man in the crowd, and Mary thought she recognized Rich Tucker's voice. His wife, Jayne, had created the Watermelon Mint Sherbet.

Blake waved to the heckler. "Well, we're ready. We've got participation ribbons for all the creamers who created these eight luscious flavors, and special awards for the first-, second-, and third-place winners. I'd like all eight of the contest entrants to come up here and give you folks a look at them."

Mary glanced at Henry. "I wasn't planning on this."

"Go on," he said with a grin. "You deserve a little acknowledgment."

The other contestants were making their way through the crowd. Megan jogged eagerly toward the gazebo in her cut-off jeans and striped T-shirt, while the older contestants approached more slowly, responding to the greetings and encouragement of well-wishers in the throng. Mary rose reluctantly and walked over to stand between Todd Milton and her friend Jill Sanderson. Paige and Jamie came forward and gave each one a small envelope.

"Each of our contestants is receiving a gift certificate to Bailey's for six half-gallons of ice cream," Blake announced.

Everyone clapped, and a few enthusiastic spectators whistled.

"Thank you," Blake said. "Now for the winner. The way we judged this is based solely on how much you folks ate of each flavor. Every time you ordered a flavor, you were voting for the person who came up with that delectable taste sensation."

Laughter rippled over the crowd, and Mary smiled. Blake was milking this for all it was worth, but she didn't mind. Community events like this were great for Ivy Bay and would keep tourists coming back into the downtown area.

Blake continued, "The more ice cream you kept coming back for, the more votes you were casting. So I'll give you a hint: In no particular order, the three that we had to make extra batches of were Megan Winslow's Ultimate S'more, Deena Hancock's Cherry Pie Dream, and Mary Fisher's Frosty McIntosh Pie."

The crowd erupted in cheers and applause. Blake waited until everyone calmed down and held up both hands.

"And now we'd like to present the third-place award."

Tess hurried over and handed Blake a bundle. He held up a white bib apron emblazoned with the words *I Placed Third in the American Flavor Ice Cream Taste-Off.* "This special apron and the white ribbon rosette goes to…" He paused and gazed out over the crowd for a moment with a teasing smile on his face.

"Deena Hancock."

Again, the people cheered. Deena smiled widely as she went to the gazebo steps and accepted her apron and ribbon.

"Thank you! I'm glad so many people enjoyed my flavor."

"I know *I* enjoyed it," Blake said. "Now, folks, that means that the first- and second-place winners are Megan Winslow and Mary Fisher. The second-place winner will receive an apron and a red ribbon. The first-place winner gets a cash prize of one hundred dollars and a blue ribbon, as well as her apron. And we're going to offer all of the top three flavors for the rest of July at the store, but the winning flavor will be the featured flavor of the month."

The crowd cheered, but Mary hoped she didn't win. Suddenly she wanted very much for Megan to have the excitement of winning that prize.

"Why don't the two of you come up here, where everyone can see you?" Blake said.

There was no help for it, so Mary walked up the steps and turned to stand between Blake and Megan while the onlookers clapped and the other contestants went to join their families and friends in the audience. From the front row, Megan's parents and her grandmother Bea Winslow beamed at her with pride.

Megan reached over and grasped Mary's hand. "Good luck, Mrs. Fisher!"

"Thanks. You too, dear. I loved your ice cream."

"All right, just imagine a drumroll," Blake said, holding up an index card. "The winner of the American Flavor Ice Cream Taste-Off is...Megan Winslow!"

Megan let out a little shriek and covered her face with her hands. Mary chuckled and reached out to hug her as the crowd roared, whistled, and applauded.

"Congratulations, Megan. Well deserved," Mary said in her ear.

"Thank you! I can't believe I actually won!"

Grinning, Blake said, "Come on over and get your prizes, Megan. And one more thing. We're going to have your name engraved on a plaque that we'll hang in the store. We'd like to make this an annual event and add the winner's name each year."

While the crowd again clapped and Johanna Montgomery stepped up to photograph Megan and Blake for the *Bugle*, Mary calmly accepted her prizes from Paige and slipped off to join Henry.

"Well, now. Second place," Henry said, squeezing her hand.

"I'm glad Megan won," Mary said. "She'll probably put the money in her college fund, and it's so much fun watching her."

"I know what you mean." Henry clapped loudly along with the rest.

As the teenager made her way down the steps, Blake said, "Thank you all for coming and participating. Stick around now—I'm told there'll be some string music at five o'clock sharp." He glanced at his watch. "That's only twelve minutes from now. And don't forget—we've still got plenty of ice cream."

Henry grinned and gave Mary a quick squeeze. "Well done."

"Thanks. What's the plan now?"

"I thought maybe a drive along the coast before supper?"

"That sounds nice." Mary folded her chair, prepared to carry it to the car, but Henry reached for it.

"Let me carry that."

"Well, hello," said a deep, strong voice.

Mary looked up into Benjamin McArthur's smiling face.

"Chief McArthur! Welcome back."

"Thanks." He shifted his ice-cream cone to his other hand, so he could shake her hand and Henry's. "How are you folks doing? Henry, I heard you had a little excitement while I was away."

"I'm fine now," Henry assured him.

"Good. Glad to hear it. You're looking well. And you, Mary." The chief eyed her with mock severity. "You dared to solve a case when I wasn't here?"

"Someone had to," Henry said, and the chief laughed.

"How was your vacation?" Mary asked.

"Not bad." Chief McArthur smiled sheepishly. "It took me a week to relax and let go of work, to be honest. But the second week was a lot of fun."

Mary smiled. That was about what she would expect from him. "I can't tell you how glad I am that you're back."

Chief McArthur held up his ice-cream cone, and Mary noticed that he had chosen her Frosty McIntosh Pie.

"Oh, I don't know, Mary." He winked at her. "Maybe I do have an inkling."

ABOUT THE AUTHOR

Susan Page Davis is the author of more than forty novels in the romance, mystery, suspense, and historical romance genres. A Maine native, she now lives in western Kentucky. She is a past winner of the Carol Award, the Will Rogers Medallion for Western Fiction, and the Inspirational Readers' Choice Award. Visit her Web site at susanpagedavis.com.

CORNFLAKE MACAROONS

◆◆◆

1 egg white
8 tablespoons sugar, divided
1 cup cornflakes
½ cup coconut
¼ teaspoon almond extract
¼ teaspoon vanilla
Dash of salt

In a mixing bowl, beat egg white, gradually adding two tablespoons of sugar. Beat until stiff. Stir in the rest of the sugar and remaining ingredients. Place by rounded spoonfuls on a greased cookie sheet. Bake at 350 degrees for ten minutes or until golden brown.

FROM THE GUIDEPOSTS ARCHIVES

❖◆❖

When I sit in darkness, the Lord shall be a light unto me.
—Micah 7:8 (KJV)

My college physics teacher once asked the class this question: "Can you see farther in the daytime or at night?" Most of us replied very quickly, "In the daytime, of course." But we were wrong. Professor Baines then explained that the most distant object we can see in the daytime is the sun, but that at night we can see stars that are millions of light-years farther away.

Sometimes, when my own private world seems to go dark, I think about that. A few years ago, our oldest son, Paul, had a very serious car accident. It was one of the darkest periods of my life, but sometime during that first long night, while Paul was in a coma in intensive care, I found my way to the hospital chapel. There in the darkness, as I prayed for my son, I felt a warmth, a reassurance, a peace that was the light of Christ's presence.

Paul, thank God, is now fully recovered. The sun shines again—in his life and in mine—but the glimpse of heavenly light that pierced that dark night will be with me always.

Lord, in my darkest hours, let Your light shine into my heart like a star. —Marilyn Morgan King

A NOTE FROM THE EDITORS

We hope you enjoy Secrets of Mary's Bookshop, created by the Books and Inspirational Media Division of Guideposts, a nonprofit organization. In all of our books, magazines and outreach efforts, we aim to deliver inspiration and encouragement, help you grow in your faith, and celebrate God's love in every aspect of your daily life.

Thank you for making a difference with your purchase of this book, which helps fund our many outreach programs to the military, prisons, hospitals, nursing homes and schools. To learn more, visit GuidepostsFoundation.org.

We also maintain many useful and uplifting online resources. Visit Guideposts.org to read true stories of hope and inspiration, access OurPrayer network, sign up for free newsletters, download free e-books, join our Facebook community, and follow our stimulating blogs.

To learn about other Guideposts publications, including the best-selling devotional *Daily Guideposts*, go to ShopGuideposts.org, call (800) 932-2145 or write to Guideposts, PO Box 5815, Harlan, Iowa 51593.